Doctor January

Doctor January

Rhoda Baxter

Published 2014 by Choc Lit Limited
Penrose House, Crawley Drive, Camberley, Surrey GU15 2AB, UK
www.choc-lit.com

A CIP catalogue record for this book is available
from the British Library

ISBN 978-1-78189-124-7

Printed and bound by CPI Group (UK) Ltd, Croydon, CR0 4YY

To my family

Acknowledgements

There are so many people to thank
that it's hard to be selective.

This book started out being about why women
with PhDs left science and ended up being about
emotional abuse. Thank you to Dr Hayley Wickens
(beta reader extraordinaire) and Dr Emma Byrne
for long discussions about workplace bullying,
emotional abuse and the difficulty of helping
someone who doesn't want your help.

Thank you also to Jen Hicks, for her thorough critiques
– without her this book would have been more rambling
and contained a lot more of Mrs Tait; to the lovely
team at Choc Lit for making this book even better;
to the RNA for the support and invaluable advice.

Last of all, thanks to my family for … well,
everything. I couldn't do this without you.

Chapter One

Beth removed her cycle helmet and fluffed up her hair before she punched in the security code to get into the labs. As soon as she entered the corridor, she heard the shouting. Since she hadn't had a card or text from Gordon, she was hoping she'd at least get a couple of cards and 'happy birthdays' from her colleagues, but it looked like she got to witness some sort of argument instead.

Vik, her fellow PhD student, was standing beside the door to the lab, apparently listening.

A female voice wailed, 'You care more about those bloody bacteria than you do about me!'

Beth shot Vik a questioning glance. He put a finger to his lips, so she stopped outside the door too.

Hibs said something, his voice too low for Beth to make out the words.

'Well, I've changed my mind,' the woman said. 'You can keep your experiments. I've had enough. We're finished.' Footsteps stamped towards the door.

Beth pulled back, flattening herself against the wall.

'Wait,' Hibs said, and the footsteps stopped. 'You forgot your scarf.'

The girl made a strangled *ugh* noise and stormed out of the door. Beth tried to look like she hadn't been listening outside as the girl gave another *ugh*, marched down the corridor and slammed the security door behind her.

Beth entered the lab to find Hibs concentrating on his computer screen. 'Are you okay?'

Hibs tied back his long hair and shrugged. He was tall and slim and moved like something on the hunt. A

Japanese ancestor a few generations back meant he had a faint, high-cheekboned exoticism about him. Beth was so comfortable hanging out with him as a friend, it sometimes surprised her that he was such a success with women. On the other hand, he was so phenomenally bad at keeping hold of the ones he bedded, that being his friend was a far better long-term option.

'That one lasted … what, two weeks?' Beth asked as she hung up her coat.

'Ten days,' said Hibs as he returned his attention to the computer.

Beth shook her head. 'Anyone would think you don't really want a girlfriend.'

'Why would I want a girlfriend? They just get in the way and make you go to dinner parties,' he said, without turning away from the screen.

'Not all of them.'

Hibs grinned. 'Enough pleasantries, come look at this.'

A Plexiglas partition separated the lab into two zones – a dry area with desks and computers and, beyond it, the 'wet' area, where the lab benches were. Beth tossed her bags under her desk and went to stand next to Hibs. He pointed to some red and green pictures on the screen.

'Oh cool. Are those your glow-in-the-dark bacteria?'

'Uh huh. GFP – green fluorescent protein.' He clicked a button and the images overlaid each other to show little black ovals with green spots. 'The green is my protein. Look, you can see where it clusters in the cell.'

Beth nudged him out of the way and leaned closer to look at the images, which showed a bacterium with two glowing green patches. 'That's cool,' she said. Her finger traced the pattern of green. 'So, if we compared these to images of your mutant bacteria and my mutant bacteria …'

'We could see if yours holds the other proteins together.' Hibs finished off her sentence.

'Can we do it in time for Roger's presentation next month? We've got six weeks.' It was their supervisor's turn to present the research done in his lab to the microbiology department's annual symposium. But Beth felt that the slides she'd contributed to the talk were not very interesting – they didn't show any conclusions as to what the protein she was studying actually did.

Hibs frowned. 'Not sure.'

Beth pulled her diary out and started marking off the days. 'Let's see. We each need to make the strains ... at least six sets of images each ...' She crossed off days until she ran out.

'We don't have time.' Hibs's voice was full of disappointment. 'Bugger. It would have been really good. Lots of nice pictures you could have used in your thesis.'

Beth stared glumly at the diary covered in pencil marks. If she could produce data that told a nice, solid story, then Roger would have to show her some respect. And she could get a decent research paper out of it. 'We can still do the experiments,' she said. 'It just won't be done in time.'

'What are you two looking so pissed off about?' Vik came in carrying a small bucket of ice chips. When he'd first arrived, they'd tried to use his full name – Kaushalya Vikramarathne – but ever since their first trip to the pub, he'd been known simply as Vik.

Beth outlined the problem and Vik pulled a face. 'Why don't you use the microscopes downstairs?'

Hibs shook his head. 'Booked solid for three months. They're only free at night.'

For a moment, they were all silent as Beth stood in

between the two men. There was a nice symmetry to it, she thought – her, small and blonde, in between two guys who were both tall and dark. Beth and her boys.

'Shame you're not nocturnal,' Vik said.

Nocturnal. Working at night had not occurred to her, but now Vik had mentioned it, it was an obvious solution. She looked at Hibs to see if he was thinking the same thing.

He was. 'We *could* run the experiments at night,' Hibs said. 'It would probably be better, come to think of it. Less chance of someone knocking the microscope out of frame.'

'We could run our two experiments simultaneously …' said Beth, excitement rising in her chest. 'And take it in turns to do the night shift …'

They looked at the diary again.

'It'll be a close call,' said Hibs. 'We'd have to work every night to get it done in time.' He tapped a staccato rhythm with his pen. 'What do you think?'

'I'm up for it if you are,' Beth said.

'You know me,' said Hibs. 'I'm always up for it.'

Beth gave him a mock punch on the shoulder. 'Seriously though, it would take up lots of time. And neither of us would be able to have a social life.'

Hibs shrugged. 'I don't care. I'm single.'

Beth glanced at him to see if he was going to comment on the limbo status of her own relationship with Gordon but, thankfully, he said nothing. Vik shook his head and headed off to the other end of the lab.

'I'm going to ask Roger at the lab meeting,' said Beth. 'When he sees that my results don't support his theory, he's bound to let me try and prove mine.'

* * *

Beth felt she did well in her presentation, putting up slides of DNA sequences and bar charts to show what the mutant bacteria did. At the start of her PhD, standing here in front of even three people would have terrified her into stuttering. Now she was able to talk with more confidence.

'So,' she said in conclusion. 'There are two possibilities: either my protein acts as an "on" switch for the rest of the proteins, or it holds them together so that they can communicate. Judging by these results, I think it's the second explanation.'

'Let's have a look at those graphs again.' Roger, her supervisor, crossed his arms over his belly. He raised his eyebrows, making them ride up into his thinning curls. 'It looks like they support the first hypothesis.'

Beth flicked back to the right slide. 'Yes, but the data points are scattered. There isn't a significant effect.' Roger glared at her for just long enough to tell her that he did not appreciate being contradicted. Beth looked away.

'No, I think you're wrong,' Roger said. 'You just need more data.' He leaned back in his seat and tapped the end of his pen on the table. 'Do me some slides. I'm going to throw some of this stuff into my departmental presentation. The highlight will be Hibs's pictures, of course.'

'Actually,' said Beth. 'I'm hoping to put Hibs's GFP proteins into mutants that are missing my protein. If my protein is holding them together, removing it will make the green end up scattered instead of nicely packed into clusters. I've already started making—'

'Is this true?' Roger turned to Hibs, who looked surprised.

Beth bristled. Why did he need to ask Hibs for confirmation? Roger always did this –pretended that she was incapable of independent thought. If he didn't think she should be in science, then why on earth had he taken her on as a PhD student?

'Yes,' Hibs said. 'Beth has started making the strains. As she just said.' He nodded to Beth.

'Well, I think you should concentrate on getting those graphs sorted out,' Roger said. 'I need those slides by the end of the month. You need a couple of extra data sets so you'll have to get a move on.'

'But the images—'

'Okay. Is there anything else?' Roger looked round the table. Vik and Hibs both shook their heads. 'Right,' said Roger. 'I'll see you next week.' He turned to Beth. 'Keep me posted on how that data set is coming along. Now, I've got a meeting to go to.' He swept out.

Beth slapped the laptop shut, muttering under her breath. She had been working in Roger's lab for two years now and it was always the same. He undermined her at every step. It wasn't as though he was even a good supervisor. She wouldn't get any real direction on her project if it weren't for Hibs.

'Hey, steady on,' said Hibs. 'It's not the computer's fault that our boss is an arse.'

'How come you don't get this kind of crap?' Beth said to Vik, who was in his first year of a PhD and seemed to be getting an easy ride of it so far.

Vik shrugged. 'Maybe it takes him a while to work up a vat of bile.'

'I think it's because he doesn't like women in the lab.' The minute she said it, doubt niggled. It was all very well bringing out the sexism card, but was it true? Could she be sure it wasn't just her that Roger didn't rate?

'He's a bully,' said Hibs. 'You really should stand up

for yourself a bit more, Beth. You're good at what you do. You know that.'

The environment at her work was so stifling, with its hierarchies and politics. It made her so angry. There must be less confrontational places to work. 'Yeah, well, just wait until I get enough data to write up my thesis. I am *so* going to get into industry.'

Hibs poured out fresh teas and coffees for all three of them. 'What makes you think it's any better out there?' he asked as he put the drinks on a tray. 'Get the door for me, will you, Vik.'

They trooped upstairs, past Roger's office and into the lab. Beth paused to check her pigeonhole for post. A card from Mum and Dad. A couple from friends from undergrad days, most of them joking about being a quarter of a century old. She raced through them, scanning to see who they were from and checking the envelopes twice, in case Gordon had sent the card home for someone to post. Nothing.

Beth stomped into the office and plugged the laptop in to charge. Then she dropped into a chair and started to check her e-mail – maybe he'd got in touch while she was in the lab meeting.

There were messages from a number of friends. A few posts on her Facebook wall. Nothing from Gordon.

Had he really forgotten her birthday? They had agreed to stay in touch when he left, but after the first few e-mails, there had been nothing. Beth sighed. Why couldn't she just get over Gordon? She missed him so much it hurt. It wasn't just the comfort of having a boyfriend. She missed the way he looked at her, as though nothing and no one else mattered. When he really made time for her, it was incredible. Just thinking about it made her pulse quicken.

Gordon could make her feel sexy and alive in ways that no one else had done. It was as though they connected at a deeper level than normal. Without him, everything seemed duller.

She banged out a couple of responses to old friends. She didn't really have much to say to them nowadays. They'd grown up and grown apart.

'What's up?' Hibs came up behind her.

'Nothing,' she said as she closed down her Facebook page.

She waited for him to squeeze past her chair and go over to his desk, but he remained standing behind her shoulder. 'Still bothered about Roger?'

'Yeah. Sort of.' And another thing – neither of the guys had mentioned her birthday either. Well, that wasn't fair. She always remembered theirs. She even organised the collections and bought them presents. It was official. This was the lousiest birthday ever.

Hibs patted her on the shoulder. 'Nothing like a bit of work to get your mind off things. Come on, Miss Tyler. To your bench.'

She shrugged his hand off and stood up. 'Sod off, Hibs.'

'Now that's no way to talk to your favourite postdoc.' He pulled a disappointed face.

He was right. Just because Gordon had forgotten, she shouldn't take it out on Hibs and Vik. 'Sorry.' She pushed her hair back. 'It's not your fault. I'm sorry.' Mind you, she thought, Vik and Hibs had forgotten too. That hurt. She'd thought they were friends she could rely on.

'Apology accepted. Now, to work.' He made shooing motions with his hands. Puzzled, Beth started towards her bench.

The benches were laid out so that the lab was divided

into a series of bays, with a walkway at the end separating them from the communal equipment. It was a small enough facility that Beth and Hibs had to share a bay. Roger had commandeered the first bay for himself, even though he rarely made it into the lab any more. Hibs had started using it to store various boxes of kit.

Vik was loitering at the end of Beth's work area. As the newest member of the lab, he got the smallest bench, tucked away in the back next to the solvent cupboard. There was no reason for him to be near her bench. Suspicion crept in. 'What's going on?'

'Okay, time to close your eyes.' Hibs was grinning. 'Go on. Close them. Otherwise I'll have to put my hands over your eyes.'

'Ugh, no way. I don't know where they've been.' She closed her eyes. Hibs's hand closed round her elbow and he guided her towards her bench. The warmth of the contact felt strange. She reminded herself that this was only Hibs. They worked in such a small space that they could almost bump into each other if they turned round too quickly. So, sharing space with Hibs shouldn't bother her in the slightest. Except, today it did. Maybe she was just missing Gordon so much that physical contact with anyone was a big deal. She had to pull herself together.

'Open your eyes.' His voice was warm in her ear.

As she opened them, both men shouted, 'Happy Birthday!'

They'd made a garland out of Eppendorf tubes and strung it along her bench. Someone had filled up several days' worth of yellow tip boxes and drawn big bows on the autoclave tape that sealed them shut. Putting fiddly yellow pipette tips in the racks was one of the most boring chores in the lab and they'd saved her having to do any that week. In the middle of her tidy work area was a parcel, wrapped up messily, as only boys could do.

'Oh. How lovely. Thanks guys.' She really was touched. The heavy sadness that had been settling on her lifted. They'd remembered: she was loved.

'You thought we'd forgotten, didn't you?' Vik was practically bouncing with excitement. 'Go on. Open the present. Open the present.'

Beth tore open the wrapping. Inside was a gift voucher for the camera shop in town and a T-shirt. She lifted it out – it was a skinny top with 'It's okay Pluto, I'm not a planet either' written on it.

'Is it the right size?' Vik said. 'Hibs guessed.'

'Of course it's the right size,' said Hibs. He was leaning back against his own bench, on the other side of the small bay. 'I'm good at guessing stuff like that.'

Beth held it against herself. It would be a snug fit, but yes, it was the right size. It was kind of weird that Hibs had guessed her size so accurately, but then, maybe he'd seen enough women's bodies to become an expert on them. Because he'd never made a move on her, she'd assumed that he'd not bothered noticing hers. It felt unsettling to think that he had.

She picked up the birthday card. It had a Far Side print of two bacteria on it and she laughed. 'That's made my day!'

Hibs watched Beth examining her gifts with pleasure. It had taken him ages to find the right presents for her and it was gratifying to see that she loved them.

His lips twitched into a little smile. They always did that when he saw Beth. He couldn't think when she'd first started having this effect on him. Certainly, when he'd first met her, he'd thought she was cute, sure, but nothing much more than that. He might have even found her attractive, but she'd displayed her appalling lack of taste by opting to go out with Gordon the Git, which made Hibs think of her as some sort of pretty idiot for a while. He knew now that she wasn't an idiot – just a girl with terrible taste in men. Over the past few years they'd got to know each other well, like you do when you work opposite each other day in day out, and now she was a friend. Almost off-limits. But whenever he saw her, he felt like he'd become a better person just by looking at her.

It had been a few months since Gordon the Git had flitted off to America, and Beth had finally stopped coming into work with red-rimmed eyes now. Maybe she was getting over him. Maybe if he approached her ... but then if she wasn't ready he'd have ruined a perfectly good friendship. Hibs sighed. Better to leave things as they were for now.

Beth looked up and smiled. He stopped staring at her. *Just a friend. Just a friend.*

'You guys are the best.' She leapt off her seat and, to his delight, gave him a quick peck on the cheek. He watched Vik tense as Beth stepped towards him. She hesitated and touched Vik's arm instead. 'Thank you. I love them.'

Hibs tried not to touch the spot on his cheek where Beth's lips had touched it. She felt comfortable enough to kiss him on the cheek, but not Vik. It didn't mean anything, of course, but he couldn't help feeling pleased.

Beth folded the vouchers inside the T-shirt and stowed them in her bag. 'So, pub tonight then?'

'Of course,' said Vik.

'Naturally,' said Hibs. 'Now, perhaps we should all get back to work? Before Roger comes in and accuses us of not being serious scientists.'

Chapter Two

Hibs was disappointed to see that the bar was manned by a skinny guy with dodgy facial hair, rather than the new Aussie barmaid. Oh well, couldn't be helped. The kid was busy taking someone else's order, so Hibs leaned on the varnished wood of the bar to wait.

From where he was standing he could see into the anteroom, where Beth was checking her phone while pretending to talk to Vik. She was still waiting for Gordon to call. It was past six in the evening. If he hadn't called all day, it was unlikely he was going to now. Bloody Gordon. Seeing Beth all screwed up like this almost made Hibs wish the bastard would phone, just to put a smile back on her face. But Beth needed to get over this. If a day of obsessively checking for a birthday message that never showed was what it took …

Maybe if Beth got properly, ridiculously drunk, it would help her break through this mental barrier that made her think that Gordon was actually a decent human being. Hibs had spent hours looking up advice on how to handle the situation. He knew that until she admitted to herself that Gordon was bad for her, she couldn't accept help. Until that day came, Beth needed a friend more than she needed a boyfriend. He would have to be patient and not wreck the relationship they had right now. It was difficult having to wait, but wait he would. It wasn't like he wasn't able to have fun in the meantime.

The kid behind the bar asked what he wanted. He ordered three pints.

There was a blast of cold air as someone entered the bar.

Hibs turned to see a slim girl, dressed far too formally for the pub. Spiky hair, nose stud. Multiple earrings. Figure-hugging dress showing off a flat stomach. A swing to the hips that was really rather special. He prided himself in knowing the enthusiastic from the skilled when it came to the bedroom, and he would be prepared to wager that this girl was the latter. Suddenly she turned and caught him looking at her. She held his gaze and raised an eyebrow. Oh. Yes. Definitely.

Hibs picked up his drinks and went over to the girl. 'Hello. Are you lost? Can I help?'

She gave him a glance and a little smile. 'I'm looking for someone.' Her eyes honed in on him again. 'Not you.' Fabulous sparkly green eyes.

'That's a shame. Are your friends not here yet?'

'Actually, I don't really know them that well. It's my new flatmate's birthday today. She said she'd be here. I just wanted to pop in and say hello before I went somewhere else.'

'That's a coincidence. I'm here celebrating someone's birthday. We're just in the next room.' He indicated the door to the anteroom, careful not to spill the drinks. 'Want to join me?'

She laughed. 'I'm Anna.'

'I'm Hibs. I'd shake your hand, but …'

'Lead on, Hibs.'

He was willing to bet anything that this was Beth's new flatmate. As they entered, Beth looked up. Her eyes flicked from him to Anna and back again. A look of something like annoyance flitted across her face.

'Anna. I thought you had an archaeology thing tonight.'

'I don't need to be there until later, so I thought I'd pop in and say hi.'

'Everyone, this is Anna.' Beth's eyes settled on Hibs. 'She's my new flatmate,' she said, meaningfully.

Hibs knew she was trying to tell him to back off. She didn't want him to make things awkward for her by bedding her flatmate. Fair enough. He understood, but it didn't mean he had to make it easy for her. He had a reputation to protect. He grinned at her. 'Anna and I have already met.' He slid the drinks over the table, avoiding eye contact with Beth. He knew she hated that.

It took a few minutes for the conversation to flow. Hibs kept his tone pleasant and conversational. Next to him, he felt Beth relax as it became obvious that he hadn't turned on the charm. Vik was trying to make small talk, but wasn't doing a great job.

Anna turned to Hibs. 'So, what sort of a name is Hibs?'

He held her gaze without flinching. 'A nickname.'

'Have you got a real name too?' Anna asked

Beth looked from one to the other. 'His name's James,' she said. 'James Hibbotson.'

'My brothers were at the same school,' Hibs said. 'So I got to be Hibs – the shorter Hibbotson. I think I got off lightly – the alternative was Hobbitson.'

Anna leaned forward on her long slim arms. 'Sounds like you were bullied.'

Hibs laughed. 'No, I wasn't.'

She looked sceptical.

Hibs leaned forward too. 'Do you want to know why? Because I was captain of the karate team.'

Anna made an impressed face.

'Sounds dangerous.'

'Only if you don't know what you're doing.'

'And do you … know what you're doing?' said Anna.

Her eyes were dancing, inviting. Hibs had no doubt that she could be a lot of fun.

'Of course.'

Beth huffed. 'Anna's starting work at the Archaeology department next week,' she said, loudly.

Hibs turned to look at her, breaking his eye contact with Anna. Beth was getting annoyed. Winding Beth up was one of his favourite pastimes, but he would never go so far as to actually upset her. Besides, it would be far too weird to hang around Beth's flat with Anna. He leaned back in his chair. 'Archaeology huh? So, what are you working on?'

Anna glanced round at her audience and started to explain her project. She was interrupted by a loud beeping

'Sorry,' said Hibs. 'That's me.' He unclipped his laboratory timer from his pocket.

'You've brought a timer to the pub?' said Anna, incredulously.

Beth, Hibs and Vik all looked at her, surprised. They often brought lab timers to the pub. Especially if they were there at lunchtime.

'Science is a cruel mistress,' said Hibs. 'I'll be back in a bit.' He threw back the rest of his drink and pulled on his coat. 'Beth, did you need me to set up your cultures for tomorrow?'

Beth shook her head. 'I did them before I left.'

'Tomorrow? It's Saturday tomorrow,' said Anna.

'We've got a bit of a rush on,' said Beth. 'We don't always work Saturdays.'

'Well, Hibs does,' said Vik.

'That's because I'm a sad git,' said Hibs. 'Right then, boys and girls, I'll leave you now. It was good to meet you, Anna. I'm sure we'll see you again.'

Her eyes locked on to his. 'Oh, I'm sure you will.'

After Anna left to go to her dinner, there was only Beth and Vik left. While Vik was telling her about his aunt's latest attempt to fix him up with a wife, Beth sneaked another look at her phone. Still nothing from Gordon. She did a quick calculation. He would have been up and about for hours now. Plenty of time for him to send an e-mail or text. She sighed and slipped the phone back into her pocket.

'What's up?' said Vik.

'Nothing.'

Vik raised his eyebrows. Whatever he was going to say was interrupted by Hibs's return.

'Everything okay in the lab?' Beth asked.

'Yes,' Hibs said, shrugging off his jacket. 'What are you talking about?'

'Beth's waiting for a call,' said Vik.

Hibs slid into his seat. 'I take it Gordon hasn't called to wish you a happy birthday then?'

Beth said nothing and took a sip of beer. The tang was welcome on her tongue. Gordon didn't like her drinking beer because he thought she looked silly holding a pint glass in her small hands. 'Beth, you need to let it go.'

'I don't know what you're talking about,' she said. Hibs had never liked Gordon. The two men had always sniped at each other on the few occasions they'd been in the same room. Now Hibs was constantly going on about how she should get over Gordon and move on.

'Don't give me that,' said Hibs. 'It's been, what, six months since you split up? Has he called you in that time? Or e-mailed?'

Not for months. 'He's probably busy.'

'I thought he dumped you,' said Vik.

'It's not like that,' she replied, weakly. Wasn't it? All this time, she'd been giving him the benefit of the doubt – he was busy, the time difference was awkward – but it would really have taken no time at all to write her an e-mail. He had the perfect excuse to call her on her birthday and he still hadn't.

'I don't know why you let him do this to you, Beth,' said Hibs. 'He treats you like crap.'

'He doesn't. Didn't.'

'Really? When you were going out with him, when did you last do something that you wanted to do? You even stopped doing your photography because he disapproved,' said Hibs. 'He bullied you.' He frowned and took a long sip from his pint.

'He didn't bully me. He never touched me.'

'There is such a thing as emotional abuse, you know.'

'Like you'd know anything about it,' Beth snapped. 'Sometimes you can be a really immature.' Okay, so Gordon didn't like her doing her photography, but it was only because he wanted them to spend their spare time together. Hibs had never been with one woman long enough to fall in love. He could never understand what she'd had with Gordon.

'I'm not the one pining after some guy who hasn't been in touch for six months.' Hibs leaned forward, daring her to contradict him.

'Hey. Come on guys.' Vik held up his palms. 'Calm down.'

They both glowered at him.

'Anyway,' said Beth. 'It's not like you're qualified to lecture me about relationships. It's not like either of you have had a serious relationship, ever.'

The men both stared at her like she'd gone mad. Annoyed now, Beth carried on.

'Vik, have you ever had a proper relationship? Not just a one-off date who ended up not returning your calls?'

Vik looked at his pint. 'There was a girl once. Back home. We went to the cinema a couple of times. Held hands. Does that count?'

Beth stared. Did that count? It wasn't what she'd call a long-term relationship, but it was rather sweet. Vik was looking at her with his big puppy dog eyes. She looked at Hibs, who shrugged one shoulder.

Hibs made a little noise as though he was trying not to laugh. Beth turned. 'Shut your face, Mr Superior. When was the last time you had a serious relationship?'

His smile disappeared. 'Define "serious".'

'Where you were faithful to them and went out with them for a decent length of time.'

Hibs frowned. 'I'm always faithful.'

'Not difficult when you change women every other day,' said Beth.

'To be fair, he does only sleep with one woman at a time,' said Vik.

'Thank you, Vik.' Hibs raised his glass to his colleague.

'You're avoiding the question.'

'No, you're avoiding mine. What qualifies as a "decent" length of time.'

Beth stared at him. He stared back, the corners of his mouth curling into the beginnings of a smile. He was laughing at her. Git. 'A month,' she said.

'Oh yes. Definitely. I was afraid you'd say something difficult, like a year.'

'Really?' said Beth. 'When was that?' This was an insight into Hibs's life that she hadn't had before. As his long-time friend, she was surprised she didn't know about this already. She'd thought she knew all about Hibs's chequered love life. Or sex life. He seemed to think the two were the same.

'Oh, a long time ago. I was eighteen.' Hibs waved his glass vaguely. 'It was fun. Lasted almost a whole summer.'

'Why did you split up?'

'I went to university.'

Beth narrowed her eyes. He clearly didn't want to go into details. But she couldn't let it go. 'This girl was the last person you showed any commitment to. She must have been very special.'

Hibs grinned. 'Oh, she was. Very special.'

'You've got to tell us more, now,' said Vik.

'No. We're not talking about me this evening. We're talking about Beth. Now then, how about you cheer up a bit, birthday girl? You've been walking around with a face like a smacked arse all day. That's not right. Is there anything we can do to pep you up?'

Beth considered saying that telling her about his ex would cheer her up, but the glint in Hibs's eye told her she wasn't going to get anywhere with that.

'You know what I do when I'm a bit miserable?' said Hibs.

'Get laid?' said Beth. Vik sniggered.

'I was going to say, get drunk,' said Hibs. 'So, with that in mind, would you like another drink?'

'I haven't finished this one yet.'

'I didn't mean another pint. I meant something stronger.'

Beth's hand closed around her phone, in her pocket. It was still silent. Hibs was right. Gordon wasn't going to phone. She was just torturing herself waiting for him. She had to forget Gordon and move on. 'Oh, what the hell,' she said.

'Good. A round of whiskies coming right up.'

By the end of the evening, Beth was drunk and giggly. So was Vik. Hibs, quite merry himself, but more in control than the other two, decided it was time he got them home.

'If we hurry, we can get Vik on the last bus.' He watched Beth try to get her coat on and miss entirely. He caught her arm and gently guided it to the right place.

'You were nearly coatless,' said Vik, grinning. His eyes looked very round in the pub lights.

''Armless,' said Beth and they both started giggling.

A barmaid came over. Not the new Aussie one, Hibs noted, but one he already knew. He couldn't remember her name but he remembered other details about her. Tattoo on the top of her hip. A tendency to make squeaking noises when aroused. He grinned at her.

She winked at him and gathered up the glasses.

Beth was watching him, her eyes going from him to the barmaid and back again.

'Ooh, Hibs, you didn't,' she said.

'Come on. We'll be late for the bus. Then we'll have to find him a taxi.' Hibs ushered the pair of them out like they were little children. Beth veered off to the left but he caught her hand and set her trajectory for the door.

'Yes, Mother,' said Vik, making himself and Beth giggle all over again.

The fresh air was a shock. All three stopped and stood blinking for a moment before Hibs got them moving again.

'D'you know,' said Beth as they walked down to Vik's bus stop. 'You're right.'

'About what?' Her hand was still in his but she didn't seem to notice. Hibs gave her hand a squeeze to see if she'd respond. Nothing. She was just using him to keep herself upright. He suppressed a sigh and reminded himself he was being a supportive friend. Literally.

'About the alcohol. It doesn't hurt so much any more.' She pressed her free hand to her sternum. 'Here. It normally hurts here.'

Hibs looked at her, suddenly sober. He hated that Gordon had this hold on her. Why would someone who was normally so cheerful and confident let herself be treated like a possession?

He wished he could do something. He wanted more than anything in the world to help her, but he didn't know how. Sometimes he thought it would be easier if Gordon had actually hit her. At least then she could see him for the bully he was. At least then Hibs would have an excuse to go for him. But Gordon was sly in his bullying. He always provided ways for Beth to excuse him. Bastard.

'Bus!' said Vik. He started to run, not quite in a straight line, towards the bus stop. The bus pulled up and opened its doors to the waiting queue.

'Come on,' said Hibs. Still holding Beth's hand, he started to run.

Vik reached the bus just in time.

As they stood there waving, Beth slowly leaned against Hibs, closer and closer until he had to let go of her hand and get her around the waist.

'I'm shoo drunk,' she murmured into his collar.

Hibs fought the urge to put both his arms around her and cradle her. If he kissed her now, he guessed she'd let him, but that was wrong. He hadn't got her drunk to take advantage. He'd hoped that breaking her out of her normal routine would shake her into realising that Gordon wasn't the be all and end all of things. There were other men out there. She was too good for him.

'Let's go get you a coffee,' said Hibs. 'And a glass of water.'

Beth shook her head. 'Take me home, Hibs. Please.' She looked up. To his horror, there were tears in her eyes. As he watched, one loosened itself and meandered down her cheek.

'Oh Beth. He's not worth it, you know. Really. He's not.' He reached out and wiped the tear away with his thumb. 'He's not going to call you. He left. You're going to have to learn to accept that.'

'I know. I know. You're right. I'm so stupid.'

'You're not stupid. You're just …' What? Misguided? Naive? Trusting? Gorgeous. He shook his head to get rid of the thought. Focus, Hibbotson, focus. 'You just fell for the wrong guy.' Arse. Where did that come from? He must have been watching too much late night TV. 'You're a nice person. You expect other people to be nice and play fair. Some of them don't.' They started walking, Beth leaning heavily against his arm. Her footsteps were erratic so he used his arm around her waist to straighten her up and tried not to think about the warm press of her hips against his.

'I'm a doofus.'

'No you're not. You just made a mistake. You need to get over it and move on. Now you know, you won't make that mistake again.'

Beth blinked. 'You're really clever,' she said. 'You're like that guy with the hat and the beard.'

'Terry Pratchett?'

'No, silly. The other one. Gandalf.'

Hibs stopped. Beth nearly fell over. 'Gandalf?!' He was only a few years older than her! 'I'm only twenty-nine.'

Beth giggled. 'I mean wise like Gandalf. Not all beardy like him.'

'Well that's a relief. Wise, I can deal with.' They started walking again. He was glad he had made her laugh. At least she had snapped out of her morose mood. Beth giggled again and laid her head briefly on his shoulder as they walked and Hibs felt happier still.

When they got to Beth's apartment block, they took the lift. Beth leaned her head against Hibs again and by the time they got to the right floor, she was asleep, her head resting on his shoulder. As the lift doors slid open, Hibs sighed and picked her up. Her head lolled back. Well, if he had been trying to get her drunk and have his wicked way with her, he would have done a lousy job.

He got to the door and realised that he would have to look through Beth's pockets to find her keys. Carrying her home was one thing. Rooting through her pockets was tantamount to sexual harassment. Hibs sighed. With some effort he hitched her up a bit, redistributing her weight so that he could reach the doorbell. As she settled back into his arms, she started to snore quietly.

The door opened and Beth's flatmate, the cute one from the pub earlier, stood there. What was her name? He quickly ran through past conversations. Ah yes. 'Hi, Anna. I've … er … brought Beth home.'

Anna looked down at the sleeping Beth and opened the door wider. 'Come in. Is she okay?'

'She's fine. Just a bit drunk.'

'A bit?' said Anna. 'What did you do to her?'

'Whisky.' He moved carefully round the coats, taking care not to bang Beth's head or feet on the wall. 'Shall I put her on her bed?'

'Sure. It's the second room.'

Hibs already knew his way around Beth's flat – he'd been round before. The last time had been her old flatmate's leaving party. He took Beth into her room and laid her gently on the bed. Kneeling on the floor, he slipped her shoes off, and then sat back on his heels to look at her. She looked so very peaceful.

He leaned towards her. She smelled of alcohol and, more faintly, of that perfume she wore that reminded him of moss and woodland. Her hair was tousled and falling over her face. He moved it off her cheek with a forefinger. When had he fallen in love with her? He didn't know. It had happened so slowly, that creeping attraction. Until one day he looked at her and felt his heartbeat in his ears.

But she was his friend now. And she was still in love with Gordon. Even if she weren't a friend and colleague, she had no interest in him, whatsoever. He sighed and stood up. Turning, he found Anna in the doorway.

'She okay?' She nodded towards Beth, who curled up into a ball with a sigh.

'She'll have a hangover in the morning.' He left the room, shutting the door softly behind him. 'You might want to put a glass of water by her bed.'

Anna followed him. 'Can I get you a coffee or anything?'

Hibs hesitated. Anna was wearing cotton pyjamas and a little top with spaghetti straps. He could see the piercing in her navel. She'd had plenty of time to go and get a jumper, if she'd wanted to. She folded her arms over her breasts and smiled at him. Interesting.

'Actually, a glass of water would be great.' He leaned on the countertop. There was a stack of birthday cards, opened and carelessly discarded. 'We were celebrating Beth finally admitting that things were over with Gordon.'

'Oh yeah. Gordon the golden ex.' Anna handed him the glass and leaned on the counter next to him. 'I've heard a lot about him.' She was standing very close. Too close, he noted with amusement. 'So what prompted her to finally accept it?'

'He didn't send her a birthday card.'

Anna made a tutting sound. 'Tit.'

Hibs's eyes automatically flicked to her chest. When his brain caught up with him, he looked back up to see she was smiling.

'You did that on purpose,' he said.

Anna raised an eyebrow. 'And?'

Hibs stared at her for a moment, seriously tempted. But that would annoy Beth … and it would be really awkward tomorrow. Besides, his head was starting feel like it was stuffed with lead. He needed to go home, drink a huge amount of water and go to bed, or he wouldn't be able to function in the morning.

'I should go,' he said. His eyes didn't leave her face. 'It was nice to see you again, Anna.'

'Likewise.' She moved away. 'I'm sure I'll see you again, soon.'

Chapter Three

Beth woke up in a foul mood. Her head was full of thunder and the taste in her mouth was unspeakable. She rolled out of bed. What had she done last night? Someone had thoughtfully left a glass of water by the bed. She took a couple of sips before sinking down on the floor with her head in her hands. There was an insistent keening in her head. Dear god, what was that? It took her a while to realise it was her alarm clock. Groaning, she turned it off. It was definitely morning. Maybe a shower would make her feel more human.

A shower, clean clothes and clean teeth made her feel a bit better, but not much. She walked gingerly to the kitchen, where Anna was eating cornflakes and reading a book. She looked up as Beth approached. 'Hey. How're you feeling this morning?'

Beth made it to a chair. 'Awful.'

Anna grinned and poured her a coffee. 'Here you go.' She slid it across to Beth's hand. 'He said you were drinking whisky. I'm not surprised you've got a hangover.'

'He? Who was that?' She tried to remember, but couldn't place anything beyond being in the pub with Hibs and Vik.

'That gorgeous bloke from your lab.'

'What gorgeous bloke?' Had she managed to pick up a gorgeous bloke and not remember it? If so, where was he now? She felt an irrational stab of guilt.

'With the long hair.'

'Hibs?' Beth peered at Anna. There were many words she could think of to describe Hibs – kind, thoughtful, dependable, irritating, bossy, but not gorgeous. 'He's not gorgeous. He's just … Hibs.'

Anna laughed. 'You've been hanging out with him too long. You've stopped looking.' She paused, her spoon poised above her cornflakes. 'Have you seen the way he moves … and those beautiful long fingers …'

'He's got stupid long hair.'

'He seems to look after it though. It's all glossy and thick.'

Beth considered it. 'I suppose.' She didn't particularly like long hair. She preferred her men to have buzz cuts and muscles in the right places. Like Gordon.

'I'd love to get my hands on that,' said Anna, still staring into space. 'And on that body.'

Beth tried to think of what Hibs's body was like, but couldn't really bring to mind much beyond a lab coat. 'What? *Hibs?*'

Anna stared at her. 'What? You haven't noticed? He hasn't got an ounce of fat on him. He's all toned and … yummy.'

Beth sighed. Hibs had this effect on women. She wasn't sure how he achieved it. It was probably some mesmerising technique he'd learned with his martial arts or something. 'He's not really boyfriend material, you know,' she said.

Anna looked surprised. 'What do you mean?'

'His idea of a long-term relationship is, like, two weeks.'

'So?'

'What do you mean "So"?' She was clearly missing part of the conversation. It was probably drowned out by the pounding in her head. 'He's this massive commitment-phobe.'

'That's only a problem if you're after more than just sex,' said Anna. 'Besides, people change.'

'Not Hibs.'

There was the sound of post landing on the mat and Anna went to fetch it. Beth looked up, a tiny spark of hope flaring in her queasy stomach.

'Is there anything—'

'From America? No.' Anna pulled a face. 'I'm sorry, Beth.'

So, definitely nothing from Gordon then. Beth swallowed another sip of coffee and felt the hot liquid rebel and come back the other way.

'Beth?'

Beth stood up and lurched towards the bathroom. 'Going to be sick.'

It was nearly lunchtime before she made it into the lab. Her head still hurt and her vision seemed to be lagging behind real events by a few seconds. Her stomach had settled down now and her nausea was replaced by anger. Anger at Gordon for being such a bastard. Anger at Hibs for being right. Anger at herself for caring.

It was Hibs's comment about photography that really got to her. There was a time when she had really enjoyed photographing people. But Gordon had frowned on the idea. She wasn't sure what it was exactly that he disapproved of, but she had sensed his annoyance. At first she'd just stopped telling him about the photos she'd taken. Then, as she spent more and more time in his arms, she'd stopped entirely. Almost without her noticing, her favourite hobby had simply faded out of her life.

Perhaps she should take it up again, see if the buzz was still the same. There were those vouchers the boys had given her – she could use that and the cheque from her parents to get some supplies. It would make a change from taking pictures of bacteria.

She slammed her way into the office and stomped to her bench. There was a Post-it note saying, 'I've set up cultures for you to do your experiment tomorrow. Hibs.' She scrunched it up. She had lost the morning. The only way she could catch up was to work through until late.

'Afternoon,' said Hibs.

She turned, slowly, so that she didn't overbalance. 'What?'

'Good afternoon, Hibs. Thanks for getting me home and putting me to bed last night, Hibs,' he prompted.

'Did you?'

'What, take you home? Of course I did, you ninny. You fell asleep on me.'

Beth frowned. 'Did I?' She couldn't remember anything. She hoped she hadn't embarrassed herself. At least she had been fully dressed when she'd woken up, so she hadn't done something truly idiotic like succumb to Hibs's seduction voodoo.

Hibs came over and stood next to her. The bay was narrow, so they were only inches apart. He looked so utterly like his normal self that she relaxed a little. He peered at her. 'You look like crap.'

'Thanks.'

'Go home, Beth. You're probably still drunk.'

She shook her head, but then wished she hadn't. She put her hands up to her head to stop it reverberating.

Hibs put a hand on her shoulder. It felt like a ton of lead. 'I'll cover for you with Roger. Vik didn't make it in either, so it's not just you.'

Beth ignored him. 'My flatmate fancies you,' she said, accusingly.

Hibs grinned. 'I know.'

'You're not going to do anything about it, are you?'

'Do you want me to?'

'No. Definitely not. She's my housemate. She's new to town. Have mercy.'

'Mercy,' said Hibs, 'is definitely *not* what she wants.'

'You know what I mean. It would be weird. I don't want to see you wandering around in your pants while I'm having my breakfast.' The very idea made her feel light-headed. Clearly, her hangover was worse than she'd thought.

Hibs laughed. 'I don't do that.' He took her elbow. 'Now go home and sleep it off.'

She shrugged him off and stalked to her bench. She tried to pick out a pair of gloves and managed to knock a box of pipette tips on the floor. Yellow plastic tubes sprayed everywhere. She stared at the mess for a moment before kneeling on the floor and trying to gather the tips and slot them back into the holes on the box.

'You can't use those now: they're covered in crap,' said Hibs. 'Just bin them.' He started to scoop them up. 'And, Beth. Go. Home.'

Beth stood up. 'Okay, okay.' She set off towards the door. As she paused to wash her hands, she looked over her shoulder. 'Hibs?'

'Yes?' He was standing by the bin, wearing his white lab coat. He had blue latex gloves on and a pair of safety goggles on his head. His hair was tucked into the collar of the lab coat to keep it from getting any chemicals on it. This was what she thought of when she thought of Hibs. Not the sex god creature that Anna had described.

'You were right. About Gordon. I need to get over it.'

Hibs smiled. 'I'm glad to hear it.'

'I'm going to move on with my life,' she said. 'Move on to new things.'

The smile moved off his face. He nodded. 'Good. I'll look forward to it.'

As she left, she couldn't help wondering what he meant.

Chapter Four

A couple of days later Beth dragged Anna to a Women in Science meeting. When she'd first joined, the WIS had been a fun and interesting group. But lately, the more interesting people had stopped coming and had left a group of women who spent ninety per cent of their time moaning about how it was hard being a woman and the other ten per cent talking about science. The only person she actually enjoyed seeing was her friend Lara.

Beth had started going to these meetings before she met Gordon. Gordon disapproved of the WIS, but she'd carried on going, mainly because it was a chance to catch up with Lara.

The meeting was in the staff club, which had collections of tables and chairs in the bar area. In the evening, when it was full, it felt like a pub. During the day it felt oddly lifeless, like it was trying too hard to have fun. Having got drinks for herself and Anna, Beth looked around, spotted Lara sitting at a table at the far end, and waved.

Lara was wearing jeans and a shirt, but everything was so well ironed that it looked smart on her. Even her neat, sensible bob looked like it had been ironed into place. 'I saved you a seat,' she said, as she gathered up the handbag and coat that she'd placed on the chairs around her.

Beth introduced Lara to Anna. 'Lara and I met at the first WIS meeting I came to.'

'So, what happens exactly?' Anna said, looking around.

Beth shrugged. 'We talk. People have a bitch about life.'

'But what do you *do*. What's the point of meeting?'

Beth looked at Lara, who shrugged.

'I just come to catch up with Lara.' Beth took a sip of her drink. 'And to annoy Roger, my supervisor. He thinks it's a stupid group, but feels he can't really stop me going.'

'Well he sounds like a real charmer,' said Anna.

'He's okay really. Just a bit anti-women at the moment. His wife used to be a postdoc in the lab. She ran off with a senior lecturer from the floor above. He's been a bit weird ever since.'

'That's no excuse. Just because his wife ran off with someone doesn't mean he gets to be mean to all women,' said Anna.

Lara rolled her eyes. 'I've been telling her this. Roger has a duty of care towards his students.'

'Oh come on, guys, he's not that bad. I feel a bit sorry for him, really.'

Before Anna could answer, a stocky woman with a mane of black hair and too much jewellery came and joined them. Beth smiled. 'Hi, Clarissa.'

'Beth, isn't it?' Clarissa was the president of the society. She looked Anna up and down. There was a small pause as she looked from Anna to Beth and back again. 'I'm Clarissa,' she said to Anna. 'Who are you?'

'I'm Dr Anna Lightcliffe. I've just started working in the Archaeology department.'

Clarissa nodded, making her necklaces rattle. 'Welcome on board, Anna.' She turned to Lara. 'Madam treasurer, would you collect the subs, please? We're about to start.'

Once Lara had collected the money, Clarissa called the meeting to order. There were the usual boring announcements and discussion of issues.

While Clarissa droned on, being self-important, Beth thought about her plans to buy new photography equipment. She was surprised to find that the decision to take her hobby up again seemed to have kicked a switch in her brain. She was already looking at the world differently, framing it in her mind. It seemed to make everything seem that much more beautiful.

Clarissa moved onto another topic and Beth tried to focus on what she was saying. 'There's a drive on to attract more young women into science,' she read off the paper in her hand. 'We should get involved with this. Anyone got any suggestions?'

Her mind still full of photography, Beth looked around the room. The light filtering into the room fell on the women, all clever, all hard-working, but all so very different. What would these women be attracted to? Other than science itself? Could they do a photo montage of something? Or ... 'How about a calendar?' she said.

'A calendar,' said Clarissa. 'Of great women scientists?'

Anna pulled a face. Beth said, 'No.' Her mind raced and she had a sudden image of something Hibs and Vik had said about eye candy. 'No, of the most attractive male scientists we can find. We could do a local one. We must have twelve attractive men working here at the university.' She could take the photos. It would be a nice project to get her teeth into. She felt a rising sense of excitement at the idea. She loved photography. How had she let Gordon talk her out of it?

'Like the Studmuffins of Science calendar in the nineties,' Lara piped up. 'I like the idea.'

There was a smattering of laughter.

Clarissa stared at her, the corners of her mouth pinched with annoyance. 'That's a ridiculous idea.' She turned away.

Something stirred in Beth's mind. Clarissa was dismissing her, just like Roger did. How dare she?

Ordinarily, Beth would have let it slide, but today, with determination still burning, she wasn't going to put up with that.

'Hang on a minute,' she said, loud enough to make Clarissa half turn to look at her. 'Why is it a ridiculous idea?'

'What?'

'Why ridiculous? It's been done before, with great success. If you're trying to advertise science to teenaged girls, pictures of hunky men can't hurt.'

'Well ...' Clarissa blustered. 'It's demeaning.'

'To whom?' She was on a roll now. 'The guys? We'd be celebrating them as clever and attractive. What's demeaning about that?'

'But they'd be naked.'

'Woah, will they?' Anna asked, suddenly attentive.

'Who said anything about naked?' said Beth.

'But you ...'

'I didn't say anything about naked.' Beth was enjoying herself. She should do this more often. 'I just said calendar.'

'That's right,' said Lara. 'I think the nudity is in your imagination, Clarissa.'

Clarissa scowled. 'Okay,' she said. 'Now you're being silly.'

'Well, shall we put it to a vote?' said Beth. She glanced around the room. Most people seemed to be trying hard not to laugh. She wondered if everyone found Clarissa annoying. Would they be annoyed enough with Clarissa to vote in her suggestion? Clarissa pressed her lips together for a moment. 'Fine,' she snapped. 'All those in favour?'

Beth's hand shot up. So did Anna's. Lara joined them. There was a hush as people avoided eye contact.

'Okay,' said Clarissa with relish.

Someone cleared their throat and raised their hand. One by one a few more hands went up.

Anna counted. 'I make that ten to six in favour of Beth's calendar.'

Result! She was good at portraits. Even though Gordon had told her she'd do better with still life. She really, really hoped she still had the eye for it.

Clarissa looked like she was going to explode. 'There's no budget,' she said.

'Oh, it wouldn't take much,' said Lara. 'I can sort out the layouts. Beth can do the photos. Can't you, Beth?'

Beth nodded. 'For free,' she added.

'Are you any good?' said Clarissa.

'She's good enough,' said Anna. 'I'll help you do the interviews and things. I've got a good eye for a fit bloke.' Again, more laughter.

'We need a print budget.' Beth looked at Lara.

'I'll see what I can do,' said Lara. 'It won't be huge, but should be enough.'

When Beth told Hibs about the project, he laughed out loud. 'That's brilliant. I didn't know you had it in you.'

'Neither did I.' They were sitting in the tea room, with the leftovers from Beth's birthday cake between them. The feeling of triumph she'd had was starting to dissipate, and she was beginning to doubt herself. 'I didn't think anyone would vote for the idea.'

'I guess you underestimated your own brilliance,' Hibs said as he took a slice of cake.

'I underestimated how much everyone hates Clarissa, more like.' Beth found a piece of cake which was smaller than the others and picked it up. 'Or me.'

'I thought you liked taking photos of people.' Vik peered into the cake box. 'Is there anything with icing left on it?'

'Hibs had all the corner bits.'

Vik sighed and helped himself to a largish slice.

'He's got a point,' said Hibs. 'I've seen those portrait shots you did of your mum. They're really good.'

'I got lucky with the light that day,' said Beth. 'Anyway, I'm out of practise. I'm not sure I can manage the quality they need.' Then there was the fact that she didn't actually know any of the men that she would be photographing. She would have to get them to pose. It would be a completely different experience to taking candid photos of friends and family.

'You don't know until you try. What are you afraid of, Tyler?' said Hibs.

'Nothing. I'm just … not sure I want to take photos of complete strangers.'

'They wouldn't be strangers if you've interviewed them first,' Vik pointed out.

'Anna's interviewing them.'

Hibs laughed again. 'Is she helping you shortlist as well, by any chance?' When Beth nodded, he said, 'She's a force to reckoned with, that girl. I like it.'

'She said it was a good excuse to filter through photos of fit men without having to pay a subscription. She's shameless.'

'She sounds like she'd be your sort of girl, Hibs,' said Vik.

Hibs said nothing.

'I've been out spending my birthday money,' said Beth, when she got back to the lab.

'Excellent, what did you get?' Hibs was at his bench, pipetting out solutions from a Qiagen kit.

'New camera stuff.' She extracted the lens from its box and put it on the camera. 'I've got a zoom now.'

'Is that an old-fashioned camera?' Vik looked at it.

'Digital SLR.' She lifted it up and showed him. 'It lets me do some of the stuff you can do with an SLR camera, but with digital storage. Best of both worlds.' She held it up to frame Hibs and took a photo. 'Say cheese.'

'Sod off,' said Hibs.

'Oh, go on. Let's have a shot of the Man at Work in the lab.' She looked at Vik. 'Go on, you too.'

Hibs pretended to ignore her and get on with his work, while Vik stood behind him grinning and making thumbs up signs. Beth took a few photos.

'Oh, come on, Hibs. Would it kill you to smile?'

He gave her a pinched grimace. 'I'm working.'

'Uh huh.'

He rolled his eyes and carried on with his work. She could tell from the way his mouth kept twitching that he was trying hard not to smile. She moved in closer and took another photo.

'How about this?' said Vik, sitting on a stool and striking the Thinker pose.

'Nice.' She took a shot of him too.

Vik struck another pose, pointing into the distance like a catalogue model. 'Hey,' he said. 'Could I be in your calendar?'

'Oh, honey, I'm sorry. You need a PhD.'

'Ah.' Vik shrugged. 'Maybe in a couple of years then.'

'Now Hibs on the other hand ...' Beth pointed the camera back at him and took a few more.

He gave her an amused smile and half turned away.

Suddenly, his smile faded and he looked directly at her. 'You'd better not try to put me in your calendar.'

'Why not?' She was still taking photos – it was fun winding Hibs up.

'Because I don't want to be in a calendar. It's … cheesy.'

'Thanks.' She took another shot. She would have been offended if the comment had come from anybody else, but Hibs was always supportive of her. From him, she could take a joke.

'You know what I mean.' He returned to his work, frowning. 'It just seems a bit wankerish to say, "Hey look at me, I'm so attractive." Besides, who'd want a picture of me on their wall?'

'Er … Anna, my flatmate.'

Hibs acknowledged that with a shrug. 'Besides her.' He looked over his shoulder. 'Seriously, Beth. Can you stop that please? You're starting to annoy me.'

'Only starting?' said Vik. 'You need to try harder, Beth.'

'Clearly.' Beth took one last photo of Hibs and put the camera down. 'There. I've stopped. Happy now?'

'Yes, thanks.'

The sound of footsteps made her turn round.

'What's going on here?' Roger looked at the boys in their lab coats and Beth, standing at the end of the bay, holding a camera. 'Pissing around as usual, Beth?'

'I'm on my lunch,' she said. 'And my gels are staining.' She pointed to the timer, counting down on her bench.

'Hmm.' Roger looked her up and down with an expression of contempt. 'Hibs, have you got a minute? I need to talk to you about the revisions to that grant application.'

'Give me five minutes,' said Hibs. 'I'll just put the samples in to digest.'

'Good. Good. I'll see you in a few minutes then.' Roger turned to go, but then looked at Beth again. 'Get back to work, Beth.'

Beth stuck her tongue out at his retreating back, but put the camera back in its case anyway.

'That was crap timing,' said Hibs.

'Isn't it always.' She stowed the camera bag under her desk and pulled out her lab coat with a sigh. 'I'm destined to always be caught not working whenever Roger comes around.' She lit her Bunsen burner and dejectedly started to label flasks. 'It's not fair. He's never around when I'm doing the night shift.'

Chapter Five

Beth and Anna designed a simple poster and ran off a few copies. Lara called round to Beth's lab the next day to collect them.

'Morning,' Lara said, when Beth let her in through the security door. 'Is it safe to come in?'

'Roger's teaching, so yes.' She led the way into the dry area of the lab. Reaching under her desk, she pulled out a wodge of posters.

Lara leaned against the desk. 'So, how's it going?'

Hibs came into the dry area, tossing his gloves into the bin en route. 'Hello, gorgeous lady,' he said to Lara. 'How're you?'

'All the better for seeing you, Hibs.'

'How's The Man?'

There was the briefest of pauses before Lara said, 'He's fine too, thanks.' Beth looked up, sensing something amiss, but Lara wasn't looking at her.

'So, which month are you going to be then?' Lara asked Hibs as she put the posters into her bag.

'What? In Beth's calendar? I'm not doing that.'

Lara looked at Beth, but she shrugged. They'd discussed it; he'd refused. She wasn't going to argue with him. She could tell by the set of his mouth that this was something he wasn't going to back down on.

'Why not?' Lara asked. 'You've got a PhD. You're not bad-looking. There's nothing obviously wrong with you.'

'Thanks. From you, that's high praise.'

'Seriously, why not?'

'He's too cool,' said Beth.

'No,' said Hibs patiently. 'I'm too shy.'

Both women laughed.

'I am,' he protested. 'I really don't like the idea of being hung on some woman's wall and being ogled. It feels ... wrong.'

Beth said, 'I thought you *liked* women ogling you.'

Hibs shrugged. 'Not really. I think of it as a sort of service. They want sex. I want sex. It all works out.'

Lara shook her head. 'You astonish me. By rights you should be totally repellent.'

'It's part of my charm,' he said. 'That's why you love me.'

Lara looked at Beth, who pulled a face. 'Don't look at me,' Beth said. 'I don't get it either. My housemate fancies him. She's always going on about the way he moves.'

'What about the way he moves?' said Lara. She put her head to one side and examined him. 'What's so special about it?'

'Do you mind? I can hear you.' Hibs threw himself into his chair.

'Hibs, walk around a bit, will you,' said Lara.

He ignored them. After a while, he rubbed the bridge of his nose. 'Stop looking at me. You're making me nervous.'

Beth grinned. 'I'm just trying to work out what all these women see in you.'

His shoulders stiffened and he rubbed his nose again. 'Well, please don't.'

'You can't stop me.'

'I can.' He stood up and stamped out. 'Bye, Lara.'

'Bye, Hibs.' Lara watched him leave. She turned to Beth 'Does he always stomp about like that?'

'No,' said Beth. 'He's normally a lot more graceful.'

She wheeled her chair across to where she could peer into the main lab, and watched him pull on his lab coat.

'He does have a nice arse though,' said Lara.

'I can still hear you,' Hibs called over his shoulder.

Beth and Lara grinned at each other.

At half past five in the morning Hibs stood in the middle of his living room. The neighbours hadn't woken up yet, so he couldn't hear their footsteps or radios through the shared walls. It was about the only time of day his little house was quiet enough for him to do his meditation. It was his favourite time in the morning.

His few items of furniture were placed so that there was a space in the middle. There was just enough room for him to practise his kata if he concentrated and maintained control. Most people didn't realise that karate wasn't about speed: it was about control. Lately, his control had been shocking. If he carried on like this, he was going to hurt himself. Or worse, someone else.

Hibs sighed, shook his arms to loosen them and stretched. He knew why he was having problems: he wasn't focusing properly, letting thoughts of Beth distract him when he was supposed to be concentrating. The fact that he'd been working nights meant that he slept through his kata time every other day, and trying to meditate when the hubbub of daily life was in full swing was just a disaster. He had to get back into it. He owed it to his students. They were going to a competition soon and they needed him to be there for them: they were a good bunch and they deserved a decent Sensei.

He put his movement yoga CD on and turned the volume down so that he didn't wake the neighbours. He stood in neutral position, turning his attention inward, until he was aware of all his muscles. Focusing intently, he found his core. Only then did he start to move.

Beth checked her pigeonhole and found one snail mail submission for the calendar. She glanced at the photo – not bad – and wondered if Anna had had many entries.

They had put the posters up wherever they could and asked all the women from the group to spread the word, but the take-up had been fairly low. At the rate they were going, they would only have about eight months' worth of candidates.

'What's that?' Roger's voice in her ear made her jump.

Beth tried to stuff the documents into her bag, but Roger grabbed it out of her hands. He lifted the photo and looked at the text underneath. 'I heard there was some calendar being done. I didn't realise you were involved.' He looked at her and back at the document in his hand. 'What exactly is your role in all this?'

'I'm … helping out a bit. Nothing major.' She would have tried to move away, but the pigeonholes took up a lot of room, making the corridor very narrow at that point. There was no way she was going to get round Roger.

'And how much of your time are you wasting on this project?'

'None. I'm still working the same hours as before. I have been working nights a lot lately.' Did Hibs have to justify his time like this? Or perhaps being a postdoc was a job whereas being a PhD student was more of a lifestyle choice.

'Hmm.' Roger stared thoughtfully at the guy in the photo. 'So, what sort of people are you looking for? For this calendar.'

'Men with PhDs in science,' she began. Beth eyed Roger. He was okay-looking for a middle-aged guy. He was certainly in better shape than the guy his wife had run off with. She had a creeping suspicion of what was coming next. 'I'm not sure, but I think there's an age cut-off of thirty-five.'

'Why?'

'Well, it's meant to attract girls into science, in a tongue-in-cheek sort of way. So the ... er ... committee decided it was best to have an upper age limit. Keep the models young. You know.'

Roger frowned. 'Sounds very short-sighted. George Clooney is an older man and very popular.'

Beth nodded. 'True.' Any minute now Roger was going to ask if he could be in the calendar. She didn't want to hurt his feelings, but ... she cast another glance at him. Please don't ask. Please don't ask.

'Would you like me to ...'

Oh no. Too late. If she let on that she had any role in the decision, Roger would lean on her. She didn't want any more reasons for conflict between them. 'You could send your photo in. The committee won't be deciding for another couple of days.'

'Surely I don't need to do that. You know me.'

Beth shook her head. 'I can't do that. It wouldn't be fair. Besides, I don't get to decide. The others do that.'

Roger gave her a suspicious look. Vik appeared round the corner, carrying a sandwich. 'Hi.' He looked from Roger to Beth. 'What's going on?'

'Nothing.' Roger thrust the papers back towards Beth. 'Beth was just telling me about her stupid calendar idea.'

'Why is it stupid?' Vik looked genuinely puzzled. 'I thought it sounded like fun.'

Beth lowered her head. If she looked up now, she would laugh.

'Trying to attract women into science by parading men at them. It's ridiculous.'

'It's no sillier than Miss World,' said Beth, fighting to keep her voice steady.

'Yes, well, if I'd suggested doing a calendar with some young women scientists in it, there'd be uproar.'

'What would that achieve? We don't need to attract more men into science,' said Beth. 'There are plenty already.'

Roger snorted. 'I don't suppose there are that many attractive female scientists anyway,' he said.

'Hey, I resent that,' said Beth.

'You don't count. You're not a real scientist until you have your PhD.' Roger turned away. 'I have a lecture to prepare.'

'Mind you,' said Vik, his face all innocence. 'The calendar could help attract young gay men to the profession too.'

Roger paused. 'I think you two should stop messing around and get back to work.' He went into his office and slammed the door.

Beth shook her head and went into the lab. She would have preferred not to hurt Roger's feelings. He could be a total pain, but that was probably because he was lonely. She felt a little bit bad for being mean to him.

As she was heading to her bench, the phone rang.

'Beth, it's Anna.'

'Hey, what's up?' She started to roll up her sleeves, the phone tucked by her shoulder.

'Have you had any more entries come through for the calendar?'

'One.'

'Any good?'

Beth picked up the photo from her desk and looked at it again. 'Not bad. How about you?'

'I've had a few, but I don't think we've got enough for a calendar'

'How many have we got?'

'I've had about twenty e-mails, but not many suitable ones. At a push, seven maybe. That's assuming your new one's any good.'

Beth felt that was a little unfair – perhaps Anna was setting the bar too high. 'So, what are we going to do? We need to get started soon or we won't be able to get it done in time for the next meeting. Clarissa will have a field day.'

'There's nothing else for it. We'll have to keep an eye out for fit men and ask them if they'll take part.'

'We can't do that. We'll look like nutters. They'll probably call the police.' Beth thought of Roger's animosity. 'I don't think that would go down too well with my supervisor. I'm on thin ice as it is.'

'Well, I'll do it then. Just make sure you have your camera with you at all times.'

Beth shifted the phone to her other shoulder. She didn't like the idea of taking people's photos without asking. 'We'll have to get their permission.'

'You can get them to agree after you've taken the shot. You can always show them you're deleting them if they say no.'

It still didn't sound right. 'I don't know, Anna. There must be another way. Is there an advertising avenue we've missed?'

'I don't think so. I've even been hawking it around on

Twitter. That got me some obscene messages, I can tell you. That's after I specified that they *had* to be wearing clothes.'

Beth sighed. 'Okay. When do you want to start interviewing the people you've already got on the list?' She heard Roger's footsteps. 'I've got to go, Anna. See you later.' She rang off and turned round.

'Still not doing any work, Miss Tyler?' He emphasised 'Miss' as though it were an insult.

'I am, thanks,' said Beth. 'Can I help you with anything?'

'I'm looking for Hibs, actually.'

'He won't be in until later today. He did the late shift last night.' Beth gathered up some papers.

'Late shift?'

'We're taking it in turns to work nights, as I mentioned earlier. We're running two sets of experiments in parallel so that we can use both microscopes at once. At night.'

'What sort of experiments?'

'Time courses. We're looking at how the GFP-tagged proteins behave over time.'

Roger folded his arms. 'I asked you to concentrate on repeating the tests you did before.'

'I'm doing those as well.' She was finding it surprisingly easy to work in the night, when the lab was quiet. As long as she'd set her bacterial cultures growing the day before, so that they were ready by the evening, she could get on with the experiments without interruptions from anyone. She rather enjoyed it.

Roger snorted. 'Just make sure you have the results I want ready in time.'

'I will. Don't worry.' Seeing him turn to go, she added, 'How can you be so sure that my hypothesis is wrong?'

Was she missing something obvious? Some key fact that Roger knew but she had overlooked?

'Because if you've been doing this stuff as long as I have, you have a good understanding of the background work. Your protein will not make any difference to the way the tagged proteins localise. It looks like a signalling protein, not a structural protein.' Roger glared at her. 'I don't expect you to know everything, Beth, but I expect a basic understanding of the fundamentals. Clearly, you don't even have that. I don't know why I bothered taking you on as a PhD student. It looks bad on me when you fail.' He turned and walked off.

Beth stared at Roger's retreating back, too astounded to speak. To criticise her science was one thing, but to attack her personally like that? It just wasn't on.

Vik came up from the far end of the lab. 'Harsh.'

Beth leaned against the desk. 'Yeah.' What was it about her that got Roger's back up like that? Was it simply that she was a woman? Or was there more to it than that? She looked up at Vik. 'Do you ever get this sort of thing from Roger?'

'What? Abuse?' said Vik. 'No.' He paused. 'At least, not as much as you do.'

Beth shook her head. 'If I was wasting time, Hibs would have said.'

Vik shrugged. 'I should think so.'

Beth stared thoughtfully at the floor. Roger was entitled to his opinion, but there was no excuse for his behaviour. How much trouble would she get into if she made a complaint about bullying? She could count on some people from WIS to support her. Hibs would back her up too. Except … her PhD rested in Roger's hands. He could really mess with her chances of completing it. She'd put up with it for this long, so maybe she would be better off just sticking it out until the end of the year, when she could write up and get her PhD.

'Hey,' Vik said. 'Cheer up. He's probably just sore that you didn't ask him to be in your calendar.'

Beth gave him a grateful smile. She didn't believe it for a moment, but it was nice of Vik to say so. 'Thanks, Vik.' She sighed. 'I suppose I'd better get on with some work.'

Hibs's phone rang and the caller ID flashed up 'Mrs Tait', though she much preferred for him to call her Winifred. He'd put her in his phone as Mrs Tait twelve years ago, when he'd started doing her gardening in the summer holidays, and had never changed it. He tugged off his gloves to answer it.

'James, darling. How are you?' Winifred Tait's voice was quiet and businesslike.

'I'm fine, Winn. To what do I owe the pleasure?'

'I'm in the area next Tuesday. I was wondering if you'd join me for a spot of lunch. My treat, naturally.'

Hibs hesitated. Lunch invites from Mrs Tait were always more than they seemed. He didn't mind when he was at home, but he wasn't sure he really wanted to mix the two worlds.

'Just lunch. No strings attached,' Winn added.

Hibs imagined her sitting in her office, in that big chair that reclined all the way back. No strings. She always said that. He didn't have to do anything he didn't want to, but Winifred Tait, the most glamorous woman he knew, was taking him to lunch, in a hotel where she had a room for the night, no doubt. No strings. Unless he wanted there to be.

'Lunch would be lovely, Winn. When and where shall I meet you?'

'I've heard Le Manoir is good. Stockton says traffic in the city centre is dreadful, so where do you suggest we pick you up? I'll be coming from Lechlade.'

Le Manoir! Winn liked to do things in style.

They arranged a time and place for her driver to pick him up. 'I'm looking forward to it.' He genuinely meant it. He got on well with Winifred and he missed talking to her. They hadn't intended to keep in touch once he went to university, but they still met from time to time. Over the years, they'd become friends.

'Me too, darling; me too.' He could tell from her voice that she was smiling. 'I'll see you next week. And, James, wear a suit.'

'Will do.' He hung up. If anyone could help take his mind off Beth, it would be Winn. And lunch at Le Manoir was too good to miss. He hummed to himself as he went back to work.

Anna, Lara and Beth met in the staff club for lunch to compare the entries for the calendar and even Beth had to reluctantly agree that they were struggling to fill it. It wasn't so much that the men weren't good-looking – they were – but there just weren't that many entries. A few guys who were still students had entered: they were disqualified regardless of how gorgeous they were.

Soon they were left with a small selection of photos. They spread them out on the table.

'Not bad,' said Lara. 'I'd say we've got ten, at best. We need a couple more.'

'Roger wanted to enter,' said Beth and Lara laughed. 'I told him I didn't decide who went in the calendar. You did.'

Lara put her head to one side. 'You do get a say in it, you know.'

'I'm not sure I *can* choose between these guys. They're all gorgeous and every single one would photograph well. I'm happy for you guys to choose.'

'If you had to take just one of them home tonight, which one would you choose?' said Anna.

Beth refused to rise to the bait. Anna was seeing this whole thing as an extended dating service, while Beth was more interested in the photographs than the men. She should have been interested in the men, she supposed, but really none of them appealed. She shrugged. 'They're all nice, I'm sure, but I'm not particularly interested in any of them'.

'Is that because none of them is Gordon? You said you were moving on,' said Lara.

'I am!' Why did they not believe her?

'Well, you're not moving very fast ...'

'It's not like I've had lots of opportunity,' Beth protested. 'I've been working most evenings. I don't exactly have a chance to go out.'

'Working. As in hanging out with the gorgeous Hibs.' Anna grinned.

Beth rolled her eyes and Lara laughed. Anna said, 'Honestly, you can't tell me you haven't noticed him. Seriously? Are you blind?'

'No,' said Beth. 'I just don't get what you see in him.' She started to gather up the bits of paper. Since Anna had started going on about him, she had started to really look at Hibs. He was kind and caring, she already knew that. What she hadn't realised was that he was also slim and elegant in a streamlined sort of a way. She preferred her men more muscular, like Gordon. But she had to admit slim and elegant was attractive too.

'Huh,' said Anna. 'This Gordon must have been something incredible.'

Beth ignored the comment and said, 'Shall we sort out the photos and interviews for the guys we've got? Maybe some other candidates will turn up in the next couple of weeks.' Thankfully, Lara had squashed Anna's idea of accosting random people in the street.

'I don't see that we have much choice,' said Lara.

'Well, he was interesting,' said Beth. 'Once he put his clothes back on.'

She and Anna were walking back across the Museum Garden after visiting one of the men for the calendar. Despite their best efforts at clarity, he had answered the door wearing nothing but a dressing gown, which he'd dropped when Beth picked up her camera. Following a hasty explanation, and a few minutes standing outside in the corridor trying not to laugh hysterically while he made himself decent, Anna had interviewed him, flirting outrageously all the while and Beth had taken a few photos. His office had been in one of the lovely old buildings, so she'd had lots of light from the tall windows. She was quietly pleased with the results. They had shown the photos to the guy and he'd asked for a copy to put on his personal webpage.

'Yeah,' said Anna. 'He was. And he gave me his number. Bonus – did you see the size of his—'

'I didn't look!' Beth said. 'And you're still not supposed to hit on the candidates.'

Anna waved a hand. 'It'd be such a waste not to.'

They walked along for a moment, each busy with their own thoughts. It was pleasant and cool under the trees and Beth was in no particular hurry to get back to the lab. Suddenly, something thumped down from a large tree ahead and someone swore from up in the branches.

Anna and Beth paused and looked at each other. Beth undid the case on her camera and got it ready, just in case. A leg appeared from the tree, and then there was a grunt as a man swung down, his body hanging from well-muscled arms before he dropped to the ground.

Beth took a series of photos as the man stood up, brushing the dirt off his hands. He looked suspiciously at them. He had a shock of black hair and sideburns that framed a handsome face with startling blue eyes.

'Er ... hi,' said Anna.

'Did you just take a photo of me?' He glared at Beth's camera.

'Yes. Would you like to see?' She turned it around to show him. 'I'm Beth. This is Anna. We're working on a calendar of attractive men in science. You don't happen to have a PhD in a scientific discipline, do you?' She scrolled through the pictures. Even at first glance some of them looked very dramatic.

'Dr Dan Blackwood,' he said and held out a big hand to Beth and then Anna.

'Would you like to be in the calendar?' Anna asked. 'I think you'd make a fantastic Dr August.'

Dan Blackwood looked taken aback. 'I'd heard about this. It sounds very enterprising, but I don't think my wife would approve.'

'Why ever not,' said Anna. 'It's not like we're making a "free and single" calendar. It'll be nice to have some married men in it to show that scientists aren't sad cases who can't find a partner. We could mention your wife in the blurb.'

Dan looked uncomfortable. 'I'm not sure ...'

'Tell you what, why don't you check with your wife and let us know. If she says no, we promise we'll delete the photos we took of you,' said Anna. 'I'll write you a note to say so, if you like. Like an IOU.'

'I suppose ...'

'Can I ask a few questions, while we've got you here?'

He shrugged. The piece of equipment that had fallen from the tree lay nearby. He picked it up and examined it. 'I think it's okay.'

'What is it?'

'It's a mini camera.' He showed it to them. 'I think there's an unusual species of beetle arrived in there recently. It's quite possibly invasive. I'm trying to get some pictures to make sure I've got the right one.' He looked up, his eyes bright. 'Have you heard of *Acillus blackwoodii*?'

Both women shook their heads.

'Oh.' He looked disappointed. 'I discovered it. Never mind.'

'We'll look it up when we get back to the lab,' said Beth.

'Dan, what's your specialism?' Anna was scribbling notes.

'Beetles,' he said. He went on to explain about his projects and once he started talking Anna quite easily got him to answer her questions.

'Thank you so much, Dan,' Anna said. 'It was great to meet you.'

'Let us know what your wife says,' said Beth. She handed him a piece of paper with her and Anna's e-mail addresses on. 'I'm sure she won't mind telling the world that she's got a husband with looks as well as brains.'

Dan smiled. 'When you put it that way, I suppose she won't.' He looked back at his tree. 'I'd better get back up there and install this thing. I'll let you know what she says.'

'Do you need a leg up or something?' said Beth, even though she wasn't sure how you went about giving one.

'No need,' said Dan. 'I managed before.' He looked at them. 'Although you guys are making me a little self-conscious.'

'Sorry. We'll be off.' Beth started walking and Anna came after her. A few paces on, they turned to see Dan jump, grab a branch, walk his legs up the trunk and then haul himself up into the leaves.

'He was nice,' said Beth.

'Shame he's married,' said Anna. 'I wonder if he has a brother.'

Anna followed Beth into the tea room. Hibs, who was reading the newspaper while eating his baguette, nodded at Anna and smiled at Beth. 'So, how did you get on?'

'Pretty good, actually,' said Anna, sliding into a chair opposite Hibs.

Beth grinned. 'It's not every day a handsome man just falls out of a tree.'

Hibs looked from one woman to the other. 'Dare I ask?'

'We were walking along and this guy literally came down from a tree,' said Anna. 'Beth's got photos to prove it.'

Beth passed the camera over and Anna scooted round and stood by Hibs's shoulder. As Anna leaned over, pressing the buttons on the camera, Beth felt a wave of annoyance. Anna had placed herself so that her breasts were right in Hibs's eyeline. There was no need to help – Hibs was perfectly capable of handling the camera himself.

She tried to concentrate on making tea, but the

knowledge that Anna was flirting with Hibs made the hair on the back of her neck prickle. She fought the urge to turn around. The lab was the only place where Hibs didn't turn on the charm – she and Vik were the only ones who got to see Hibs as he really was. It was, somehow, special. She didn't mind sharing her home with Anna, but she didn't want to have to share her work space and all her friends as well.

She turned with Anna's tea just in time to see Hibs's gaze dart to Anna's chest and back again. He caught Beth's eye and had the decency to look embarrassed; then he turned back to the photos. 'Hey, I know him. That's the beetle guy from zoology.'

'That's right.' Beth thumped Anna's tea down and held her hand out for the camera. Anna finally moved her breasts away from Hibs's face.

'Did you just accost him in the park?' Hibs asked as he picked up his baguette and bit into it.

'Yes,' said Beth. She looked at the photo – there was a particularly good shot of him just dropping down from the tree. 'He's going to ask his wife if she minds him being in it.'

'I thought you only wanted single blokes.'

'What gave you that idea?' said Anna.

'Well, you did.' He looked at her.

'I personally prefer single men.' Anna winked at him. 'But for the calendar, any man will do, so long as he's drop-dead gorgeous.'

Hibs was staring at her, a small smile pulling at the corner of his mouth. 'Really? Did you find many?'

'There are some who just refuse to have their photo taken,' said Anna. 'Like you, for example.'

'Me?'

'Beth tells me you were … reluctant.'

'Did she now?'

Beth was starting to feel left out of the conversation. If they were going to continue flirting, she might have to excuse herself and go upstairs to the lab. 'I did ask you,' she said, trying not to sound peevish. 'You said no.'

'I wonder why?' said Anna. 'Are you afraid you photograph badly?'

'No.' Hibs finished his sandwich and balled up the cling film. 'I just don't want to be in the calendar.'

'That's not very nice.' Anna pouted.

Hibs gave her a wicked smile. 'Bite me.'

'Only if you ask, really, really nicely.'

Beth looked from one to the other.

Anna fancied Hibs. Hibs fancied Anna. They would end up together, briefly. Then they'd split up. Anna would be cross; Hibs would be unrepentant. Everything would be awkward. Beth sighed at the inevitability of it all.

Chapter Six

Hibs put on the suit his parents had bought him for graduation and was pleased to find it still fit. He paced round his living room, wondering what to do between now and noon. Unable to think of anything, he decided to go into the lab.

'Morning.' He threw his coat on his chair, went to his bench, pulled open his notepad and started transferring notes into his lab book. After a few minutes, he felt he was being watched. Looking up he found Beth and Vik standing at the entrance to the bay, staring at him.

'What?' he said.

'You're wearing a suit,' said Beth, not quite looking him in the eye. '*Why* are you wearing a suit?'

'I've got a lunch date.'

'A lunch date that requires a suit?' said Vik.

'Sort of.' Hibs was enjoying himself. It wasn't often he got admiring attention from Beth. He pressed his advantage. 'I'm going to Le Manoir aux Quat'Saisons. That requires a suit.'

'Le Manoir, wow.' Beth's eyes were wide.

She looked so impressed that Hibs decided that he would take her there one day. If he could find a decent excuse to take her out for a posh lunch. If she accepted. He looked away, the happy daydream punctured. She considered him a friend and nothing more. Most of the time she probably even forgot that he was male.

'So, who's taking you for lunch in the most expensive restaurant in the area?' said Beth. 'It's too pricey for normal people.'

'Winifred Tait. She's a friend of the family.' Hibs paused. 'Well, sort of. She plays bridge with my mum.'

The other two were both silent for a minute. 'So, a little old lady is taking you to lunch at Le Manoir?' said Vik, sounding puzzled.

Hibs laughed. 'Winifred Tait is no little old lady,' he said. 'She'd probably brain you with a stiletto heel if you called her that.'

Beth narrowed her eyes and wandered off without saying anything.

'Why?' said Vik.

'She likes me.' Hibs grinned.

'Do you think she wants to get you drunk and have her wicked way with you?' Vik leaned on his elbows – he always seemed to find Hibs's relationships with woman fascinating.

Hibs smiled. She didn't bother to get him drunk when she wanted to have her wicked way with him. 'No. She promised she wouldn't.' At the other end of the lab he could hear a clatter of computer keys. He guessed that was Beth Googling Winn. 'Tait's spelt T-A-I-T,' he shouted down the lab.

'What do you mean, she promised she wouldn't? You mean she tried it on once?' Vik was still looking for gossip.

Hibs grinned. 'Taught me everything I know.'

Vik gaped. 'You shagged a little old lady?'

'I told you, she's not a little old lady. She's only about ten years older than me. And it was all a long time ago. I was eighteen.'

There was a gasp from Beth. Hibs peered between the racks and could just make out the back of her head in front of the computer screen. 'Did you find her?'

'Vik, come here,' said Beth.

Hibs put his lab book away and went to stand behind her. There was a picture of Winn in her heyday, all long legs and sexy curves. 'Yeah, that's her,' he said. 'She used to be a model. She did some work for old Mr Tait and he married her.'

'Wow,' said Beth. 'Does she still look like that?'

Hibs put his head to one side. 'More or less,' he said. 'A bit older, obviously. But yeah. Pretty much. Still stunning.'

'What are you lot doing? Not more nonsense about calendars I hope.' Roger stomped in. 'If you put half as much work into your PhD as you do on your side projects, Beth, you'd have finished by now.'

'I *am* putting that much work into my PhD—' Beth began.

'Are you diversifying and putting women in your calendar?' said Roger. 'Who's she? I'd buy that.' He caught sight of Hibs. 'Why are you in a suit? Have you got a court appearance?'

Hibs rolled his eyes.

'Hibs has got a lunch date with that lady,' said Vik.

Roger took a closer look at the screen. 'Scroll down,' he ordered Beth.

Beth did so.

'She now runs the Tait textile empire ...' Roger read. He looked at Hibs. 'Is she loaded then?'

Hibs thought of the house and the enormous lawn and the scandal when old man Tait left everything to his young widow. 'I guess.'

'And you're having lunch with her because ...?'

'She's a friend. Of the family.'

'You could try persuading her that she wants to contribute to the advancement of science.'

'She's in textiles, Roger. Why would she want to work with a microbiology unit?'

'I don't know, maybe pictures of bacteria …'

'I can't anyway,' said Hibs. 'This is purely personal.' He wondered why Roger was there. 'Is there anything we can help you with, Roger?'

Roger seemed to be captivated by the pictures of Winn. 'Oh. Yes. I was after Vik, actually. Can you step into my office for a minute? I've got some paperwork I need you to sign.'

After Vik and Roger departed, Hibs watched over Beth's shoulder as she clicked through picture after picture. When she finally turned away from the screen, she shot him a curious look.

Hibs looked at his watch. 'I'd better go,' he said as he grabbed his coat. 'I'll be back to take over for the evening shift, okay?'

Beth nodded, her attention back on the screen, but as he reached the door she called him. He turned and she looked at him as though seeing him properly for the first time. 'You look good,' she said.

Hibs felt a little kick of happiness in his stomach.

After Hibs had left, Beth turned back to the photos of Winifred Tait. Vik returned and stood behind her. 'Wow. He's right. She's no little old lady. Look, she's got her own Wikipedia entry.' He pointed to the link.

Beth clicked through, curious to know more, and Vik read over her shoulder.

'Says here she married a guy who was forty years older than her and he died of a heart attack within a couple of years,' she said.

'I'm not surprised,' said Vik. 'She probably wore him out.'

'Gosh, her husband died nearly fifteen years ago. She must be nearly forty now.' She scrolled through and read the rest of the entry. 'Sounds like she's quite a businesswoman though.'

'Brains as well as beauty. No wonder Hibs went for her.'

Beth turned to look at him. 'What do you mean "went for her"?'

'They had a thing a while back. I guess you were over here when he was talking about it. He said he was only eighteen and she taught him everything he knew.'

Beth ran another search, this time with the year in it. It pulled up a recent press release showing Winifred Tait shaking hands with a businessman. She looked older, but still incredibly attractive. 'Wow.'

'He's a dark horse, our Hibs,' Vik said with admiration in his voice.

'Being seduced by an older woman isn't an achievement,' said Beth far more sharply than she'd intended.

'Being seduced by that woman is,' said Vik.

The thought suddenly struck her. 'I wonder if that's the same woman he said he had a relationship with. He said it lasted a summer and then he went to uni.' She looked back through the images. Hibs's girlfriends usually flitted through his life so fast that they were irrelevant. This woman was the last person to have connected with Hibs in any meaningful fashion. And she was beautiful, rich and sophisticated.

Beth felt a twinge of irritation and killed the browser. 'I'd better get back to work.' As she went back to her bench, she rationalised that she was merely annoyed because Hibs had kept something so important hidden from her. She'd assumed she knew everything about him. Clearly, she didn't. She flipped open her own lab book. She hadn't, for instance, seen him in a suit before. He looked different. Hot.

She filed that information away to think about later.

Hibs wasn't usually impressed with overpriced food, but he couldn't help but appreciate the cuisine at Le Manoir. Everything was prepared to perfection and, although the portions looked small, they were just enough.

As they ate, Winn brought him up to speed on gossip from home, told him about her new William Morris-inspired collection and asked him about his work. He told her about Beth and Anna and their calendar and she laughed, causing a ripple of interest among the other diners. He looked round to see people return to their own conversations. This often happened when he was out with Winn – wherever she went, people turned to look at her. She was just that sort of woman. He glanced at her, and she winked at him and leaned forward.

'It does my reputation good to be seen in public with a handsome young man,' she whispered. She laid a hand on his arm. Hibs looked down at the slim manicured fingers and suddenly he was eighteen again and the impossibly glamorous Mrs Tait, the woman all the men in the village, including his father, fancied, had stopped discussing the rhododendrons and put her hand on his thigh.

Her hand lingered on his arm and Hibs looked up at her. Over the years he'd recognised that there was more to her than the legs, the curves and the beautiful face. There was power, intelligence, determination. All the things that made her fit to run the empire her husband left to her. Mrs Tait was a wonderful, sophisticated woman and she wanted him. Just that alone was a powerful turn-on that never failed.

But this time felt different. He thought of Beth, with her jeans and T-shirt and flyaway hair. Next to Winn she was small and vulnerable and messy … and so effortlessly sexy.

As he made eye contact, Winn raised an eyebrow at him, just a tiny bit. This was his cue, but he knew he wouldn't take it. He gently moved her hand off his arm.

If he'd needed confirmation that he was in love with Beth, he had it. He'd never thought he'd see a day when he didn't fancy Mrs Tait.

Clearly Winn hadn't either: her eyebrow rose a fraction higher. 'I see,' she said.

Hibs focused on his plate and felt awful. He genuinely liked Winn's company. He had turned her down before, for various reasons, but there had always been the understanding that next time things could be different. This time, he knew it was permanent. 'I'm sorry.'

'Don't be.' She drank the last of her wine. A waitress appeared as if by magic and refilled her glass.

'So,' she said. 'Which of the two young ladies has taken your heart?'

'Pardon?'

'Oh, come on, James. How long have I known you? One of those two ladies you just mentioned means something to you. I can tell from your face and your voice. Now tell me.'

'Well … Anna fancies me,' Hibs said.

'Naturally.' Winn waved her wine glass as though to say that was a given. 'And the other one?'

'Beth. She … is a friend.'

'This would be the same Beth who was your friend last year? And the year before that?'

'Yes.'

'And you would like her to be more than a friend, I take it.'

He sighed. 'Yes. I would.'

'But?'

'But she's my friend.' He looked up at Winn, who had put down her glass and was watching him carefully. What was he doing, talking to Winifred about Beth? 'I'm sorry, Winn, I feel really weird talking to you about this.'

She laughed and leaned forward. 'What? You think I didn't know this day would come, James? No strings. That was the deal. This is lunch now. That's all.' She smiled, a genuine smile that reached her eyes. 'Oh relax, darling. You don't owe me anything.' She gave his hand a quick pat and leaned back in her seat. 'Now. Tell me. You want this girl, but you can't have her. Why not?'

Hibs stared at his hands for a moment. He had to tell someone or his head would explode with thinking about it. 'She used to have this boyfriend, Gordon. He was a real shit to her. He had to know exactly where she was at all times, that sort of thing. He was horrible, but she didn't see it.'

Winn held up a finger. 'You said "used to have". Is she no longer with him?'

'No, they split up a few months ago when he went to the US. He dumped her, just like that. She was devastated.'

'Okay. Why is he relevant now?'

'She's not over him. She was waiting for him to send her a birthday card which, obviously, he didn't. Then she was all cut up about it.'

'Right.' Winn nodded slowly and took a sip of wine. 'Perhaps she needs someone to help her move on. Why don't you …'

Hibs sighed. 'That's the problem. I can't,' he said.

'What do you mean, you can't? You've never had any trouble approaching girls before? I've heard all about your exploits at the hunt ball, young man. I know you're not shy.'

'It's not the same. Beth is … she's special. When she looks at me properly …' He thought about her compliment as he'd left the lab. 'Like today, she said I looked nice in my suit and I was so happy I didn't know what to say. It was like I was a twelve-year-old bag of hormones again. I don't know what's happening to me. It's ridiculous.'

'Oh, James.' Winn shook her head. 'Darling boy, you're in love. That's all.'

He frowned. He knew that, but was it so obvious to everyone else? Was everyone laughing at him? Did Beth know? What did she think of him if she did?

'Let's see.' She leaned forward and put her perfectly manicured fingers together. 'Everything you see reminds you of her. If she says something remotely personal, you analyse it over and over until you don't know what it means any more. You could have anything in the whole world, but nothing would compare to one small smile from her. You're in love.'

'How come you know so much about it?'

She pulled a face. 'I was in love once, you know,' she said. 'A long time ago now.'

'With whom?' He knew it wasn't him. There were other conquests though; perhaps it was one of them.

'Oh, you know how it is. Gold-digger meets sugar daddy. Gold-digger marries sugar daddy. Gold-digger falls in love with sugar daddy.'

'You were in love with *old man Tait*?'

'Oh don't look so horrified, darling. Reginald Tait was

one of the kindest, gentlest, funniest, most intelligent men I've ever met. Not the sort I'd normally go for physically, but as soul mates go, there was never anyone more perfect.' She touched the wedding ring she still wore on her finger. 'I loved him more than I thought possible. And when he died … When he died, I was lonely.' She smiled. 'And you, of all people, know how a lonely widow gets her kicks.'

Hibs gaped, still thinking about old man Tait. He couldn't remember much beyond the smell of cigars and a funeral. 'Er … right.'

'Anyway, darling, back to your problem. You're in love with this girl and you find your legendary charm has deserted you when you need it most.'

Hibs nodded. 'I can talk and joke with her like normal. It's just that I'm afraid to come on to her like I would with any other girl. I don't want her to think she's just another … She's special.'

'Well, why don't you ask her out?'

Hibs thought about it. 'I don't know,' he said. 'She might just laugh in my face and then I'll have ruined the friendship we have.'

'Is that what you're afraid of?'

'Yes. I think it is.'

'Hmm …' Winn frowned and took a sip of her drink. 'I hate to tell you this, darling, but if you don't at least *try* to ask this girl out, you're going to end up losing her.'

Hibs tapped a forefinger thoughtfully on the table. 'But what if she turns me down?'

She gave a one-shoulder shrug. 'You never know until you try.'

Chapter Seven

Hibs changed out of his suit before he returned to the lab for the evening. He took his time getting there: spring was bursting into summer and the city was beautiful. He spent so much time rushing between work, home and dojo that it was nice to be able to savour the outdoors. It also gave him space to think.

The Biochemistry building loomed ahead, the concrete turning orange in the evening glow. Beth had sent him a text to say she'd set up the microscopes for him so it was all ready for him to take photos of the bacteria every four hours. They worked well together, him and Beth.

Hibs touched his card to the sensor and let himself into the building. Night time security was faintly irritating. An hour earlier he would have been able to just walk in. Now he needed to beep his way through several safety doors.

He tramped up the stairs rather than take the lift and when he got to the lab, he was surprised to see that Beth was still there. 'Hello,' he said, as he hung up his coat. 'What are you doing here?'

'I work here,' she said, not looking up. 'How was your lunch?'

'Very nice.'

'Did the old lady make you pay for your meal in kind?'

'No. It was a no-strings-attached lunch with a friend. That's all.' He pulled on his lab coat. 'Seriously, what are you doing here? Didn't you trust me to come back in time to do the readings?'

Beth finally turned round. 'I promised Lara I'd get the calendar mocked up with the photos that we have.' She turned back to the computer. 'I'm nearly done. I'll be heading off in a few minutes.'

Hibs glanced at the screen, which had a headshot of some bloke on it. 'I'll go look at the bacteria. Back in a minute.'

The microscopes were set up so that a small number of bacteria were framed by the viewing window. Hibs used the computer to run through light flashes at different frequencies, and then waited for the protein to glow. When the glowing images appeared, he photographed them and e-mailed them to the lab. By taking photos of these cells at regular intervals, they could use time-lapse images to see how the glowing patches moved as the cells grew and multiplied.

Once he was back in the light, he peeled off his gloves and washed his hands thoughtfully.

He had no real excuse for not admitting to Beth how he felt. He kept telling himself that the time wasn't right, but the real reason was that he was scared. Scared of her rejecting him. Scared of losing the friendship that had grown so comfortable. He rubbed the bridge of his nose. Beth was acting more normally now and seemed to be getting over Gordon. Why not now?

'Come on, Hibs,' he muttered to himself as he took the stairs two at a time. 'What's the worst that can happen?'

Beth dropped the final photo, cropped and perfectly framed, into the calendar template and rubbed her eyes. It was getting late. Technically, it was her night off from the experiments, but Anna was out and she didn't fancy sitting in the flat by herself.

She did one last check before saving the file. The guys looked good. There were eleven men now. Anna was still on the hunt for the last one. Beth had done her best to capture them as handsome and sexy, without diminishing them to mere models. Some of the men were photographed in their offices, a couple in their labs. Her favourite was still the one of Dan Blackwood, in the act of landing on the ground, his blue eyes glaring straight into the camera like some sort of chino-wearing Tarzan.

Idly she flicked back to the folder of photos, scrolling through them. She was pleased with her work. In the privacy of her own mind, she admitted that they were good, very good. She hadn't lost her touch: if anything, her eye for detail had matured since she'd last taken photos seriously. She couldn't believe she'd let her interest drop like that. It was a mistake she wouldn't make again.

Beth paused at the photos of Hibs that she'd taken in jest. It was a shame he didn't want to be in the calendar, because he was so photogenic. In most of the pictures he was ignoring the camera in a slightly self-conscious manner. She scrolled though more images, and suddenly there was one where he wasn't looking away. He looked out of the screen at her, brow slightly furrowed, his lips parted as though he was in the middle of word.

She stared.

It was Hibs, but different. It was as though some of the familiarity had been stripped away, leaving behind a beautifully defined face with high cheekbones and serious grey eyes. Was this really the guy she worked next to and joked with every day?

Perhaps this was what Anna saw when she looked at him. Beth clicked ahead to the next image and the regular Hibs was back, looking reassuringly like his normal self. Beth flicked between the photos. Sexy. Normal. Sexy. Normal. Sexy. He was very good-looking – how the hell had she not noticed before? Had being with Gordon made her blind or something?

The sound of footsteps made her jump. She quickly closed down the album, just as Hibs walked in the door.

'Haven't you got a home to go to?' He went over to his desk and wrote something down.

'I was just finishing off.'

'Let's have a look.' He leaned on the desk next to her and suddenly she was very conscious of how close he was. She felt blood rush to her cheeks and hoped he didn't notice she was blushing. She pulled up the file.

'Those are really good,' said Hibs. He punched her gently on the shoulder. 'Well done, Tyler. If you ever decide to give up on science, you've got a promising career as a photographer.'

Beth sighed. 'Yeah. Good job too, the way things are going.'

Hibs frowned, moved some papers and sat on the desk. 'What do you mean? Something upsetting you? Beth?'

Beth rolled her chair back, so that there was distance between them. She still felt hot and flustered. This sudden new awareness of Hibs was disconcerting. 'No. Nothing really. I just sometimes wonder whether Roger's right.'

'About what?'

'About me not being a very good scientist. He's told before me that I only got the studentship because he couldn't have his first choice. I find it all really hard. I'm not sure I'm cut out for this.'

Hibs shook his head. 'You're looking at it the wrong way.'

'What do you mean?'

'Okay, first of all. You're doing a PhD: of course it's hard. It's bloody meant to be. Otherwise every stupid

Herman off the street would do one. Since you're doing something difficult, it's going to *be* difficult. It doesn't mean you're failing at it.' Hibs counted off on his long fingers. 'Second of all, so Roger says you were his second choice. You see it as you not being good enough to be his first choice. What it also means is that Roger's first choice got a better offer and turned Roger down. Third of all ...' He lowered his voice. 'Roger's a tosser.'

Beth stared at the rectangle of black window behind Hibs. 'I guess,' she said. 'But what about my results? Why are they so inconclusive?'

Hibs shrugged. 'Because bacteria are little buggers. If we knew what results we were going to get, we wouldn't call it research.'

Beth shook her head. Hibs was always so sure of himself. She wished she had even half that amount of self-assurance. Suddenly, she felt exhausted. Working late every other night was taking its toll already. She stifled a yawn.

'Go home,' said Hibs. 'Get some sleep. You look knackered.' He pushed away from the desk. 'I would offer to do an extra night tomorrow, but I've got to take my class to their tournament.'

'Do you think you'll win?'

'No idea,' said Hibs. 'They've been working very hard, so it would be a shame if they didn't.'

'How can you be so calm? I'd be a nervous wreck.' Beth shook her head. 'How come nothing ever ruffles you?'

'Because I'm worth it.' He grinned and pretended to flick his hair back.

Beth laughed. 'You mean you're so laid-back because of shampoo?'

Hibs rolled his eyes. 'No. I mean I'm so laid-back

because I believe in my own worth.' He waved a hand. 'Let me give you an example. When you told your parents you were going to do a PhD, what did they say?'

Beth winced. 'You know what they said.' He knew, because she'd told him.

'Tell me again.'

'My dad said I was wasting my time doing a PhD because I'd never manage it and I was trying too hard to look clever.'

Hibs pulled a face. 'Nice man, your dad.'

'He doesn't mean it like that. He's had to fight to get where he is today. He just doesn't see things the way other people do.' And he wanted a son who could take on the family business and build stuff, not a daughter who decided to go and work in a lab doing things he didn't understand.

Hibs narrowed his eyes and looked about to comment. Then he shook his head. 'Okay. So, let's just say he wasn't supportive. Yet here you are. Doing a PhD and still on speaking terms with your father. How come?'

'I persuaded him that it would lead to a better job later. I showed him some stats from somewhere that showed PhDs got better salaries.'

'So what does that tell you? You saw a problem and you worked out how to get round it.' Hibs leaned forward. 'You should have more faith in yourself.'

Beth looked at her feet. She wasn't so sure. What her father had actually said was, 'Fine, go ahead. Don't come back to me asking for money when you can't find a real job.' Not exactly a ringing endorsement.

Hibs slid off the desk and she could feel the change in the air as he moved. She looked up to find him crouched in front of her; her gaze met his eyes. They seemed to be looking right into her.

'You shouldn't undervalue yourself, Beth. You're clever, you're talented and you're beautiful. Don't let anyone tell you differently.'

Beth felt like she was falling into his eyes. He was so near she could smell his shampoo. Her gaze drifted down to his lips – he had nice lips; they looked as if they'd be soft if she were to kiss them. Then she noticed that he'd stopped speaking. What had he just said? In a panic, she looked up, only to meet his eyes again. She looked away. What was wrong with her? This was ridiculous. She'd known this man for years. He was her friend. She really shouldn't be fantasising about kissing him. That's what other women did with Hibs. She didn't want to be reduced to one of them.

'I've got to go.' She stood up abruptly, making Hibs fall backwards. Grabbing her coat, she turned to see him standing up, dusting his hands on his jeans.

'Sorry. I didn't mean to ...' She backed away from him as she pulled her coat on.

'No harm done.' He was frowning. He took a step towards her.

Beth snatched her bag off the desk. If he came near her again she might just cave in and try to kiss him or something. That would be wrong. Just wrong. 'You're right. I need to get to bed.' Did that sound suggestive? 'By myself. To sleep, I mean.' That was worse. 'Bye.' She turned and fled.

'Beth!'

She was halfway down the corridor when Hibs shouted out to her. She paused, half turned. He stood in the doorway to the lab, looking impossibly tall and beautiful. Beth felt her pulse in her throat.

'I won't be in tomorrow,' he said. 'Tournament, remember.'

'Oh. Right. Okay.'

Beth took advantage of the pause to get to the end of the corridor. She ran down the stairs and out. Once she got to her bike, she put her cycle helmet on and rested her head against the brickwork. This was insane. She had just run away from poor Hibs. All he'd done was try to be nice to her and she'd come over all flustered like some sort of great big idiot. She groaned. She'd just run out with no explanation and she hadn't even wished him luck for his tournament. 'Bugger.'

In the lab, Hibs swore. That hadn't gone well. He'd come on too strong and frightened her off. Returning to the desks, he noticed Beth's computer was on. A touch of the mouse brought up pictures of the guys on the calendar. Hibs shook his head and logged Beth off the computer.

He was busy checking his e-mail when a text arrived.

Sorry about before. I'm a bit tired, that's all. Good luck with the tournament tomorrow.

Hibs stared at his phone. Right. So what did that mean? He tapped his fingers on the desk. Beth had obviously decided that she wasn't quite as freaked out as she was initially. He leaned back in his chair and closed his eyes. Beth's image sprang into his head: her eyes wide, the way her gaze flicked between his eyes and his lips. He had been too close. She'd thought he was going to kiss her. Which had frightened her. He sighed and rubbed the bridge of his nose. He needed to be more careful with Beth. He couldn't just come on to her like any other girl. She knew him better than anyone. He had to take it much more slowly. If he moved too quickly he risked losing the comfortable connection he had with her and might alienate her completely.

Thanks. Sorry if I upset you. Didn't mean to.

He put the phone down and started saving image files, ready for analysing later. His phone beeped again. It was Beth.

No. My fault. Not enough sleep, I reckon. Sorry again.

Don't worry about it. Night night.

Night night.

Hibs stared at the phone for a few minutes before he put it away. There was something nice about a goodnight text. Like a virtual kiss on the cheek. He caught himself mid-thought. What a load of crap. She was going to bed. That was all. He was just being a soppy arse.

He put the phone in his pocket and went back to saving files. He was still smiling.

Chapter Eight

The following night, Beth was working downstairs on the microscope when the text arrived. Not wanting to risk jogging the microscope slide, she ignored it.

Once she got back to her own lab, she dug out her phone to check the message.

We won! Celebratory drinks in the Queen's Head. Shld be getting there around 7.

She smiled. Hibs sounded happy; he had been training his 'kids' hard. She leaned out from her desk to shout down the lab to Vik, who was still finishing off his work. 'Hibs and the gang won. They'll be in the Queen's Head later. You going?'

Vik appeared at the end of his bench, pulling off his gloves. 'Of course. I can't not congratulate my buddy on his win.'

'To say nothing for any pissed-up girls from his karate class?'

'Not so much. Most of Hibs's students are blokes. The few girls are a bit scary, frankly.'

'Not all of them. I think little Jenna quite likes you.'

Vik shook his head. 'No, she likes Hibs. But he won't touch his students.'

'Rightly so.'

'He's funny, Hibs. On the one hand he has no scruples whatsoever when it comes to picking up random women. On the other hand, with students and colleagues, he's all moral.'

Beth paused. 'Colleagues? Which colleagues has he turned down?'

Vik gave her a funny look. 'He just said once about students and colleagues being out of bounds.'

That was interesting to know. She hadn't given it much thought before, but he had never had a one-night stand with someone who worked on the same floor. People in labs in other areas, yes, but never anyone he worked with or saw every day. That ought to be reassuring. So why did she feel disappointed?

'He never tried to pull you, did he?' said Vik.

Beth was about to deny it when she thought about the night before and how close she'd come to kissing him. What would he have done? He probably would have kissed her back. This was Hibs after all – he was a walking one-night stand.

Other than that, he'd never come close to hitting on her. She'd been going out with Gordon from pretty much day one of her starting her PhD. Maybe if things had been different ...

'Beth?' Vik was still waiting for an answer.

'No,' she said to Vik. 'Never. We're just work mates.'

She was being silly. She and Hibs were good friends. She was probably closer to him than any other woman. You couldn't spend so many hours of each day together without building up some sort of special relationship.

Her phone beeped as another message came through. It was from Anna saying she'd pop by the Queen's Head after her late lecture.

'Hibs didn't say anything about housemates of colleagues, did he?'

By the time Beth got there, the karate club had been drinking for quite a while. The pub was noisy and busy and they were all crammed into one of the alcoves, crowded round the table in the middle. Hibs waved to her. His eyes were shining and he had the biggest smile on his face. He moved up to make space next to him on the seat.

'Congratulations,' she said, giving him a friendly poke on the shoulder. 'Well done, you lot.' She looked around at the rest of the gang. She knew a few of the older ones from going to karate club socials before. The fresh-faced kids must be new this year.

'I've got you a drink already.' Hibs slid a glass of Coke across to her. 'I bought it a while ago so it's gone a bit flat.' He pulled a face. 'I didn't know you were going to be this late.'

'It's only eight.'

'Really?' He made a show of checking his watch.

'You don't wear a watch,' she reminded him, laughing.

'Oh yeah.' He took her wrist and checked hers instead. 'Huh. I thought it was later than that.'

His fingers were warm on her wrist and suddenly Beth was very aware of her own pulse. She was sure that Hibs had checked her watch, holding her wrist in exactly the same way, before. She hadn't minded then so why did it feel so strange now? Was it simply that being single had made her somehow more aware of men in general? She looked up to find him watching her, frowning slightly. She glanced down at her wrist, which was still in his hand. He let go immediately.

'So, tell us details,' said Vik, as he squeezed in on the other side of Beth.

Beth picked up her drink and moved up next to Hibs, uncomfortably aware of how close he was.

Anna arrived in the middle of an anecdote about why martial artists shouldn't wear glasses. Beth looked up to see that Anna was wearing a tiny strappy top and more make-up than usual. Great – she was on the pull. People squished up to make room for her and Beth ended up thigh to thigh with Hibs.

He looked at her and smiled. 'Okay?'

She nodded. She was so close to him she could feel the muscles in his arm move when he lifted his drink to his mouth. If she looked up now, she would be looking straight into his eyes.

'Are you sure? You've been quiet all night.'

She looked up. He was even closer than she'd thought. He had beautiful eyes. How had she not realised before? Dammit. Why was she even noticing now?

He held her gaze for a second and Beth thought that if just one of them moved their heads, they could end up kissing. Hibs's eyebrow twitched as though the same thought had just occurred to him. He drew a breath and looked away.

Anna shouted her congratulations across the room. Hibs grinned back and asked her if she knew everyone. When she shook her head, he started making introductions.

Beth looked at her drink. This was mad. He was her friend. They'd been friends for years. Now she was all flustered just from sitting next to him. What was wrong with her?

Perhaps she was missing Gordon more than she'd realised. Was this what sexual frustration felt like? She sneaked a quick glance at Hibs, who was busy chatting to the guy sitting next to him. Thank goodness he hadn't noticed the effect he was having on her.

Beth couldn't concentrate. Anna was talking to her about the calendar, but it was taking all her focus not to jump whenever Hibs moved. Luckily, it was loud in the pub and Anna didn't seem to mind repeating herself.

'I think I've found Dr December.' Anna slid a photo across to her and Beth leaned forward to look. She was so wedged in, the movement caused her to be pushed further than she'd intended.

The man in the photo was nice enough and Beth nodded to Anna. 'We'll interview him in the next couple of days. Then we'll have the full set to take to the WIS meeting next week.'

Beth leaned back into her space and found herself leaning against Hibs's arm. While she was talking to Anna, he had encroached onto her space. She froze. Should she move forward again, and have to spend the rest of the evening doing that? Or should she go with the flow and risk things being a little too cosy? The thought of cosy was attractive. But then …

Hibs turned to look at her. She thought he was going to apologise and remove his arm. Instead he raised an eyebrow and said, 'Comfortable?'

His gaze met hers and something deep inside her glowed in response. She was suddenly acutely aware of her own breathing slowing down. Something had changed. She knew for absolute certain that she was going to let him leave his arm exactly where it was. She was going to spend the evening feeling the warmth from his lean body. Sitting too close for friendship. She had no intention of being another notch on his bedpost, but it was nice to have someone flirt with her. At the end of the night, she was sure this brief flirtation would end and things would go back to the way they had been. Until then, she may as well enjoy it. 'Yes,' she said. 'Very.'

Hibs smiled and little creases appeared by his eyes.

She'd noticed them before, but now she realised they made his eyes more gentle.

'Excellent,' he said.

Beth grinned back.

Someone said something and Hibs's attention was taken away from her. It was as though a lighthouse beam had swept past and plunged her back into darkness. Behind her back, Hibs's thumb slowly drew circles on her back. She looked across at him and he gave her a glance full of humour before he turned back to his conversation. Hibs was playing with her. So this was how he pulled in all those girls. He made them feel like they were special. The only ones in on a private joke between them. Beth smiled and turned to talk to Vik. She'd never been party to his secret before – she realised she liked it. His thumb traced another lazy circle on her back. Oh yes. She definitely liked it.

Hibs drew another circle on Beth's spine. He couldn't look at her now. If he did, his resolve might break and he would have to kiss her right there in front of everyone and Beth wouldn't thank him for that. He could tell she thought his flirting with her was just a joke.

The kid next to him was still talking about the tournament and Hibs nodded on autopilot, not really listening. Dear god, how had it come to this? He was touching up his friend. How sad was that?

She laughed at something Vik said and her head touched his shoulder. Well, she wasn't objecting. Maybe he was reading this situation all wrong. Maybe she was interested. Certainly, she'd stopped going on about Gordon. Maybe she was finally ready for someone else. He stole a glance at her. Maybe. He could ask her out.

His heart rate increased. He frowned, nervous. Nervous about asking a girl out? That hadn't happen in years. Come to think of it, he hadn't asked a girl out in years. They usually just came to him. His gaze flicked across to Anna, who had been looking at him all evening. Just like that.

Beth's lab timer, which had been set on the table amongst the glasses, went off. She jumped. 'I'd better go,' she said, giving Hibs an apologetic glance. People started to move to let her out. Bugger. That bloody timer had ruined the atmosphere. It had all been going so well up to then. He had to regain that feeling of intimacy somehow. If he let her disappear now, he might never get another chance like that.

'Will you be okay going back by yourself? Do you want me to walk with you?' Hibs said. He needed to talk to her. He couldn't treat her like any other girl. This was Beth.

'It's okay, I've got my b—' Beth started to say, but she stopped. 'Actually, that would be good. I'm not sure I have bike lights.'

'Right. Give me a minute to nip to the loo and I'll be right with you.'

Beth nodded as they both left the table. She seemed a little flushed, Hibs thought. It made her look like she was glowing. 'I won't be a minute,' he said and dashed off.

'I can't believe you brought your lab timer to the pub,' Anna said.

'It's my turn to do the night shift.' Beth pulled on her coat and her bike lights clinked in her pocket. She hoped Hibs didn't notice them when he walked her to the lab. She could have got back quicker on her bike, but she didn't want to leave Hibs right now. Not when things were starting to get interesting.

Her back tingled where his thumb had been. It wasn't a big deal that he'd offered to walk her to the lab. He always did that if she was walking anywhere alone at night. She had thought it was sweet. But what if it led to something more? There was definitely something in the air that night. If he kissed her, would she object? She thought about the creases by his eyes and how solid he'd felt next to her and she had butterflies in her stomach. No. She wouldn't object. Not at all.

In a corner of her mind, a voice reminded her about Gordon. It was unfair to muddy the waters with her friend when her heart was still bruised. But this sort of flirting meant nothing to Hibs. He would carry on as normal tomorrow. All she had to do was do the same. Besides, she reminded herself sternly, she was over Gordon. It would all be fine

She fidgeted, full of nervous energy. If she didn't get a move on, she'd be late for her next time point. 'Tell Hibs I'm heading off. He can catch up with me.' She started walking across the pub.

'Beth.'

The voice connected to something in her hind-brain and her heart picked up speed. She caught her breath – she would know that voice anywhere. Gordon. But how?

Someone caught her round the waist and spun her. 'Babe, I've missed you so much.'

Before she could say anything, Gordon kissed her. For the briefest moment she thought to protest, but her body responded to the familiar taste of him. His arms tightened around her, pressing her to him and it all felt so like old times, so right. She had missed him so much. Without pausing to think, she kissed him back.

When he finally drew away, thoughts tumbled in her head. What was he doing here? When had he come back? Why was he kissing her? 'Gordon. You ... I ... Why aren't you in America?'

'I missed you,' said Gordon, with one arm still holding her to him. He moved a wisp of hair off her cheek and her skin tingled at his touch.

She wanted to say she'd missed him too. But if he'd missed her that much, how come she hadn't heard from him in six months. Beth frowned. 'You didn't call. Or e-mail.'

He smiled, lifted her hand to his face and kissed it. 'I thought it might be too painful for you.'

He was wrong, but it was sweet that he'd worried. It didn't matter. He was back. Her heart lifted. His kiss left her so breathless and giddy, she couldn't believe she'd ever thought it was wrong to be with him. She made a last effort to get answers out of him. 'You didn't send me a birthday card.'

'I did!'

She raised her eyebrows at him.

'Didn't it arrive? I posted it in good time.'

'No.'

'Oh, babe, I'm so sorry. Did you think I'd forgotten? How could I forget?' Gordon looked so concerned that her heart melted. He was still holding her round the waist. She realised suddenly that she was not over him. She was *so* not over him.

'Beth, you didn't seriously believe I'd forget your birthday, did you? Oh, babe.' He gave her a quick kiss on the lips.

Beth didn't know what to think. 'I ... We'd split up,' she said. She suddenly remembered Hibs and flushed deeper. She shouldn't have led him on like that.

'Only because it was for the best. We were so far apart, we thought it would be best if we tried to get on with our lives,' he said, slowly, as though talking to a child. 'Remember?'

'We? You decided.'

'You agreed with me.' Gordon shook his head, as though saddened by how she'd forgotten that. 'Listen, let's not quibble about that now.'

Beth didn't want to quibble either. She wanted to kiss him and hold him and make up for all the months she'd spent without him. But how long was he back for? Was this one night, before he disappeared again? 'Are you back for good?' she asked, wishing ardently that's he'd given up on the US and decided to come back to her. Where he belonged.

'I'm back for a few months. Got seconded to a lab here. Cool, huh?'

Hallelujah! A few months wasn't as good as forever, but it was better than nothing. 'Can we go somewhere a little quieter?' Gordon cast a disapproving glance at the table where the rest of the gang were sitting. He leaned closer. 'Who are these guys anyway? They're not the usual lo— guys from the lab.'

Beth remembered why she was wearing her coat. 'I need to get back to the lab. I've got to take some photos.' Oh no – Hibs. He was expecting to walk her back.

'At this time of night?'

'It's a long story. Come on. I don't want to miss my time point.' She struggled out of his arms and made for the door. Hibs would understand. He would just move on and find someone else to chat up, like he always did.

Harmless flirting. That was all it had been. She would apologise to him later. Maybe buy her way back into his good books with cake. Cake usually worked with Hibs.

'How did you know I'd be here?' she asked, over her shoulder.

'I tried the lab and your place; you weren't there. Where else would you be?'

Which just went to show how little life she had when Gordon wasn't around.

As she hurried out she caught sight of Hibs staring at her and Gordon, scowling like fury. She gave him an apologetic smile. He was going to give her a hard time about Gordon. He never did get on with him.

Hibs stared after Beth as she and Gordon disappeared. What the hell had just happened? He had emerged from the loo to see Beth standing in the middle of the pub snogging Gordon the Git.

He felt like he'd been kneed in the stomach. Where had he come from? Things had been going so well with Beth. It looked like there was a real possibility of something happening that evening. For the first time ever she'd noticed him as something other than a friend, and then that fuckwit had somehow materialised to ruin everything. He wanted to run after them and tear him away from her. He wanted to—

'So, who was that?' A voice interrupted his furious thoughts.

Hibs returned to surroundings. 'What?' He found Anna standing next to him, her hands in her back pockets, breasts thrust out towards him.

'That guy who just kissed Beth. Let me guess … it was Gordon.'

'What happened?' he said. 'I thought she was going to the lab.'

'She said she was setting off because you were taking too long and then this bloke walks up to her and kisses her.' Anna looked thoughtfully at the door. 'It was quite romantic in a weird sort of way.'

'He just grabbed her and kissed her? Just like that?'

Anna nodded, grinning at him. 'I can show you how, if you like.'

Hibs stared at her and suddenly realised how annoyed he must look. His gaze took in his karate students, who were whispering amongst themselves, and Vik, who was watching him carefully. He couldn't lose his cool in front of them. 'Sorry,' he said. 'Gordon rubs me up the wrong way, that's all.'

'I get it.' Anna put a hand on his arm. 'I could rub you the other way, if it would help you feel better.'

Hibs tried to focus on her. There was no doubting he was in there. Anna raised her cute eyebrows at him and winked.

'Anna, I'm sorry. I don't really need a relationship right now.'

Anna shrugged. 'Excellent.' She slid a hand over his shoulder. 'That makes two of us.'

What the hell. It wasn't as though he was going to get a better offer. He forced a smile. 'I need to spend a bit more time with my friends,' he said. 'You're welcome to stay.'

'I'd love to.' She slipped her arm through his and went back to the table. When the guys shuffled up to make a space for him, she sat on his lap.

Chapter Nine

'I'll be about five minutes,' Beth said as she pulled on latex gloves and grabbed a lab book.

'Okay. I'll wait here.' Gordon flung himself into a chair and put his feet on her desk. He grabbed a draft paper that Hibs was proofreading and started to skim though it.

Beth paused. 'Don't touch anything.'

Gordon gave her an injured look and carried on reading.

Beth hurried down to the microscope room, turning lights on as she went. She shut the door to the room behind her, leaned against it and let out a deep breath. Gordon was back. On the walk over from the pub, he had slipped his arm around her waist like he had always done and they caught up with what had been happening while they'd been apart – in Beth's case, not much; in Gordon's, a whole lot.

She couldn't believe that he had come back. He was back for a whole six months and he still wanted to be with her. Rolling back her sleeve, she pinched herself. Ow. Yes, it was definitely happening. A huge smile tugged at her mouth. Once she'd taken these photos, she'd have four hours to spend with him before she had to take the next set. Four whole hours to catch up with Gordon. She was so happy she felt she could fly. She took another deep breath and tried to force herself calm. She had to keep a steady hand for these photos.

After a few more breaths she had her emotions under control. She checked that there was nothing lying around to trip her up and turned out the main lights. In the eerie red light, she found the first of the microscopes, turned the camera on as carefully as possible and grabbed the image.

She practically flew back upstairs to Gordon. He was leaning forward, looking through something else on her desk.

'I'm done for another few hours,' she said as she binned her gloves and washed her hands.

'What's this?' Gordon held up a list of names.

'Those are the guys who responded to our advert for the calendar.'

'Calendar?'

She told him what it was about.

He frowned. 'That sounds like you're desperate to find a man.'

'I'm not looking for a man.' She felt a stab of guilt that she'd even been thinking about snogging Hibs. It had made sense at the time, when she'd thought that she and Gordon had no hope. It was clear to her now that she'd been wrong. He wouldn't have kissed her like that if they were over. 'Technically,' she said, cautiously, 'I am single.'

'No you're not. You've got me.' He came over to her and touched her cheek. 'Beth, when I told you earlier that I was afraid it would be painful for you if we were in touch ... I lied. I didn't call or text because it was too painful for me.' He took both her hands in his big warm ones. The sensation awoke more memories of happy times with him. His eyes met hers, so beautiful they were almost hypnotic.

Gordon continued, 'I really thought I loved the job more than I loved you, but it hurt me being away from you. I thought going cold turkey was the best way to get over it, but I was wrong. There wasn't a day that went by when I didn't think about you … us. We made a stupid, stupid mistake splitting up. I … would like us to try again. If you …' He placed her hands over his heart. 'If you'll have me.'

It was as though Gordon's thoughts had been linked to her own. He had just articulated everything she'd felt during their separation. Any residual anger at the lack of contact evaporated. Her heart sang. Her Gordon was back. Happiness broke over her, making her tingle. All was right with the world again. 'I missed you too,' she said. 'I'm glad you're back.'

Anna kissed Hibs when they got into the lift up to Beth's flat. Kissing Anna made him forget that he wasn't kissing Beth. By the time the doors pinged open, her top was in his hands. She managed to open the flat with one hand while the other was still inside his shirt. Hibs was impressed. They tumbled into the flat, kissing furiously and tearing clothes off each other. The kitchen light was on and, as they passed, Hibs dimly registered that Gordon's jacket was on the table. He pushed the thought to the back of his mind and followed Anna into her room.

Afterwards, he lay in the dark, his fingers idly ruffling Anna's spiky hair. He had been right about her. Skilled. She was currently asleep, with her leg thrown across him. She had jumped him, without much encouragement. He liked that. He never had to work hard on women, but it was still flattering to have an attractive woman just grab him.

He thought about Gordon and Beth. If only he'd made his move sooner. Beth would have been with him and Gordon would have had to bugger off. Just ten minutes and things would have worked out differently. Hibs sighed. There was no point thinking about what might have been. He had to face the fact that it was Gordon that was in Beth's bed now and he was in Anna's.

Anna was Beth's housemate ... which could make things awkward. He had been so angry about Gordon's reappearance that he'd gone with Anna when she propositioned him, almost out of revenge. Which was, even by his own standards, a stupid thing to have done.

Now he couldn't come back to Beth's house for a while. Anna stirred and her hand came up and rested on his nipple. Hibs smiled – she wouldn't take long to get over it. Her fingers moved, caressing him, and he realised she wasn't asleep at all. He looked down at her and she smiled, her eyes still closed. Okay. It may have been a mistake to sleep with her, but now was not the time to dwell on it.

Beth opened her eyes and the first thing she saw was Gordon. A sliver of sunlight sneaked in through the gap in the curtains and fell on his golden brown hair, making it glow. She pinched herself again to check she wasn't dreaming. Ouch. No. He really was back. She propped herself up on her elbow and watched his smooth, well-muscled chest rise and fall. She had dreamed about this so often in the past six months, and here he was again. Back where he belonged. To think she had almost thrown it all away. If Gordon had turned up five minutes later, she would have been walking to the lab, flirting with Hibs.

The thought of Hibs brought a small tingle to the base of her spine. She cast a guilty glance at Gordon. She was so lonely she had even been thinking she might kiss Hibs. What a disaster that would have been. She would have missed Gordon and ruined a perfectly good friendship with Hibs just because she'd let her frustrations get the better of her. Well, that was a lesson learned. She should have trusted her instincts and waited for Gordon to come back to her.

There were muffled noises from the next room. Anna must have pulled some unsuspecting bloke last night. The thought that it might be Hibs crossed her mind and she frowned. It was quite likely to be Hibs, now that she thought of it. Anna definitely fancied him. Well, that could make things awkward. But if they made each other happy … A sudden wash of annoyance and hurt surprised her. Pulling random people was what Hibs did. She shouldn't let it bother her. Besides, if she'd wanted to be one of his floozies, she'd had the opportunity yesterday. Thank goodness Gordon had returned and saved her from making a stupid mistake. She shifted position to look back at him sleeping peacefully beside her.

Gordon's breathing changed and he opened his eyes. Beth decided she was too happy to care about Hibs or Anna.

'Good morning.' She planted a kiss on his shoulder.

'Morning. What time is it?' His voice was still slurred with sleep.

'Only about seven.'

He smiled. 'I don't need to be at the department until nine. Which gives us plenty of time.'

Beth smiled back. 'Plenty of time for …?'

'Come here, you.' He kissed her, pulling her to him, and Beth melted. She had missed this so much. She could go on kissing him forever.

Chapter Ten

'So he just grabbed you and kissed you? Just like that? Before he even said hello?' Lara put down her cup.

'Yes,' said Beth. 'Isn't it romantic?'

'Presumptuous, more like. What if you had a boyfriend?'

'But I don't.'

Lara rolled her eyes. 'But if you had. He could have caused a major problem for you, just kissing you like that.'

Beth considered. Lara might have a point, but it was pretty irrelevant. If she'd had a boyfriend, she would have been with him and Gordon would have had the sense to leave her alone. 'Yes, but it's no big deal. Because I don't have a boyfriend.'

'He didn't know that though. He just marched in and grabbed you, regardless. I call that thoughtless at best.'

Beth was disappointed. She had expected Lara to be supportive or, at least, marginally happy for her. All the time that Beth had been depressed about breaking up with Gordon, Lara had listened and made soothing comments, gently urging her to move on and meet other people. Now that Beth finally had what she was longing for, she had expected Lara to be as happy as she was.

Beth regarded her friend over the rim of her coffee. Lara looked tired. Maybe that was why she was being so unlike her usual supportive self. Perhaps it was time to change the subject. 'So, what are you and Chris up to this weekend? Anything fun?'

Lara didn't answer and stared at her coffee.

'Lara? Is there something wrong?' Beth thought about Lara's hesitation when Hibs had asked about Chris the other day. 'Is something going on with Chris?'

Lara faltered in the act of picking up a flapjack. 'What?' She avoided looking at Beth.

'You're acting really strange. Are you sure you're okay?' Beth waited, watching Lara. Lara wasn't given to outpourings of emotion, so it was hard to be sure, but she knew something wasn't right. The trouble with extremely rational people was that they were often the last people to admit they needed help.

Lara carefully put her cappuccino down and sucked in her top lip to get the foam off it. 'No,' she said, finally. 'I'm not sure I am.' When she looked up, there were tears gathering in her eyes. 'I think Chris is having an affair.'

'Oh, Lara, no. Are you sure it's not a misunderstanding? What makes you think that?' Beth pictured Chris. He seemed quite nice, but then, didn't they all. She remembered the leap of faith it had taken for Lara to admit that she'd fallen in love with him. He had been so desperate to be with her. It was impossible to imagine that he could cheat on her.

Lara shook her head. 'I've suspected for some time,' she said. 'He's been working funny hours. Coming home really late most nights …'

'But he's always done that,' said Beth. 'He works in London. It is a long commute.'

'Yes, but he used to tell me about his day. Now he just says, "Oh, the usual," and changes the subject. And he jumps in the shower as soon as he gets home. I mean, literally. He's in the door and straight upstairs for a shower. I asked him about it and he said he couldn't bear the grime in London.'

'It is pretty grimy ...'

A tear rolled down Lara's cheek. 'He's started locking his phone. He said it was because he didn't want to it unlocked at work in case someone played a silly joke on him. I found it on the bed last night. He'd forgotten to lock it and I looked at his text messages ...' She scraped the tear away with the side of her hand. 'He's definitely having an affair.'

Beth put her hand over Lara's. 'Oh, Lara.'

Lara turned her hand over and gripped Beth's. They sat there in silence for a moment as Beth tried frantically to think of a reason for Chris to have compromising text messages on his phone. There had to be some other explanation.

'It wasn't a joke or something?'

'No. The texts were pretty explicit,' said Lara. There was a peculiar flatness to her tone as she stirred her drink with fierce concentration.

'Maybe—'

'Beth.' Lara dropped her hand. 'I know what I read, okay? I know you don't like to believe bad stuff happens, but it does. It happens to everyone. Now it's happening to me.' Lara pushed her hair back with both her hands.

Beth was silent for a minute, taken aback by Lara's outburst. She had only been trying to help. But this wasn't about her. It was about Lara. Lara had given up a lot to be with Chris because she loved him. She didn't deserve for this to happen to her.

'What are you going to do?'

Lara shook her head. 'I don't know.' She picked up her napkin and dabbed away another tear.

Beth squeezed Lara's other hand. 'What did he say when he realised you'd seen the texts?'

'He doesn't know. I locked the phone and left it where I found it.'

'And this morning?'

'He flew past me on his way out to catch the train, just like every morning.' Lara looked at her hands. 'I guess we haven't really been communicating for some time now.'

'Lots of couples are like that.'

Lara shrugged. 'It used to be okay. We used to do stuff together at the weekend. Now he works Saturdays and Sundays and he never seems to want to do anything with me.' She sighed and blew her nose. 'I can't carry on like this. I'm going to have to say something.'

'What sort of something?'

'I'm going to have to ask him to choose. Her or me.' Lara stared ahead. 'I bet he chooses her.'

'He won't. He'd have to be an idiot to lose you.'

Lara shook her head. 'He's already lost me. I'll never trust him again. If he chooses her, I know what to do then. It's almost worse if he chooses me. We'd have to figure out a way to salvage this relationship and I don't know how to do that. I almost *want* him to choose her.'

'But he might not. He might realise that what you have is worth fighting for.'

Lara shook her head. 'I don't know that it is. What we have isn't a relationship. It's a habit.'

'But you can change that if you work on it. Some things are important and worth fighting for.'

'Beth, I know you're trying to help, but please shut up. The only good reason for staying with someone is if your life is happier with them than without them. Chris and I … I'm not sure he makes me happy any more.'

Beth didn't know what to say. Lara and Chris had been a constant in her adult life. They were supposed to always be there, like her parents were. She tried to imagine Lara single and on the pull like Anna, and failed completely. No. Lara and Chris were Lara and Chris. She looked at her friend, who had regained some of her composure and was lining the sugar sachets up in an immaculate row. Lara was in pain and she wished there was something she could do to help.

'I can ask Hibs to beat him up for you,' she suggested, only half joking. Hibs would probably say no, but then he liked Lara, so maybe ...

Lara gave her a long look before managing a weak smile. 'Thanks. That's sweet. I think.'

Hibs knocked over a conical flask and spilled growth media all over his bench. He swore, pulled a handful of blue paper towel from the dispenser and started to mop it up before the stuff went everywhere. He was stuffing the soggy paper into the bin, still swearing, when Beth came back. He ignored her and carried on cleaning up.

'What happened?' Beth shrugged on her lab coat as she entered the bay.

'Spillage. It's fine. I've got it under control.'

'You're sure you don't need a hand?'

He still couldn't look at her. He wasn't sure what made him angry. The fact that he'd been sure he was getting somewhere with her and then she'd gone off with someone else, or the fact that she'd let that wanker Gordon take her for a ride again. Unfortunate choice of words. He closed his eyes. It had to be the latter reason. He'd spent ages slowly trying to get her out of the destructive rut that Gordon had put her into and now, in one night, Gordon had waltzed in and put her right back again. Yes. That was why he was feeling so angry. Definitely.

They worked in frosty silence for a while. Hibs tried to

focus on the cultures he was setting up, but his thoughts kept drifting back to the sight of Beth and Gordon kissing. The very thought made him queasy. He remembered Anna and felt marginally guilty. It was a revenge shag, but Anna was aware of the fact and didn't seem that bothered by it. His kind of girl. He liked Anna. He could be happily not-committed to her for a while.

He lit his Bunsen burner and held a wire loop in the flame to sterilise it. As he watched it, it grew hotter and hotter, glowing first red hot, then white.

'Hibs.' Beth's voice made him jump. 'Is something wrong?'

He turned to find her standing behind him, arms crossed, brow furrowed. Everything about her said she was annoyed. At what? He hadn't done anything.

'Actually,' he said, 'something is. Gordon. That's what's wrong.'

'What about Gordon?' Her chin rose: she was ready to defend her precious Gordon.

Hibs smacked down the inoculating loop he'd been heating. It hit the desk with a sizzle. 'I can't believe you let him waltz back into your life like that. After all the crap he put you through.'

'He didn't put me through any crap. He was away.' Her voice was taut.

'Yes and while he was away he didn't give you a second thought. Now that he's back, he fancies a quick shag so he comes to see you. You just roll over and let him in.'

Beth's jaw dropped. 'I can't believe you just said that.'

'Well it's true.' He should stop, but he couldn't help himself. 'And you know I'm right. He didn't even text you on your birthday. Those aren't the actions of a man who's thinking about you.'

She took a small step back, away from him. 'He sent a card. It just got lost in the post. He ...' She stopped talking and scowled. 'I don't have to explain to you.'

'You don't seriously believe that crap about the post?' He was shouting now. 'Oh come on, Beth!'

'Why would he lie?' Beth glared at him. 'You're just being a git because you never liked him.'

'And you're being a blinkered idiot.' Hibs raised his hand to push his hair back but, spotting his gloves, lowered it again with a frustrated *ugh*. 'Face facts, Beth. He's using you. He used you before and he's using you again. He treats you like crap and if you can't see that, you're even stupider than Roger thinks you are!'

Beth's eyes widened. To his horror, they filled with tears. She made a choking noise and ran out of the room, tearing her lab coat off as she fled.

Hibs groaned and sank back onto his stool. He shouldn't have said that. That made him almost as bad as Gordon. Shit. He'd spent months being the supportive friend all his reading said he needed to be; trying to help her rebuild the self-esteem that Gordon had taken away. Now he'd undone it all. He kicked the bench, making the jars rattle and hurting his foot. 'Bollocks.'

Beth dried her face using the scratchy paper hand towel. Her face was all blotchy now and her eyes were puffy – she'd never managed to recover from tears gracefully. Her skin felt taut and dry but all she had at work was hand cream. That would have to do.

She went into the tea room, which was mercifully empty, to make herself a drink. As she waited for the kettle to boil, she reflected on why she felt so awful. She'd been called stupid before. Her father did it; Roger did it.

Even Gordon sometimes liked to make out she was silly in a cute way. But Hibs had always, always told her she was better than she thought she was. Whenever she was at her lowest, Hibs was the one who believed in her. Now even he thought she was stupid.

The really annoying thing was that Hibs's reasoning was … well … stupid. He didn't know the first thing about love. This was a man who had managed to sleep with lots of women, but not be in a committed relationship for ten years. He wouldn't recognise true love if it came and bit him on the backside. He couldn't be expected to understand the feeling of completion she had when she was with Gordon. That she and Gordon were meant for each other. The few months of separation had turned out to be a good test for the strength of their relationship. Gordon had tried to be away from her and he'd come back. At some level, she'd always known he would. She thought about her brief temptation towards Hibs and felt guilty. Now *that* would have been really stupid.

She sighed and picked up her mug. If Hibs was going to be an idiot about her and Gordon, that was a shame. She'd just have to find a way to deal with it.

When she got back to the lab, Hibs was at the other end, carefully pipetting samples into a gel. On her bench she found a rectangle of blue paper towel stuck to the desk with autoclave tape. It read, 'I'm sorry. I'm a total fuckwit. H'

Beth stared at it, for a moment unsure what to think. It was an apology. It didn't change the facts, but it was an apology.

'Am I forgiven?'

She turned to find him standing behind her, a sheepish expression on his face.

'I shouldn't have said that,' he said.

'No, you shouldn't. Me and Gordon, that's my business.'

'You're right. I felt, as your friend ... Well, never mind. As you say. It's none of my business.' He didn't meet her eyes. 'I'm sorry, okay?' Finally, he made eye contact. 'Still friends?'

Beth smiled, surprised to find that she felt relieved. 'Yes. Just don't do it again.'

'Scouts honour.'

She rolled her eyes. 'You were never a boy scout.'

'I was too. Not a very good one, mind. Couldn't get my head round knots. And camping. Ugh.'

She grinned. 'Wally.'

R U doing anything tonite? Dinner at mine? Anna

Hibs frowned. He had to be careful: he didn't want Anna to think he was after anything more than a one-night stand.

I can't. Am working + I don't do commitment. Very sorry if I gave you the wrong idea.

Dur. I get that. So, do you fancy a shag or not? Dinner optional.

Hibs chuckled. He liked this girl. She was like a female version of him.

When you put it like that ... Sure. Why not.

'Texting your older woman again, are you?' said Beth.

'No.' Hibs wondered if she knew that he'd spent the night with her housemate. He decided she didn't. She was bound to be annoyed with him when she found out. Perhaps it was better to tell her now. 'Beth—'

Beth's mobile rang. To Hibs's irritation, she held up a finger to tell him to hold that thought and answered it. Her features immediately changed to that insipid expression she always seemed to wear when Gordon was about.

'Hello you.' She turned her back to Hibs. 'Sure. No, I'm not working tonight. Hibs is doing the night shift.' She listened for a moment and said, 'No, we're running our experiments in tandem, so we're covering for each other. I told you.'

Hibs tried to concentrate on what he was doing, but it was impossible not to earwig. He was sure Gordon wouldn't like the idea of Beth working that closely with someone. Sure enough, Beth said, 'It's the only way we'll get things done.' At the end of the sentence, the change in volume told him she'd looked over her shoulder. 'Can we talk about this some other time? I'm in the lab.'

She made arrangements to meet him and hung up.

'Hot date?' Hibs tried, and failed, to keep the sarcasm out of his voice. 'Taking you somewhere nice?'

'Well not Le Manoir,' Beth snapped back.

'Oh, right. I'm sorry I spoke.'

Beth sighed. 'Sorry. I'm a little oversensitive since … you know. Anyway. Yes, he's taking me to that new French place.'

'That's nice. Big reunion meal, is it?'

'I guess so.'

She sounded happy. He should be glad about that, but the image of Gordon kissing Beth flashed into mind again and he felt a wave of bile.

'How about you?' said Beth. 'Was that a date for tomorrow?'

'No. Just arrangements for a quick drink tonight.'

'Karate people?'

'No. A girl I got to know last night.'

Vik, who was fiddling about with a water bath nearby, looked up. 'You mean—'

Hibs cut him off. 'Yeah. Her.'

Vik gave him a puzzled frown. When Hibs shook his head the tiniest bit, Vik looked away.

He wondered if Beth would pursue it further, but she said, 'That's nice,' and wandered off, humming to herself.

Once Beth was out of earshot, Vik came round. 'Why don't you want Beth to know you got off with Anna?'

'Because things aren't exactly amicable between me and Beth today. Can you imagine how much worse it would be if she found out I shagged her housemate, after she specifically asked me not to?'

'From where I was sitting, it looked like Anna came on to you.'

'She did.'

Vik was watching him carefully. 'Before that, I'd have said you and Beth were getting more pally than usual. What's going on there?'

'Nothing.' If only. If only. His heart squeezed with sadness. 'We're just friends. We've been friends for a long time. I was a bit drunk. You know how it is.'

Vik nodded, slowly. 'Okay.' He looked down at his hands. 'You seemed pretty pissed off when the boyfriend turned up.'

'Ex-boyfriend at the time,' said Hibs. 'He's not good to her. You weren't here the last time. You'll see what I mean soon enough.'

Chapter Eleven

Beth took care getting ready. The dress she chose was one Gordon had complimented her on before and she even painted her toenails. She wanted to look just perfect for their first date. Their second first date, if that made any sense. After a final check of her make-up, she went into the kitchen to find Anna humming a tune from *Dirty Dancing* while she put a pan of water on to boil.

'Wow!' said Anna. 'You look great.'

'Thanks.' Beth helped herself to a glass of water, taking care not to smudge her sparse lipstick. Gordon didn't like her to wear too much 'war paint' as he called it, but a little was pretty much obligatory.

'So, are you doing anything this evening?' Beth flicked through a magazine, too nervous to sit down.

'Uh huh. Hibs is coming round.'

Beth froze. 'Hibs?'

Anna grinned. 'Oh yeah, you left kinda early last night so you wouldn't know. He slept over last night.' She stared into space for a moment, smiling. 'Well, I say slept ...'

There was an acid twist in Beth's stomach. But Hibs had been flirting with *her*. Then she remembered Gordon and felt guilty for even thinking that. Hibs was a free agent and so was Anna. Why shouldn't they be together? She had to pull herself together: Anna was watching her.

'Wow,' she said. 'That's ... good.'

Anna raised her eyebrows. 'You're not impressed,' she said, flatly. 'Why is that?'

Flustered, Beth thought quickly. 'He's a great guy, but he's not really into commitment. He hasn't had a long-term relationship since he was in his teens. I ... I don't want you to get hurt.'

Anna shrugged. 'I can look after myself. I've done the long-term relationship thing and I've only just been released. I don't intend to get trapped like that for a while. He's got nothing to worry about.'

'Right,' said Beth. 'Well, in that case, it's great news.'

Anna's smile widened. 'Oh yes, it is. That guy knows some *amazing* things. And what he can do with those long fingers ...' Her eyes glazed as she stared into space again. 'He can bend his tongue right back on itself. Weird, but useful.'

Beth looked for an excuse to cut the conversation short. She really did not want to hear about Hibs's sexual skills. 'He's working tonight.'

'I know. But there's all that time between readings,' said Anna. 'You can get a lot done in an hour or two.' She was grinning again.

Beth looked away. The burn in her stomach was back. Why was she feeling like this? It wasn't like Hibs was ever single for long. She'd never cared about any of those other women. But this time he was having sex with her housemate, in her flat ... somehow that was different.

'Beth? Are you okay?'

Beth realised she must have pulled a face. She quickly forced a smile. 'Sure. Why wouldn't I be?'

'You just looked ...' Anna put her palms on the table and leaned forward. 'You are okay with this? You know, me and Hibs. You said you didn't have a problem before.'

'No, no. I don't have a problem. I'm just nervous about my date with Gordon, that's all.'

'Are you sure? 'Cause if it's a problem, we could always go to his place.'

She noticed that Anna hadn't offered to end her

dalliance with Hibs, merely to take the action elsewhere. 'Hibs doesn't take women to his place.'

'Huh? What do you mean?'

'It's one of his rules. He likes to keep his women distanced from him own space.'

Thankfully, the doorbell rang, saving her from having to say any more. Her heart rose to her throat and she rushed to let Gordon in.

Gordon was fiddling with his phone. When he looked up, his gaze started at her face and went down to her feet and back up again. She tensed, suddenly wondering if she was wearing too much make-up, or if she'd put on weight since he'd last seen her.

Beth nearly melted with relief when he smiled and said, 'Nice dress,' in an appreciative voice. He kissed her. 'You look stunning. Ready to go?'

'Yes. I'll just get my bag.'

Gordon followed her inside.

Anna was still in the kitchen, throwing handfuls of pasta into the boiling water. 'Hello,' she said. 'You must be Gordon.' She wiped her hand on a tea towel and held it out. 'I'm Anna.'

'Pleased to meet you, Anna. Do I take it you're the new flatmate?'

'I am indeed.'

'Sorry,' said Beth. 'I didn't get chance to introduce you two last night. It all happened a bit quickly.'

Gordon turned and smiled. 'It did, didn't it?' He held out his arm to her. 'Shall we go?'

Beth nodded and fell into step beside him. He wrapped his arm around her waist and pulled her to him. The familiar weight of his arm made Beth feel warm inside. She had forgotten the sheer knee-wobbling thrill of being with Gordon. She belonged with him. That thing last night with Hibs had just been an aberration.

'Have a good evening,' she said to Anna, as she left. 'Say hi to Hibs.'

Thankfully, Gordon waited until they were outside the flat before he said, 'Is Anna sleeping with Hibs?'

'Apparently,' said Beth.

Gordon laughed. 'Nice to see that Hibs hasn't changed.'

'Hmm.'

'What? Something wrong?' He frowned and the tone of his voice sharpened.

Beth felt a twinge of unease. 'No, not really. It's just awkward having my flatmate seeing my work mate.'

He gave her an odd look. 'Why should that be awkward?'

Beth shrugged. Gordon was holding a little too tightly round her waist. It made it hard to walk without tripping over. Had he always done that? 'I don't know,' she said. 'I guess it's okay now. It'll just be difficult when he dumps her in a few weeks.'

'You seem very confident that he will.'

'That's what usually happens.'

'She seems pretty lively. I'm sure she can handle him.'

They walked on. Beth decided she'd just never noticed how uncomfortable it was to walk when someone taller than you was trying to tether you to their hip. She'd not minded before. So why did she now?

She looked up at Gordon's golden features. The regal nose, the perfect mouth. God, he was gorgeous. People noticed them when they walked past. It was as though Beth was normally invisible and Gordon suddenly brought her into the light. Gordon smiled at her. That was worth a little discomfort.

* * *

Dinner was wonderful. The atmosphere was buzzing, the food was good, the wine was too. But it was the company more than anything that set Beth's heart aflame. Gordon looked so handsome and it was just wonderful to be sitting opposite him again. The painful months when she'd been apart from him faded from her mind, unable to compete with the sheer joy of having him there again.

'Shall we go to the pictures tomorrow?' Gordon said. 'There's a new movie out that I'd like to see.'

'Oh, I can't. I'm working tomorrow night.'

Gordon frowned. 'Working? At night?'

'I told you, I'm taking it in turns with Hibs to do the night shift. We're running these experiments simultaneously, remember?'

'I thought that was just a one-off.'

'No. It's every other night for the next four weeks.' She was sure she'd told him this the night before. 'I did tell you.'

Gordon's frown deepened. He appeared to be focused on his coffee. 'I see.' He looked up, the frown gone. His clear eyes looked deep into hers. 'I was just so excited to see you I must have forgotten.'

Aw. That was sweet. Beth smiled back. 'That's okay. I can see you the night after, though. Is that okay?'

'I guess so. And this is every other night for the next few weeks?' He took a sip of coffee. When she nodded, he said, 'So, what do you do when you're working at night?'

'I take a reading every four hours. Since I've got the lab to myself, I tend to do other work for a bit.' She tucked a wisp of hair behind her ear. 'I usually go home and sleep in between the two early-morning readings though.'

'Sounds like hard work.' He leaned forward and covered her hand with his. 'Poor Beth.'

She laughed. 'It's not the greatest, but it has to be done.' She explained again about Roger and the presentation. 'I think he's wrong. The results should show that.'

'Wait. You think he's wrong?' said Gordon. 'That's a bit presumptuous, isn't it? He's your supervisor.'

Beth stared. What sort of logic was that? 'What's that got to do with anything? It's my project.'

Gordon raised his hands as though surrendering. 'Hey. Don't get all defensive, babe. I don't mean that you're not good at your job. I'm just saying that Roger *is* an expert in the area. He knows an awful lot about the subject.'

'Yes, but he's not being objective. He's picked a pet theory and is trying to fit the evidence round it.'

'So are you.'

Why was Gordon taking Roger's side? He was her boyfriend. He was supposed to be supporting her. 'The pictures should show things one way or the other.' She glared at him, riled enough to risk upsetting him. 'I resent the implication that I don't know what I'm talking about.'

Gordon held up his hands. 'Woah, I never said that. I would never say that.' He squeezed her hand. 'Hey, don't frown. We don't want to ruin a perfectly nice evening by arguing over something unimportant.'

Beth let her face relax. He was right. This evening was too precious to waste talking about work. What he said still niggled, but she'd worry about it later.

'Sorry,' she said. 'You're right.'

Gordon's gaze met hers. It was as though she was floating into his eyes. The rest of the room receded.

He cleared his throat. 'I was going to wait until the end of the night, but ...' He reached into his pocket and pulled out a small parcel.

For a moment she thought he was getting out a ring

and she panicked. She wasn't prepared for marriage. Not yet.

He handed her the parcel, small but flat and wrapped in paper. Okay. Probably not a ring box then. She took it, her hand trembling a little. 'What is it?'

'Open it.'

She carefully peeled the package open. Inside was something small and heavy, wrapped in tissue paper. She released it from the paper and dropped it into her hand. A delicate silver brooch nestled in her palm. She moved it, watching the candlelight slide along its smooth lines. 'Oh, Gordon.'

'Do you like it? It's not exactly like the one you saw when we were in Devon, but it was as close as I could get.'

She looked up into his blue, blue eyes. That weekend in Devon had been magical and romantic. At a time when her PhD was particularly stressful, the long walks on the beach and candlelit picnic that Gordon arranged had been the perfect antidote. 'It's beautiful. Thank you.' Her voice gave way with emotion.

'Not nearly as beautiful as you.' Gordon took her free hand in his big warm one. 'My Beth.'

Happiness lapped at her heart. No one could make her happy like Gordon could. Life was good again.

As they walked home, Gordon still holding Beth tightly to his side, he said, 'This calendar of yours, what sort of guys do you have in it?'

'Blokes with science PhDs,' said Beth, cautious that Gordon might not approve. He could be a bit possessive and she didn't want to have to argue with him about the calendar. She had forgotten just how much she enjoyed photographing people. When she was behind the camera, she forgot everything else and her whole being was focused though the viewfinder. Unsure where his line of questioning was going, she added, 'Good-looking ones, obviously.'

'Obviously.' His mouth twitched into a half smile. 'So, whose idea was that? Anna's?'

'Mine, actually.'

'Really? You are full of surprises.' His smile seemed genuine, without any trace of annoyance.

He was being remarkably agreeable about this. Perhaps she had misunderstood when she'd thought he disapproved. Feeling slightly bolder, she sketched out how she and Anna had interviewed the men and photographed them. She even told him about the naked guy. He laughed and Beth relaxed.

'So, how many have you interviewed then? Did you have loads of men throwing themselves at your feet?'

'We were lucky to find twelve,' Beth said. 'The choice was small ...' Then, thinking of Anna and Lara's stringent criteria of who was a 'fit' man, added, 'And the judging was pretty harsh.'

'I'd be happy to be in your calendar,' Gordon said.

Beth looked up at him; he was so beautiful. 'And I'd love to photograph you,' she said. 'But we've got all the guys we need.'

'So? You could move one off.'

'I can't do that!' Beth was horrified at the thought and surprised that Gordon had suggested it as though it were nothing. 'We've already told them they're going to be in it.'

'What's the point of being in charge of a project if you can't change your mind?'

Beth felt her shoulders start to bunch up. The feeling was familiar. Why was that? She didn't remember being tense around Gordon before. She threw a quick glance at him. 'I can't change anything. Besides, I don't think it would be right to.'

There was a pause, a mere heartbeat. 'I was joking,' he said. 'Of course.' He stopped and turned to face her. 'You knew I was joking, right?' His gaze focused on her.

'Of course,' she replied.

Gordon's eyes sparkled in the neon streetlight. 'I missed you so much,' he whispered and Beth's heart sped up. Being the focus of Gordon's attention was breath-taking. This was what it felt like to be adored. She slipped her arms around his neck. 'I missed you too.'

He gathered her to him and kissed her and she felt her whole body respond with well-remembered longing.

The lab timer went off, somewhere on the floor in Anna's room. Hibs cursed and rolled out of bed, where he'd almost fallen asleep next to her. Where was the bloody thing? He groped around on the floor.

Anna turned the light on. 'What's that noise?' she said, blearily.

Hibs found the offending timer and turned it off. 'I've got to go back to the lab to do my next reading.' He gathered his clothes and started getting dressed.

'Do you have to?' She was leaning on her side, naked and dishevelled.

Hibs pulled on his T-shirt. ''Fraid so. Science is a cruel mistress.' He had to drop to the floor and search for a sock. 'Gotcha.' His hair was loose about his shoulders. He pulled it back. 'Where did my hairband go?'

Anna shrugged, dislodging the duvet so it fell to her

waist. 'I'd offer to lend you one of mine, but I don't use them.'

Hibs smiled and ran his fingertips through her short spiky hair. She wound a strand of his hair in her fingers. 'It suits you that way,' she said. She pulled him down to her and kissed him. 'You can take my keys and let yourself back in, if you like.'

Hibs hesitated. He wasn't sure he wanted to get that far into a relationship with Anna. He liked her. She was fun and adventurous in bed. But, well, he didn't want to be stuck with her.

'I'll see you later.' He slid off the bed and went to the door.

'Science isn't your mistress,' Anna said.

Hibs paused, his hand on the door handle. 'Pardon?'

'Science isn't your mistress,' Anna repeated. 'It's your wife. I'm your mistress. Me and all the other girls who flit through your life.'

Oh shit. Despite her assurances that this was just a hook up, Anna seemed to think there was more to their relationship than that. Hibs retraced a couple of steps until he could see her face.

But she didn't seem upset. In fact, she smiled at him. 'Don't worry,' she said. 'I get it. You don't do relationships because it gets in the way of work. Much more fun to have the odd shag and switch it off when you need to get back to the lab.'

He stared. She did get it. Sort of. 'I'm sorry.'

'Nothing to be sorry about.' Anna pulled the duvet up. 'You're still welcome to come back,' she said. 'But there's no need to commit either way.'

He grinned back. 'Just the way I like it.'

He took the keys.

Chapter Twelve

'We're heading off to the pub; you coming?' Hibs asked as he pulled on his faded denim jacket.

Beth looked at her computer screen and pulled a face. 'I can't.'

'Why not? You haven't got to take another reading for ... what? Three hours?'

'I'm running a gel.'

'Like that's an excuse,' said Vik. 'Come on, Beth. It's Friday.' He leaned in closer. 'And I don't want to be a gooseberry while the barmaid flirts with Hibs. You know he'll only encourage her, even though he has a girlfriend.'

'She's not my girlfriend,' said Hibs.

'You're sleeping with her; you're with her when you're not at work. She's your girlfriend,' Vik said.

Beth stayed out of the conversation. It had been a few weeks now and the idea of Hibs being with Anna still brought with it a stab of resentment. She knew she had no reason to feel awkward about it, but she still did.

'Whatever,' Hibs said. 'So, Beth, will we be seeing you or not?'

'I told Gordon I'd be working ...' She was tempted: she had yet to see Hibs and Anna together and felt almost compelled to find out more. It was like the need to pick a scab. She knew it would hurt, but she really couldn't stop herself.

'But you *are* working. You'll be taking your timer to the pub,' said Vik.

He was right. And she could turn the current down on

the gel so that it ran slower. She was working, even if she took a short break to go to the pub. Gordon need never know.

'Oh what the hell,' she said. 'I'll just go turn the gel down.'

The guys waited for her and they all walked to the pub together, Beth in the middle. It felt natural to walk in between these two men, chatting about nothing in particular. Part way there, Hibs removed the rubber band that had been holding his hair back. His hair flowed thick and black onto his shoulders. '*Yeuch*,' he said, looking at the twisted piece of rubber. 'I hate these things.'

Beth giggled. 'I'm so going to buy you a set of Barbie hairbands for Christmas.' She liked to tease him about his hair. It was longer, thicker and in better condition than hers had ever been. Hair like that had no right to be on a man.

Hibs flicked his hair at her. 'Well, my usual manly black hairband is somewhere on the floor of your housemate's room.'

'How are things going with Anna?' Beth said, ignoring the churn in her stomach.

'I quite like her, actually,' said Hibs. 'She's good company. If a bit single-minded at times.'

'Single-minded about what?' said Vik.

'What do you think?'

'Oh,' Vik said. 'That's good, right?'

Hibs nodded. 'Oh yes. Although, when we're not busy doing it, Anna and I get on rather well. Which is a bit of first for me.' He paused. 'Apart from Winn, anyway.'

Beth dug her hands into her pockets and trudged along in silence. So Hibs was considering taking on a steady girlfriend after years of playing the field, and that girlfriend was her flatmate. If it worked out, she'd lose her best friend and her housemate in one go. If it all fell apart, she'd be caught in the middle.

'So, Beth,' Hibs said. 'How are things with Gorgeous Gordon?'

Beth fingered her phone in her pocket. She still felt guilty about going to the pub when she'd told him she'd be working. 'Fine.'

Hibs stopped. 'Then why are you so worried about coming to the pub?' He looked directly at her, challenging her to defend her relationship. How did he do that? Could he read her mind or something?

'Because I told him I was working. I could have told him I could come out between readings and I didn't. It was stupid of me. Okay?' She glared back.

'Okay,' said Hibs. 'Just checking.'

The pub was busy. A rugby team was taking up most of the seats near the entrance, forcing them to squeeze past loud, burly blokes to get in. Beth spotted a couple of seats in a far corner and grabbed them while the boys went to the bar.

'I meant to ask,' Hibs said when he returned with their drinks, 'what's going on with the calendar?'

'It's all ready to go to the printers now,' Beth said. 'We just need Clarissa to okay the money.'

'Is she likely to?'

'I hope so,' said Beth. 'We did an awful lot of work taking the photos and sorting out the layout. I'll have to pummel Clarissa with her own jewellery if she doesn't sign it off.'

Hibs laughed. 'I'm guessing she'll sign it off rather than risk it.'

Beth nodded.

'So where's Gordon?' Vik asked, looking behind Beth to the door.

Beth jumped and looked behind her. There was no one there but the loud rugby lads. 'He's got swimming training.' She turned back to her Coke. There was silence and she could almost feel Hibs and Vik exchanging glances.

After a few moments Vik said, 'Did you see *Britain's Got Talent* last night?'

'No,' Beth and Hibs said in unison.

They looked at each other, Beth feeling slightly embarrassed. 'Was it good?' she said, turning to Vik.

Vik pulled a face. 'Well, I watched it. With my flatmates. While eating my takeaway for one.'

Beth patted his hand. 'Poor Vik.'

'Maybe we should put a lonely hearts ad on that website ... what's it called ... the Asian dating site?' said Hibs.

'No thanks,' he said. 'My parents will do that for me when I'm done with the PhD. My aunty is busy lining up women for me to meet as it is.' He took a long sip from his pint. 'I don't need a wife. I need to meet someone for now, you know.' He looked at Hibs. 'Like you have.'

'He's not a role model, you know,' said Beth.

Her phone began to ring. 'Oh shit,' she said when she saw the screen. 'It's Gordon.'

'So?' said Vik.

'He's expecting me to be in the lab.'

They looked at the phone. It rang and rang. Eventually, it went to answerphone and Beth exhaled. She hadn't realised she'd been holding her breath. That had been close.

'I don't understand,' Hibs said. 'You told him you were

working. You are working.' He indicated the icon that said Beth's timer was running on her phone.

'I told him I'd be in the lab. Not the pub. It—' The phone started to ring – it was Gordon. Again.

'Shit,' Beth said, her heart starting to speed up.

'Take it outside,' said Hibs. 'Tell him you were in the cold room or something.'

'Right.' She grabbed the phone and ran out. The rugby lads were getting into some sort of drinking competition and she had to shove her way through them.

She answered the phone, slightly out of breath. 'Hello?'

'It's Gordon.' He sounded annoyed. 'Where were you? I've been trying for ages.'

'I was … in the cold room. I left the phone on my desk but I ran to get it when I heard it.' That should explain why she sounded breathless. Good recovery, Beth.

'Oh, okay.' He believed her, thank god. 'Listen. I was calling to check that you weren't working tomorrow.'

'No. It's Hibs's turn. Why?'

'We're going to the opera. *Don Carlos* is on at the New Theatre and I've got us two last-minute tickets.'

Beth stared at the wall opposite. She didn't particularly like opera. It was nice enough, but she hated having to read surtitles. And everything happened so slowly. Gordon loved it though. 'Sure,' she said. 'That would be lovely.' She could always switch off and go to sleep, so long as Gordon didn't notice. She mentally scanned her wardrobe for something to wear. Gordon always looked smart when they went to the theatre. She'd have to dust off another nice outfit. She smiled. It had been a while since she'd got to wear anything nice. She'd been living in her lab uniform of jeans and T-shirts for the last six months.

Someone opened the door to the pub and there was

a blast of noise. Beth turned away, afraid that Gordon would hear. Whoever it was was holding the door open. There was a roar from the rugby lads.

'What's that?' said Gordon.

'Er ... nothing.'

The rugby lads started chanting, 'Down it, down it, DOWN IT!'

'Beth?' A hard edge crept into Gordon's voice. 'You're not in the lab are you?'

Beth wondered whether to say she was watching something on YouTube, but she couldn't figure out if she'd said anything that might contradict that before. Gordon had an uncanny knack of remembering things she didn't want him to.

'Er ... I just popped out to give something to Anna,' she said. 'I've got to get back in a couple of minutes to turn my gel—'

'You said you were working.'

'I am.'

'In the pub?' His voice was incredulous now and full of ice.

'No. Yes. Well, no. I told you. I just popped in—'

'I don't like being lied to, Beth.'

'I'm not lying.' Her voice sounded plaintive. The pub door swung shut and the noise was muffled. 'I just popped down to the pub to give Anna some stuff for the calendar. I'm going right back to the lab.'

'Oh, the calendar,' said Gordon. 'I should have guessed. And I suppose Anna just happens to be hanging out with those guys from your lab now that Hibs is screwing her.'

'Gordon!'

'For heaven's sake, Beth. Sometimes I think you care more about those guys than you do about me!'

'That's not true. I love you.' This could not be happening. She had only just got Gordon back. Okay, he was possessive, but it was only because he cared. 'I really do.' Her voice caught in her throat.

There was a pause. 'Yes,' said Gordon. 'I'm sorry, babe. I shouldn't have got annoyed with you. It's just … been a hard swimming session and … look, never mind. You go back to the lab. I'll try and swing by later, okay.'

'Okay.'

'I'll see you in a bit then. Bye.'

She hung up and rushed back in, elbowing her way through the crowd by the door. 'I've got to get back to the lab,' she said, grabbing her coat. 'I'll see you tomorrow.'

'Wait, you're going?' said Vik.

'Because Gordon has decreed she must,' said Hibs. He shook his head and wouldn't meet Beth's eyes. 'See you tomorrow, Beth. Do you need someone to walk you back?'

'No, I'll be fine. It's still light.' She needed to hurry so that she was back in the lab by the time Gordon came by. 'See you later.' She elbowed her way out again and fled.

Back in the lab she carried on working, checking the clock from time to time. By the time she'd done her 10 p.m. reading, Gordon still hadn't shown up. She started clearing her bench – she was a little nervous about what Gordon might say and the work was a welcome distraction. Otherwise, she'd just be pacing and fretting, which was no good to anyone.

It was nearly eleven by the time Gordon buzzed to be allowed in.

'Babe, it's me.'

'Oh, right. Give me a minute, I'll be right down.' During the day, the doors to the department were open, but at night she had to go down to the main entrance to let him in. Rather than go all the way down and come up again, she grabbed her coat and turned the lights off in the lab.

When she got downstairs, she could see Gordon standing outside, speaking on the phone. Beth let herself through the first security door and into the glass corridor. Gordon noticed her and waved. He didn't look too angry.

Emboldened, she released the catch on the outer door.

Gordon put his phone away. 'Hello.' He gave her a kiss. 'Are you done for the next few hours?'

Okay. So he wasn't angry. She almost flopped with relief. 'I am actually. Next reading at 2 a.m., so I can go home.'

'Let's do that then,' he said. They walked back in silence and Beth started to worry again. He was quiet. Did that mean he was still thinking about the fact that she'd been in the pub when he'd thought she was in the lab? She tried to slip her hand into his, but he glanced at her and moved his hand.

'You know, you could have just told me you were going to go to the pub for a bit,' he said.

Beth tensed. 'I didn't know. It was a spur-of-the-moment thing.'

'What if I'd come round to see you instead of phoning beforehand? I would have stood outside like a lemon.'

Except he'd been at the swimming pool, training. Beth decided it was better not to say anything.

'I'm not annoyed or anything,' he said. 'I'm just hurt that you lied to me.'

'I was working. I just had a little time to spare and I needed to—'

'I guess I should expect it. You've got used to being free and single.'

Beth snorted. Single, yes. Free? 'I'm sorry. I didn't think.'

He stopped walking and turned to face her. 'I know your work is important to you. I thought I was too.'

Beth stared up at him. 'You are. How could you even doubt that? I waited for you. All that time.'

He gazed at her for a moment, his brow furrowed. 'Of course you did. I'm sorry.' He shook his head. 'I guess I'm just crazy about you and it's making me insecure.' They started walking again. 'Just please don't do it again,' he said.

'Okay.'

He slipped his arm round her waist and pulled her closer. Uncomfortable, but also relieved, she fell into step beside him.

Chapter Thirteen

It was only six o'clock on Monday morning, but it was already getting light. As she cycled home from the lab after taking the last reading, Beth breathed in the dewy air and felt light-headed with the beauty of the world. Pale morning light spilled through the trees that lined the road. There were cars about already, but nothing like the clogged-up throng that would appear in a few hours. She locked her bike and stood still for a moment, listening to the birds, before she went back into the building.

She tiptoed into the flat, not because she was afraid of waking Gordon – he was a sound sleeper – but shoes in the hallway told her that Hibs and Anna were there too. As she crept past the living room, a movement in the corner of her vision made her jump. She turned to face the open doorway. Someone was moving very slowly in there. She took a hesitant step forward and peered in.

Hibs was standing in the middle of the living room in his boxer shorts and a T-shirt. His headphones were plugged into his ears, his phone clipped into his waistband, and he was moving gracefully through a series of poses. His hair was loose and the light caught and defined his muscles. Beth watched his limbs flowing into position and recognised a few moves of his kata. He had shown her once how he used a slowed-down version of his karate to meditate. He had his eyes closed so that he could concentrate and she stood very still so that she didn't make a noise.

Where Gordon was all muscle and bulk, Hibs was slim and taut. Where Gordon was blond, Hibs was dark. He was focusing so hard that his brow was furrowed, but he was beautiful. Beth stared, knowing she should look away. She couldn't ogle him. It wasn't right. But her heart picked up, despite that. She couldn't tear herself away: watching him moving was hypnotic.

She tried to tell herself that he was her friend. She'd just fancied him for a moment, when she was lonely and frustrated. It was a momentary lapse and she had to get over it. She couldn't fancy him: he was taken. So was she.

He moved his weight on to one leg, causing the muscles to stand out. The weight of his phone tugged at the side of his shorts, exposing a hip. She had a sudden memory of his thumb drawing circles on her back and a tingle ran up her spine; the thrill was so intense that she gasped. Imagine if things had gone differently that night. Those smooth muscles would be moving against her own body. She could barely breathe at the thought.

This was insane. She had to leave before she gave in to temptation and reached out to touch him. Beth took a step back. And dropped her bike helmet on the floor.

The crash echoed round the flat; Hibs's eyes flew open.

By the time Beth had retrieved her helmet, he was standing with both feet on the ground. 'Morning,' he said. 'Are you on the way back from the lab?'

'Yes.' She had to pull herself together. She looked down the corridor. No one. Perhaps Gordon hadn't been woken by her stupid bike helmet. She turned back to Hibs, who was pulling his hair back.

'I thought you said you didn't do that?' she said, trying to keep her tone light and jokey.

'What?'

'Walk around people's flats in your underwear.'

Hibs looked down at himself. 'I'm wearing a T-shirt as well,' he pointed out.

Beth looked at his T-shirt and immediately wrenched her gaze away. 'Uh. Yeah. So you are.' She cleared her throat.

'Beth. Are you okay?' Hibs asked as he took a step towards her.

She took a step back. 'Yes. Fine. Just tired, that's all.'

'Of course, you must be knackered after the night shift. We've got the lab meeting today,' said Hibs. 'You can squeeze in a couple of hours kip before that.'

Beth yawned. 'Yeah. Sounds like a plan.'

Hibs smiled at her and little creases appeared at the corners of his eyes. She noticed he had a slight layer of stubble from having stayed over with Anna. It was rather sexy. 'Night, Beth,' he said.

'Night.' She fled back into her room, to Gordon.

Gordon muttered something and rolled over, opening one eye a crack to look at her.

'Morning.' Beth dropped a kiss on his head before stripping off her clothes and getting back into bed.

'Who were you talking to?' said Gordon, making room for her in the crook of his arm.

'Oh, Hibs was up doing his meditation thing.'

'Does that every morning, does he?' he asked, suddenly sounding less sleepy.

Beth felt the hairs on the back of her neck prickle. Could Gordon read her thoughts? Could he see that momentary desire she'd just had? 'Anna says he does,' she said, carefully.

There was a pause as Beth curled into Gordon, her cheek resting on his shoulder.

'Right,' said Gordon.

'It's only just gone six,' Beth said. 'We could get a couple more hours shut-eye before I have to go to the lab meeting.'

'Or we could do something else …'

A huge yawn threatened. Beth tried to fight it, but didn't manage. 'I'm sorry, Gordon. I'm so tired.'

'Right. Fine.' He wrapped his arm around her shoulders. 'Sleep it is, then.'

Beth closed her eyes and immediately saw an image of Hibs, moving slowly from one position to another. Think of something else. Anything else. Cats. Or Donkeys. No. Not donkeys. Gerbils maybe. Still trying to force herself to think of non-contentious things, she fell asleep.

'Are we doing lunch today?' Beth reached across for the butter, which was just out of reach. Gordon made no move to push it nearer.

'Can't today,' said Gordon. 'I'll be seeing you this evening though. You're not working tonight, are you?'

Beth stood up, retrieved the butter and sat back down. 'That's right. Hibs is doing tonight.'

As if on cue there was a giggle from Anna's room. Gordon rolled his eyes.

Hibs and Anna appeared, holding hands. Beth again felt a small stab of irritation. What was it that annoyed her so much? It wasn't like she hadn't been around Hibs's girlfriends before. Although, come to think of it, she'd never seen him hold anyone's hand. She really had to get over this awkwardness. If Hibs and Anna were going to stay together, she would have to see them together all the time. If she didn't relax about it, Gordon would notice. He wouldn't like it. Not that he had anything to worry about. She slammed another slice of bread into the toaster. Of course not.

Hibs spotted Gordon and his eyes narrowed. 'Morning,' he said to Beth. 'You're not planning on missing the lab meeting, are you?' He gestured towards her breakfast, which she'd barely begun.

'Oh, hell. I completely forgot.' She looked at her freshly buttered toast. Gordon liked to have a leisurely breakfast, but she would have to bolt it down if she wanted to make it to the meeting on time.

'What time's your meeting?' said Gordon, not bothering to acknowledge Hibs.

'In about half an hour.'

'Oh, you've got plenty of time.' He put a hand over hers. 'Don't worry, babe.' He looked into her eyes and smiled. Beth felt something flutter inside. 'It'll be fine,' he said.

Hibs shrugged. 'I'll see you there, Beth.' He grabbed Anna round the waist and gave her a kiss. 'Bye, Anna.'

Anna grinned. 'See you later.'

Beth concentrated on her toast. It was getting soggy with butter now. She scraped some of it off and Gordon looked at her curiously.

When Hibs had left, Anna gave a theatrical sigh and ran a hand through her hair. 'I'm off to have a shower,' she said to no one in particular, and ambled away.

There was a moment of silence in the kitchen. 'I'd better hurry,' Beth said as she gathered the cutlery together.

'Leave that a moment. It's not often we get time to ourselves, just the two of us.' He took her hand again. 'Let's enjoy it.'

'But ...'

'Relax,' he said. 'Hibs was just trying to show me he has some influence over you.'

Beth frowned. 'Why would he do that?'

'It's a bloke thing. He doesn't like me and it's just his way of annoying me.'

That didn't sound like Hibs. If he wanted to be rude to someone, he was just rude to them. Besides which, she knew that Hibs was right. She was going to be late.

'You know,' Gordon said, his voice dropping a notch. 'I reckon he fancies you. That's why he keeps trying all these ridiculous power games with me.' His gaze locked on to hers, faintly accusing.

Beth felt her mouth go dry. Had Gordon figured out that she was looking at Hibs with a different sort of appreciation now? She would get over it, but she needed time. Oh god.

Gordon was still looking at her. Feeling that something was required, she said, 'Huh. That's silly.'

He nodded. 'Well, you guys spend a lot of time together,' he said. 'It's understandable he's a bit confused.'

'We work together,' said Beth. 'That's why we spend time together. It can't be helped.'

'I know that, silly.' Gordon placed a kiss on the back of her hand. 'Don't mind me. I'm just jealous that I don't have you all to myself twenty-four-seven.' He looked into her eyes before dropping another kiss on the sensitive skin on the inside of her wrist. 'Who can blame me for wanting to spend as much time as possible with the most beautiful girlfriend in the world.'

Beth didn't know what to say. There was something adorable about the way he said it. She had a vague feeling she should be defending herself, but couldn't figure out against what. All he'd said was that he loved her.

'Sorry,' she said.

Gordon nodded and smiled as though acknowledging an admission of guilt. He reached out and tilted her chin up. 'You are incredible, you know,' he said.

'I ...'

He silenced her by pulling her close and kissing her. Beth felt herself melt into his arms. She loved the feeling of well-being that brought. Breakfast forgotten, she slipped her arms around his neck and kissed him back.

She knew she would be late for the meeting.

Chapter Fourteen

Beth fidgeted in her seat. The lab meetings took place in the tea room and she badly wanted to get herself a drink, but didn't want to invite the wrath of Roger. Vik had finished his presentation and Roger was quizzing him. So far, Roger had ignored her. When she had rushed in fifteen minutes late he hadn't even bothered to tell her off. Somehow that was worse than the pasting she'd been expecting.

Oddly, Hibs wasn't looking at her either. She sat up straighter and tried to listen to what was being said.

'Have you tried testing it under blue light?' Roger barked at Vik.

'That's already been done,' said Vik. 'No response.'

'That's right,' Beth chipped in. 'I did some testing under blue when I first started.' It had been a small project that failed to go anywhere and she and Hibs had persuaded Roger to abandon it.

No one paid her the slightest bit of attention.

'You should try it again,' Roger said to Vik. 'From scratch. Just to check that there wasn't any operator error.'

Beth gaped. Operator error? Was he implying that she'd somehow done it wrong? 'Wait a minute—' she started.

'When we want your opinion, we'll ask for it.' Roger didn't even look in her direction.

Beth looked at Hibs for support, but he seemed focused on Vik. She pursed her lips and glared at the floor. Vik agreed to run a small batch of tests under blue light and she couldn't believe Hibs hadn't spoken up. Did he believe that her results were unreliable? If that was the case, why was he entrusting half his experiment to her? She shot a resentful glance at him, but he didn't appear to notice.

After the meeting Roger marched off and Beth finally looked up. 'I did do those experiments two years ago,' she said to Vik.

Vik shrugged. 'I know. I'm not totally sure why they need redoing.' He looked at Hibs. 'Do they really need doing again?'

'No.' Hibs filled the kettle.

'But—'

'If the boss says to do it, sometimes it's good to humour him,' said Hibs. 'You can argue when you've been here longer.'

Vik nodded. 'I guess.' He disconnected the laptop from the projector. 'I'll take this upstairs then.' He looked from Hibs to Beth. 'I'll see you guys later.'

There was a strained silence once he'd gone. The kettle bubbled and clicked off. Hibs poured.

'Thanks for standing up for me,' Beth said with as much sarcasm as she could inject. 'You could have said something.'

'Like what, Beth?' Hibs turned round, his eyes flashing with anger. 'Oh, Roger, you can take Beth seriously. She's a good scientist. She's very dedicated. Something like that? How can I say that, Beth, when you turn up to the lab meeting late because you were *too busy getting laid*?'

Beth opened her mouth to say that he'd done it too, but realised that he hadn't. Hibs may be a slave to his libido, but he'd never, ever, let it get in the way of work. 'I ...'

'If Gordon is what's important to you, fine. Just admit it and get on with it. You need to work out where your priorities lie.' He stirred his coffee so hard that it slopped over the side of his mug. 'You can't have it both ways.' He grabbed his mug and started for the door. 'I'll see you later.'

'What? Are you saying I can't have a romantic relationship and be taken seriously as a scientist? That's just crap.'

Hibs stopped. 'No,' he said, slowly. 'I'm saying you can live for things that are important to you. Or live according to Gordon. I very much doubt you can have both.' He left, leaving the door to slam shut behind him.

Beth stared at the door for a moment, then shook her head to clear the fizz of anger. She pulled out a mug and threw a teabag into it. How dare Hibs cast judgment like that? As she poured the scalding water and watched the teabag bob helplessly in it, she wondered if he was right. Gordon had known she'd be late for the meeting. She'd told him about it, yet he'd persuaded her it didn't matter. Could she have left earlier? Probably. She dunked the teabag under with a spoon and held it there to drown. But she hadn't tried. At least, not very hard. Maybe Hibs was right; maybe she was a doormat.

On the other hand, she'd felt so guilty about fancying another man when she should have been thinking about Gordon. Her boyfriend. She'd let her guilt override her commitment to her work. Beth rescued the teabag and squeezed it on the edge of the mug. Did she really have to feel that guilty? It wasn't as though she'd done anything about it.

Beth and Hibs were sitting at their computers on opposite sides of the narrow space. Normally, they would have been talking over their shoulders to each other, but today there was nothing but the sound of keyboards clicking.

Beth knew she was being childish, sulking like she was. But she was annoyed with Hibs for being so high-handed with her. And she was angry with herself because she knew he was right.

Vik arrived and flung himself into his chair. He clattered away at the keyboard for a moment and said, 'No e-mails. Clearly, nobody loves me today.'

Beth couldn't think of anything to say.

There was the sound of wheels moving as Vik pushed his chair down between them. 'Okay, what's going on?' he said.

'What do you mean?' Beth asked.

'What's up with you two? You've been acting weird all day.'

Hibs said nothing. Beth turned to look at Vik.

'You'—Vik pointed to her—'were late for the lab meeting. Then you stomped up here with a face like thunder.' He swivelled the chair round until he was pointing at Hibs. 'And you have been in a filthy mood and haven't criticised my choice of radio station all day. Which, to my mind, is pretty much the definition of "something is up". So what's going on?'

'Nothing,' Hibs and Beth said simultaneously.

Vik rolled his eyes. 'Fine. Let me figure it out.' He narrowed his eyes and looked from one to the other.

Beth looked away from him. For one irrational moment she thought Vik might see into her head and recognise the guilt.

'I reckon,' Vik said, slowly, 'it's all gone weird because Hibs is dating your housemate, Beth. It's like a whole work/real life collision thing.' He looked pleased with himself. 'Am I right?'

Hibs finally turned round. 'Yes, Vik. That's right,' he

said, his voice heavy with sarcasm. 'I'm sleeping with Beth's housemate and it's freaked us both out so much that we can barely stand each other's company. 'Cause we're soooo delicate.' He brushed past Vik and strode out of the lab.

'If that's not it, what is it?' Vik gave Beth a puzzled look. 'I know you guys have had an argument. If it's not about Anna, then what *is* it about?'

Beth sighed. 'It's complicated, Vik, okay. Just drop it.'

'I can't. I have to work here too. It's not exactly fun at the moment. I feel like a UN peacekeeper.'

Thankfully, Beth's phone rang, rescuing her from having to explain something she wasn't even sure she understood. It was Lara.

'Hey,' Beth said. 'How's it going?'

There was a sniff at the other end of the line.

'Lara?'

'He's gone.'

'What?'

'Chris has gone, Beth. I gave him an ultimatum and he ... he left me. I don't know what I expected but ...' Soft sobs came down the line.

'Oh, Lara. Where are you? I'll come straight over.'

'What's going on?' Vik said when Beth had hung up.

'I've got to go. I'll see you tomorrow.' She paused to pat him on the arm. 'I'll try and cheer up before then, okay?'

Before she went to Lara's, she had to phone Gordon. Beth stood next to her bike, phone in hand, psyching herself up. He would be annoyed. She hated it when he was annoyed. He got all shouty. But Lara needed her so she had to go. It wasn't like she had any choice.

She took a deep breath and pressed the call button.

Gordon's phone rang a few times and went to answerphone. Beth let her shoulders relax. It always went to answerphone. Gordon claimed that mobile phone reception in his building was terrible, which is why he never picked up when she rang.

She explained that there was an emergency with Lara and that she had to cancel. 'I'm very sorry,' she added, before hanging up.

As she cycled to Lara's she wondered how long it would take him to pick up the message. How angry would he be? They were supposed to be going to the opera that evening. Gordon had tickets and everything. He was always a little more uptight about things when he had bought tickets so he wouldn't be pleased with her cancelling. She was fully expecting to get an irritated phone call from him in a bit. She hoped he would understand that Lara needed her more than he did.

Lara answered the door, her eyes and nose red from crying. Beth forgot all about Gordon and gave her friend a hug. 'You poor thing.'

Lara blew her nose and nodded. 'I'm glad you came.' She led the way into the living room. Everything looked normal, as far as Beth could tell. The only difference was the wedding photo was now face-down on the mantelpiece.

'Tell me everything,' she said.

'I should put the kettle on —'

'I'll take care of that.' Beth stopped her. 'You tell me while I make the tea.'

Lara's house was small and the kitchen led into the living room. Lara sat on a dining chair, just outside the kitchen, while Beth put the kettle on. 'There isn't a lot to tell. He came home late again last night and I confronted him. He denied it to start with, and then he said it meant nothing.' Lara blew her nose. 'I said it clearly wasn't nothing and he had to choose between her and me and ...' Her voice broke in a sob. 'He stormed off. He ... he was gone all night. Then this morning I called him. He said he needed to clear his head and think things through.' Fresh tears spilled down her face. 'When I got back from work today, all his stuff had gone.'

'Oh, honey.' Beth went over and put her arms around Lara and held her until the sobs subsided. It was a shock to see Lara, who was normally so composed, in such a state.

In Beth's pocket, her phone rang. She glanced at the clock – it was just past seven. She should have been meeting Gordon about now. She pushed the thought to the back of her mind and concentrated on Lara. 'What are you going to do?'

Lara sniffed and rubbed her cheeks with the back of her hand. 'I don't know. I have no idea what happens next.'

Beth perched on the arm of the sofa. 'If he came back, would you try again?'

Lara stared into space. 'No.' She shook her head. 'Probably not. I'm not sure.'

'He cheated on you,' said Beth. 'And then, when you found out, he just left.'

Lara nodded. 'I know. Every sensible part of me says "good riddance", but inside ...' Tears appeared again. She wiped them away with a tissue.

'Maybe you just need some time to work things out.'

In Beth's pocket the phone rang again. She ignored it, but her heart pounded. Gordon would be angry. She didn't like it when Gordon was angry.

'Should you get that?' said Lara.

'It's Gordon,' Beth said, without bothering to check the phone. 'I'll call him back. This is important.'

Lara sighed. 'Take the call. I'll be okay.'

Beth gave her a grateful smile and answered the phone. She headed to the hallway, where she was less likely to be overheard.

'Where are you?' Gordon's voice was curt. She could feel his annoyance.

'I don't think I'll be able to make it,' Beth said. 'I'm at Lara's. She's really upset. I can't leave her.'

'What do you mean you won't be able to make it? I've got tickets for the opera. The doors open in an hour.'

'I know, I know. I'm so sorry. I really am, but I can't leave Lara now. Chris has just left—'

'I don't care what Lara wants. You made a commitment, Beth. You should stick to it.'

'But—'

'But nothing. I can't believe you're standing me up! After I rushed from training to be with you. How could you do this to me? Am I not important to you?'

Beth's heart was pounding. She felt so guilty. She should have kept trying his phone, or left a longer message, so that at least she could explain before he got angry, rather than making excuses now. She was so stupid. 'I'm sorry, Gordon.'

'Sorry? *Sorry?*' Gordon was hissing down the phone now, which was somehow worse than his shouting. 'You think sorry is going to cover it? You've let me down.'

'I'll make it up to you? Tomorrow—'

'I thought you were working tomorrow. Or have you been lying to me again?'

'No. No. I am working. We can meet up between readings though. I'll cook you dinner,' she was speaking as fast as she could, so that she could say her piece before he cut her off again. 'I'll make lasagne. Your favourite.'

There was a pause as Gordon considered this.

'I'll even make crumble for pudding.' He loved crumble. Making him an apple crumble always cheered him up. She hoped it would work this time too. She hated it when he was angry with her.

'Okay. I'll see you at your flat at ten past seven.' He didn't sound so angry now and Beth breathed out in relief.

'Thank you.'

He didn't respond.

'I love you,' she said. But he had already hung up.

Beth felt weak. She put her phone back in her pocket and steadied herself against the wall for a moment. That was the first time Gordon had been angry with her since they'd got back together. He would get over it; he always did. But she had forgotten how his temper could flare. She needed to be more careful and not annoy him so much.

She went back into the kitchen and started making tea, hoping the ritual would soothe her nerves. Lara's kitchen was small and homely. It looked just like it had always done, until Beth looked closer and started noticing things. Chris's posh knives were gone: the magnetic strip only had one knife on it. The black-and-white cafetière that normally stood next to the kettle was gone too. Nothing major, just little signs of the gap in her friend's life.

Beth opened the cupboard and saw the lovely matching china mugs that Lara and Chris had received as a wedding gift. She reached around them and found a pair of mismatched porcelain mugs. Poor Lara. Lara was the important one at this moment. She needed to focus on her. Worrying about Gordon would have to wait.

When she returned to the living room Lara, looked up. 'Everything okay?'

'Yes,' Beth lied. 'Everything's fine.'

Chapter Fifteen

The next day the reception desk called up to say a bunch of flowers had arrived for Beth. She ran down to collect them. It was a bouquet of roses. Pink and red.

The little card tucked in between the flowers read, 'Sorry I got annoyed. Hope your evening went okay. I took a colleague from the dept. in the end, so got to see the opera after all. Looking forward to dinner. Gordon.'

Beth smiled and took the flowers back up to the lab.

'Flowers? Have you got a secret admirer?' said Vik.

'They're from Gordon.'

'Why? What's he done?' Hibs said.

'Nothing. He's not done anything.' Why did Hibs always assume the worst of Gordon? What was his problem? 'He just sent me flowers, okay. He's my boyfriend. It's a nice thing to do.'

Hibs snorted. 'Right. Gordon's being nice for no reason? Like that's going to happen.'

'Just because you wouldn't know romance if it came and bit you, that doesn't mean other people don't do romantic things.' She flounced off to find something to put the flowers in.

'Okay then, let's see what we've got.' Anna turned the laptop so that she could see it. 'Is that all twelve?'

It was early Sunday evening and they were in the flat, looking through the images for the calendar. The idea had been to hand them straight over to Lara, but Anna had wanted them to all to have a look at them together.

Anna flicked through the pictures and Beth and Lara

moved closer so that they could all see the screen. Beth hoped that the calendar would take Lara's mind off Chris for a bit, at least. Beth had spent the previous night at Lara's house, keeping her company, and later that evening Lara was going to meet another friend. Which was a good thing, because otherwise Beth would feel the need to call and check on her, which she knew wouldn't go down well with Gordon.

'Wow,' said Lara, who was seeing some of the photos for the first time. 'Beth, you're really good. They look very professional.'

'Thanks.' Beth felt a warm buzz from having her work admired. She'd been taking photos on and off for years, but had never really shown people, in case she was deluding herself about her skill. It was nice to see her work admired by others. The satisfaction of being *good* at something was wonderful.

Even better, Gordon was supportive of her hobby this time. Perhaps he finally understood how important it was to her. She wondered what had prompted the change. Maybe she'd been more passionate when she talked about it this time around. Last year, she had been too wrapped up in Gordon to be passionate about much else. She smiled to herself. It was nice being connected to her hobby again. It made her feel more complete.

'They all look great, but I think we might need to move them around a little bit,' said Anna, leaning back in her seat.

'Why?' Beth had spent a long time getting the pictures edited and put into a sensible order. 'What's wrong with them?'

Anna looked up. 'Nothing. The pictures are brilliant. Relax.' She gestured to the laptop. 'I just thought we might need to change the order.'

'Oh. Right.' So long as the pictures were okay, she needed this discussion to be over really soon so that she could get on with making the salad for Gordon's special meal.

Anna was watching Beth carefully. 'You okay?'

'Yes. Fine. I just need to get on with making dinner, that's all.'

'For Gordon?' Anna shot a glance at Lara, whose mouth tightened, as though she was stopping herself from speaking.

'What?'

'Nothing,' Lara said.

'We're just surprised that you haven't suggested we put Gordon in the calendar, that's all,' said Anna.

'We'd already decided the line-up before he came back.' Beth was surprised at Anna's tone of voice. Clearly Hibs had been feeding Anna his bad opinion of Gordon. She wished Anna would bother to form her own opinions rather than regurgitating Hibs's.

'I wouldn't have put it past him to ask for someone else to be dropped off the list so that he could go on,' said Lara.

Gordon had asked her to do just that. Beth felt a disloyal stab of annoyance. 'He knows I would never do that,' she said. 'So he wouldn't ask.' Okay, so he'd asked. But it was probably a joke. That didn't count. 'Let's just get on with this. What do you want to change?'

'I think the beetle man should be Dr January.' Anna scrolled up to the photo. 'This photo is brilliant. It shows a gorgeous man who looks like an action hero – and he's a brilliant scientist. What could be a better advert for the calendar?'

Lara stared at the photo. 'You're right,' she said. 'That is a pretty impressive front page.'

Anna flicked back to the naked guy, whom Beth had originally chosen to be Dr January. 'Also, I'm not sure we should give this guy's ego any more fodder than strictly necessary.'

Beth shrugged. 'Fair enough.'

'Agreed?' Anna looked at Lara, who nodded.

'Great.' Anna selected the next photo. 'This is a great photo too. Very happy and sunshiny.' She indicated a picture taken in the plant biology department. A man stood in the dappled sunlight, his eyes creasing with laughter. Beth remembered that he and Anna had got on really well and Beth had been sure that Anna would try and get his number, until he'd casually thrown in a comment about his boyfriend. 'I think we should keep this one for Dr December. It'll be a nice happy note to end on.'

'I think it works as Dr June,' said Beth.

They moved the pictures around until they had a line-up that they agreed on, and then had a final flick through.

'That's quite a good effort,' said Lara. 'Well done, girls. I'll drop them round to the printers next week.'

'Beth did all the difficult bits,' said Anna. 'I just asked them questions. They were only too happy to talk about themselves.'

Lara nodded. 'And how many of them did you ask out in the end?'

'None,' said Anna. 'I got a few numbers, but I got together with Hibs. So ...' She smiled, almost to herself.

Beth hadn't had chance to tell Anna what had happened. She glanced at Lara and caught the cloud of sadness that passed across her face.

The doorbell rang.

'That'll be Hibs.' Anna leapt up. 'I'll get it.'

'Is Hibs coming here?' Beth didn't know why she was surprised. It was his night off – he would want to spend it with his girlfriend. She and he had been avoiding each other since their argument at the lab meeting. They still spoke, but only if it was essential to keeping the experiments running. The atmosphere in the lab had been tense.

The doorbell rang again, a bit longer this time. Anna went to get it.

'Are you going to be okay?' Beth whispered to Lara.

Lara nodded. 'I've done some thinking. It's hard, but I think I did the right thing.'

Hibs sauntered in and Anna rushed off to have a shower and get ready.

'Lara,' Hibs said, spotting her. 'How are you?'

'I'm fine thanks. You?'

'Pretty good.' He glanced at Beth and slid into a seat. Beth looked away. 'How's The Man?' he said to Lara.

Beth shot a warning glare at him. Lara looked like she was about to cry.

Hibs frowned. 'What's wrong? Is everything okay?'

Lara stood up. 'Excuse me.' Then she ran off to the bathroom.

'What's going on? Is Lara okay?' Hibs finally made eye contact with Beth. This was the first time since her flowers had arrived that he'd spoken to her about something not related to work and she felt a flutter of relief in her chest. She quickly outlined what was happening.

'Ouch,' said Hibs.

'Yeah. She had to do something about it. She couldn't carry on being trapped in that relationship. It was ruining her life.'

'You're a fine one to talk,' said Hibs.

'Oh for heaven's sake, Hibs. Grow up.'

He stuck his tongue out at her, proving he was anything but grown up. She turned away from him, annoyed. For a moment, neither she nor Hibs said anything. Just when it looked like they were going to remain that way until Anna or Lara came back, Hibs sighed and Beth looked round.

'You're right,' he said. 'This is ridiculous. I'm sorry, Tyler. I was out of line.'

Beth stared at him. Was he really admitting that he'd been wrong? Really? Did men *do* that?

'What you do in your private life is your business,' Hibs continued. 'You're normally very diligent with your work and just because you were late for one meeting that doesn't mean you're not dedicated. I overreacted.'

Beth drew a deep breath. If Hibs could be big about this, so could she. If she was being honest, one of the reasons she felt so angry with him was that she knew he was right. She had to learn to prioritise. Her work was at least as important as Gordon. 'Thanks,' she said. 'I'm sorry too. I shouldn't sulk like a teenager.'

'Teenager? A child more like.' The corners of his mouth twitched upwards.

'Don't push it.' Relief washed over her. It was as though a weight had been lifted. She had her friend back.

'Wouldn't dream of it.' He held out a hand. 'Friends?'

'Friends.' She shook his hand and tried not to think about how warm it was.

'So.' Hibs leaned back in his chair. 'What are you up to this evening? Seeing Gordon between readings?'

Beth nodded. 'Don't worry. I won't miss any, no matter how persuasive Gordon's being.'

'Glad to hear it.'

Anna and Lara returned, Lara's eyes looking red. 'I'm sorry,' she said.

'Don't be,' said Hibs. 'You're going through a crap time. You're allowed to feel crap.'

Lara sniffed. 'Thanks.' She punched him on the shoulder. 'I can always rely on you to tell me I'm crap.'

'I never said that. I said you're allowed to feel crap.' Hibs rolled his eyes. 'Bloody women. Putting words in my mouth and leaking tears everywhere.'

Lara managed a weak smile.

'That's better,' said Hibs. 'Want to talk about it?'

Lara sat down. 'Not especially.'

Hibs gave her a long look. 'Fair enough. If you ever want someone to try and talk some sense into him, let me know.'

Lara raised her eyebrows at him. 'You? Talk about relationships? That'll be a first.'

Gordon arrived as Lara was leaving. She nodded to him but didn't bother to say hello. Beth paused in her task of cutting up apples for the crumble. It was sad that her friends never appreciated Gordon. Lara, like Hibs, had always told her that Gordon didn't value her. They must see they were wrong now. After all, he had come back to her after just six months apart.

Gordon kissed her before he threw himself into a chair. Beth went back to chopping apples.

'Is that the calendar?' said Gordon, looking at the open laptop. 'Is it done? Can I see?'

Anna hesitated before she said, 'Sure.'

Beth turned to watch him as he stretched across the table and took the laptop from Anna. His face was neutral as he clicked through the pictures. But Beth knew what she was looking for and she spotted the slight tightening around the eyes that said he wasn't best pleased. She should have hidden that bloody laptop before he came round. This evening was supposed to be about placating him, not needling him even more.

'Hey, isn't that Dan Blackwood?' Gordon pointed to the photo.

'You know him?' said Anna.

'A bit. His office is at the end of my corridor. We chat when we meet at the coffee machine.'

'Cosy,' Anna said.

'I'm surprised you got him to pose for this. I thought he was married.'

'It's a calendar to show that there are attractive men in science,' said Anna. 'Not a dating column. Bloody hell. Why does everyone think that?'

Gordon ignored her. 'Let's see the rest of your specimens then.'

Beth winced at the word 'specimens'. They had all been nice guys – they were certainly not specimens. She looked over her shoulder to see Anna, her lips pressed together, scrolling through the photos for Gordon. Hibs was studying the picture on the wall with apparent concentration. Who would have thought that a picture of a plate of lemons could be so fascinating?

'Very good,' said Gordon. 'Nice photos, Beth. You can hardly tell they weren't professionally done.'

There was a moment of tense silence before Anna cleared her throat. 'We were about to have a cup of tea. Would you like one, Gordon?' Her voice was pointedly polite.

'I'll make them.' Hibs jumped to his feet, put the kettle on and moved round Beth to find the mugs. 'How do you take your tea, Gordon?'

'Black. No sugar.'

Hibs threw teabags into mugs. 'Anna?'

'White, one sugar, please, my lover.'

Hibs turned and winked at her. She said, 'Mwah,' and blew him a kiss. Beth tried not to notice the twinge of annoyance she felt. What did she have to be annoyed about? She moved along a bit to give Hibs space as he poured the water. It seemed natural to share work space with him. She did it every day at the lab.

'There we go.' Hibs pushed Beth's cup towards her before he handed the others round. He didn't need to ask her how she took hers.

'Thanks,' said Anna.

Beth didn't hear Gordon say anything. There was the rustle of newspaper, and then silence again.

'So,' said Anna, brightly. 'What are you cooking, Beth? It smells delicious.'

'Lasagne.'

'Yummy.' Anna sniffed the air. 'Aren't you having garlic bread? I love garlic bread.'

'I don't,' said Gordon.

Beth loved garlic bread too. She had eaten lots of it when she'd been single. But Gordon said it made her smell like a pizzeria. So no garlic bread these days.

'Do you cook, Gordon?' Anna asked.

'Very well, thanks,' said Gordon. 'Since you ask.'

'How about you, Hibs?'

'I can follow a recipe.'

'Really?' Anna sounded amused.

'Hang on, how come you find it hard to believe that I can cook?' Hibs said. 'I can.'

'You've never cooked for me.'

'I've only known you a fortnight.' Hibs leaned back

in his chair so that he could see Beth. 'Back me up here, Beth.'

He had cooked a meal for all his friends on his birthday. Yes, he could cook. 'He doesn't do it often, but when he does, he does it well,' Beth said.

'So there.' Hibs nodded triumphantly at Anna.

'Men make better chefs than women,' Gordon observed, without looking away from his paper.

'Ooh,' said Anna. 'Those are fighting words. What about Gordon, Beth. Can he cook?'

Beth paused in her chopping and tried to remember a time when Gordon had cooked for her. She turned, knife in hand, and looked at Gordon for assistance.

'I prefer to take Beth out for meals,' he said. 'That way, I don't have to rush about preparing things and I can give Beth the attention she deserves.' He smiled at her. 'Isn't that right, babe?'

Beth turned back to her crumble. 'Yes. That's right.' That's what he had always said and she believed him. After all, why would he lie? It suddenly occurred to her that she had always cooked for him a lot. Maybe it would be nice for him to put himself out and cook her a meal, for a change. But she said nothing.

'Anyway,' said Gordon. 'What are you two up to on Hibs's night off?'

'We're going to the cinema to see a re-run of *Taxi*,' said Anna. 'The original French one, not the one with Queen Latifah.'

'That'll have subtitles,' said Gordon.

'I can read,' said Hibs.

There was a rustle as Gordon turned a page. Beth measured out the flour and sugar for the crumble. The tension in the room was grating on her nerves. She wished

Hibs and Anna would just go. She was nervous enough about this evening without having to worry about them hanging around as well.

'The cinema sounds very cosy,' said Gordon. 'Does that mean you two are a proper couple now?'

There was a pause. Beth turned round just as Anna said 'yes' and Hibs said 'no'.

Anna and Hibs stared at each other for a tense moment. Hibs's eyes were wide and slightly panic-stricken.

'You don't sound too sure,' Gordon said with amusement in his voice.

'No,' said Hibs, his eyes still on Anna. 'We're not.'

'We're just having fun together.' She turned to look at Gordon. 'Nothing serious. Just one day at a time. Right, Hibs?'

'Right.' His voice was too sharp and Beth thought he still looked frightened. To her surprise she felt a little pleased about that.

Turning, Beth noticed that Gordon was watching her. She gave him a quick smile and returned to her cooking.

'Sorry,' Gordon said, sounding anything but. 'I seem to have touched a nerve there.'

'Don't worry about it,' said Hibs. 'What time does this film start, Anna? Should we get going?'

After they'd gone, Gordon said, 'Well, I think Hibs has bitten off more than he can chew there.'

Beth took the lasagne out of the oven and dished up. She didn't want to say anything in case it gave away too much. Her awareness of Hibs was a passing thing. It wouldn't have even started if Gordon had been there. If Hibs's girlfriend hadn't been her housemate, she wouldn't have noticed who he was sleeping with. It was nothing. However, Gordon could be quite protective of her.

'Beth?'

'Hmm?' She realised she'd been staring into space, thinking. 'Sorry, what was that?'

'I said, Hibs might have met his match with Anna.'

'Looks like it,' she said. 'They've seen a lot of each other for a few weeks now. That's a pretty long time for Hibs.'

'Hmm.' Gordon prodded his lasagne. 'You know, I still think Hibs fancies you.'

Beth felt her heart rate increase. Had he somehow read her mind? 'That's silly,' she said.

'Is it? You spend a lot of time together.'

'That's only because we work together. Hibs spends a lot of time with Vik. I don't see you accusing him of fancying him.'

'Woah. Steady on. No need to snap.'

'I wasn't …' If she argued, would she be demonstrating that she cared? Would it be better to dismiss his suggestion as though it wasn't worth thinking about? 'Never mind them,' she said. 'Let's talk about something more interesting. How was your day?'

There was a pause as Gordon looked at her steadily. Beth held his gaze, her throat constricting. She took care to breathe evenly. He couldn't read her mind. She hadn't done anything wrong. Okay, she'd admired another man. A bit. She didn't mean it seriously. It wasn't a crime.

Gordon gave a small nod and broke off eye contact. 'My day?' he said. 'It was good thanks.'

Chapter Sixteen

Hibs sat in the cinema, glaring at the screen. The film was loud and lively. Normally, he would have enjoyed it, but Anna's comment about them being a couple was bothering him. If she thought that, then it was time to move on. In a way, he was disappointed. He liked Anna. She was good company and great in bed. But if she wanted more than that … well, he couldn't offer it to her.

Anna's hand had made it onto his thigh. He put his hand over hers and gripped it firmly. Then she leaned across and nipped his earlobe – he moved away slightly. The sex-on-demand thing was great, but he needed to think. And he was tired. He spent his working nights in the lab and his nights off either with Anna, or in the dojo, which meant he hadn't slept properly in weeks. Suddenly, he was unbelievably shattered. When Anna's hand moved further up his leg, he moved it back down.

'What's wrong?' Anna whispered in his ear.

'We're supposed to be watching a film,' he whispered back.

'So?'

'Well, you're the one who wanted to see it.'

Her eyes gleamed at him in the cinema light. 'What's going on with you?'

There were several *shhh*s from people around them and Hibs spread his hands in a gesture of helplessness. Anna narrowed her eyes at him and turned back to the screen, crossing her arms.

Hibs settled back in his seat. This 'date' had gone a bit wrong. Most dates did. That's why it was simpler not to go on them. On the screen two cars screamed round a track but after a few moments, his eyelids started to drop. The room was warm and dark and noisy; it lulled him to sleep.

Beth hung up her cycle helmet and coat when she got back from the lab. Gordon was still in the kitchen, reading, and didn't say anything.

'I passed Hibs and Anna walking back from the cinema,' Beth said. Almost on autopilot, she put the kettle on.

'Oh yes? Did they look coupley?'

'You shouldn't tease them like that,' she said. 'It's … mean.'

'They can take it. Besides, it's funny.'

'Hmmm.' She still thought it was mean. Beth was hot from cycling, so she pulled off her jumper and tied it round her waist. After a moment, she felt the hairs on the back of her neck prickle and turned to find Gordon watching her, his expression disapproving.

'What?'

'What's that T-shirt you're wearing?'

Beth looked down. She was wearing the skinny tee that she'd got for her birthday. 'It was a present from the guys in the lab.'

Gordon sniffed. 'It makes you look like a geek.'

Beth laughed. 'I *am* a geek.' She tossed teabags into mugs as the kettle started to boil. Before she could pour, Gordon came up behind her and kissed her, just behind her ear.

'I think,' he said, 'that it doesn't suit you and you should take it off.'

'But, I like it.'

Gordon kissed his way down her neck and wrapped his hands around her waist. 'Perhaps I can persuade you.' He turned her round to face him.

Beth slipped her arms round his neck. 'Oh yes?'

Gordon replied by kissing her lips. He tasted faintly of apple crumble and smelled of Lynx. Beth savoured the familiar sensations. The way he tasted, the warmth of his arms round her, the feel of hard swimmer's muscles against her. Tea forgotten, she kissed him back.

Gordon's fingers sneaked underneath her top and brushed her spine. Excitement tingled through her like electricity. His hands caressed gently and moved up. His kisses became more fervent. He paused, then, with a swift movement, he pulled the top over her head and tossed it into the recycle bin.

Beth gasped. 'Gordon! That was a present!' She didn't mind, really. She could retrieve it later.

He bent his head and kissed her chest. 'Mmm?' He straightened up and his mouth found hers. Beth gave up and gave into the delicious feeling.

There was a sound at the door and Beth sprang back. Anna was home – probably with Hibs. She couldn't let them see her semi-clothed. But Gordon's embrace held her firmly to him.

'Gordon. I need to get my top.'

'No you don't.'

Hearing the key in the lock, she wriggled. Gordon pinned her arms with his and kissed the swell of her breasts, still holding her tight. Her heart raced. She could feel her throat constrict in panic. She would just die of embarrassment if Hibs saw her like this. She twisted in earnest. The door handle turned. Gordon grinned and let her go. He was between her and the T-shirt, so she made a bolt for her room instead. Gordon reached after her and snapped her bra clasp. As she twisted out of his way, her breasts escaped from the delicate material. She shrieked and made it into her room just as Anna and Hibs walked in. Gordon slipped in behind her, laughing.

Beth's face flamed with embarrassment and her breath came fast. What if they had seen her? She pulled her bra back on. 'I can't believe you just did that.'

Gordon took hold of her hands. 'Hey, leave that,' he said, taking the bra off her and dropping it on the floor.

'What if they saw me?'

'So what? They're adults. They know what a topless woman looks like.' He pulled her gently onto her bed and unzipped her jeans.

Still angry, Beth moved her face as he tried to kiss her. 'But Hibs is my colleague. I won't be able to face him at work.' Why was he being so cavalier about this? Didn't he understand how mortifying it was?

Gordon tilted his head to one side. 'Oh, babe. I didn't realise you'd feel that way about it. I'm sorry.' He smiled.

For a moment, Beth was trapped between her own feelings of embarrassment and rage and confusion. Gordon raised her hand to his face and kissed the palm. He wasn't fazed by it at all. He hadn't meant to upset her. Maybe she was overreacting. It was a mistake. A bit of foreplay gone wrong. She stared at him, her indignation seeping away.

'You're getting upset over nothing, you'll see,' said Gordon gently. 'Don't be silly.'

It was silly, she supposed. He was right. They wouldn't have seen her. Gordon was just trying to liven things up a bit. Yes. Silly. She sighed.

He kissed her 'That's better. And besides.' He slipped his hand inside her jeans. 'You look so, so sexy right now.'

Beth didn't know what to say. Gordon laid her back on the bed, his fingers exploring. His kisses were deeper, more aroused than before. And Beth, her heart pounding as the adrenaline kicked in, kissed him back.

Hibs followed Anna into the kitchen just in time to see Beth, her breasts escaping from her bra, bolting into her bedroom. The world lost focus for a moment as Gordon, just behind Beth, paused at the door and grinned at Hibs.

'What was that all about?' Anna said, throwing her keys on the table. 'I thought we were the kinky ones around here.'

Hibs said nothing. The sight of a topless Beth, her slim, smooth back; the glimpse of a small, perfect breast, replayed in his mind. Unable to look at Anna, he looked around the kitchen. Something in the recycling bin caught his attention. He picked it up and recognised Beth's T-shirt. It was still warm. He carefully turned it the right side out and a picture of a crying Pluto looked back at him. He remembered Beth opening the parcel, the laughter when she pulled it out and held it against herself. The top looked tiny in his hands. Why had she thrown it away? He'd thought she liked it.

Anna was still talking and Hibs tried to concentrate. He had to get the image of Beth out of his mind or he would never be able to concentrate on anything ever again. He forced himself to look up. 'Pardon?'

'I said, what do you want to do tonight?' She put a coffee on the table, next to him.

He looked at Anna and felt very tired. He liked Anna. More than anyone he'd slept with before. But if this went on for much longer, she'd expect more from him. It was getting complicated. It always did. 'I don't know,' he said. 'There isn't an awful lot of tonight left, is there?'

Anna was looking at his hands and he realised he was

still holding the T-shirt. He dropped it on the table and held his hands up to show they were empty. He had to focus on the girl in front of him. Anna stepped into the gap between his hands and kissed him. Hibs closed his eyes. A vision of Beth running away sprang up behind his eyelids. Concentrate, he told himself. Anna's arms were around his neck now, her body close. He tried to focus on Anna, but all he could think about was Beth. This was all wrong. He broke away from her. 'Anna, we need to talk.'

She didn't move her arms from around him. 'Oh, come on. You're not still sulking about me saying we were going out, are you?'

'No.' He gently moved her arms off him.

'And you know I don't mind that you fell asleep during the film.'

'I know.'

'So, what do we need to talk about?'

He looked down at her sparkling eyes. 'I can't do this,' he said, and took a step back. 'It's been fun, Anna. You're a really great person, but I don't do relationships. And we're becoming ... a relationship.'

Anna's gaze slid down from his face to his hands and back again. 'No,' she said. 'That's not what this is about.' Her eyes met his again. He was relieved to see there was no anger in them. 'You're dumping me because you're in love with Beth.'

Hibs started. He had not been expecting that. 'What?'

Anna smiled. 'Oh come on, Hibs. It's pretty obvious. The way you look at her ... any idiot can tell how you feel about her.'

'Really?' And he'd thought he was hiding it so well.

'Actually, not any idiot. Beth can't.' Anna backed away from him and sat down. 'So, what happens now?'

'I'm sorry,' he said. He genuinely was sorry to part company with Anna, but there was no other way. He was never going to be able to get the sight of Beth out of his mind now. To carry on sleeping with Anna would just be wrong.

Anna waved his apology away. 'No need. It's not like I didn't know. I wasn't after a relationship anyway.'

'But you said we were a couple.'

'That was for Gordon's benefit. I didn't expect it to freak you out like that.'

'Oh.'

There was silence for a minute. 'Anna,' he said. 'How long have you known?'

'Since that night in the pub, when Gordon came back.' She kicked off her shoes and put her feet up on another chair.

'But you still ...'

'Came on to you? Of course I did. I fancied you. I took my chance when I saw it.' She looked up and grinned. 'You're not the only one who's a promiscuous hussy.'

Hibs smiled back. 'No, I guess I'm not.' He put his hands in his pockets. 'I guess I'll be seeing you, then.'

The next morning, when Beth and Gordon went into the kitchen for breakfast, the Pluto T-shirt was carefully folded on the table. Gordon swept it into the recycling bin before he sat down for his coffee. Beth said nothing. But when Gordon had left for work, she fished the T-shirt out of the bin and hid it under her mattress. She wasn't sure when she was going to wear it again or even why she'd hidden it, but she did it anyway. She would rationalise it later, when she had time.

Chapter Seventeen

Hibs was late coming into work, which was unusual. Beth was glad. Despite Gordon's assurances, she was sure Hibs must have seen her last night. The very idea made her face flare. It was wrong on so many levels. He was her friend, her colleague. It really shouldn't have happened. Gordon had meant it as a playful gesture and he had obviously found it arousing, but it was just so embarrassing.

'What's the matter with you today?' Vik said.

'Huh?'

Vik had been leaning on her lab bench, telling her something about a girl. She realised she hadn't heard most of it.

'I'm sorry, Vik. I was miles away. You were saying … about your friend.'

He sighed. 'It doesn't matter. It wasn't that interesting anyway.' He plonked himself on Hibs's stool. 'Are you okay? You've been kinda spaced out since you got here.'

'I'm fine. I guess the broken sleep every other night is just getting to me.' She rubbed her eyes. It was true: she was starting to fall asleep when she was with Gordon, which she knew annoyed him.

'How many more have you got to do?'

'A few more sets. So, another couple of weeks. Assuming nothing goes wrong.'

Vik glanced at the clock. 'Where's Hibs today? I wonder if Anna's detained him.'

Again, that acid twist in her stomach. She really had to get over it. She had Gordon and she didn't want anyone else. So why this fixation with Hibs's love life?

'Maybe,' she said, and turned back to her work.

Footsteps approached. Both Vik and Beth peered through the lab benches to watch Hibs stomp into the dry end of the lab and hang up his jacket.

'Afternoon,' Vik said. 'Did you sleep in?'

'Yes, thanks.'

Beth couldn't see Hibs as he sat down at his computer, but she could hear the ragged edge in his voice. She looked at Vik.

'Something's up,' Vik whispered. 'Come on.' He slid off the stool and walked across the lab. Halfway there, he turned and looked at Beth, gesturing with his head that she should come with him.

Oh well. She had to face him sometime. Beth sighed and followed.

Hibs was slumped so far down in his chair that he was practically lying down. There were blue shadows under his eyes and his lips were clamped so tightly that they were turned down at the corners.

'You look awful,' Vik said. 'What's wrong?'

'Nothing. I'm fine.' He didn't look up.

'Rough night? How was the cinema?'

'Dark.' He still wasn't looking up.

Vik looked at Beth for assistance. She shrugged. Even she was worried now. She'd expected things to be awkward after last night, but she hadn't expected belligerence.

Hibs swore at the computer. 'What does this thing run on? Goblins? Twentieth-century piece of crap. I need coffee.' He stood up, passed Beth without looking at her and stomped off down the corridor.

'Ooookay,' said Vik. 'That was weird.'

'I'm sure he'll tell us when he's ready,' Beth said. She

wasn't sure what was going on, but she didn't really want to prod Hibs when he was in a bad mood. He seemed to be in a bad mood a lot these days. Perhaps Anna wasn't all that good for him. 'I'm going back to work.'

She returned to her bench, still thinking. Anna was the sort of person who knew what she wanted and didn't hesitate to go get it. Just look at the way she got Hibs to go to the cinema the night before. Hibs was terrified of commitment. What if Hibs and Anna had fallen out? It was her fault that he and Anna had been introduced in the first place. She had been so worried about how Anna would fare with Hibs that she hadn't thought Hibs might get hurt. Damn. She'd known from the start there would be trouble if those two got together.

Hibs pulled out his notebook and stared at his plan for the day without actually noting any of it. He hadn't slept much. The whole episode with Beth and Gordon had played over and over in his mind. It was Gordon's smile that bothered him. Gordon had wanted him to see Beth topless. He knew Beth well enough to know that she would be mortified, and if he knew that, Gordon must know it too. So why would Gordon want Beth to feel humiliated?

Or was Gordon trying to prove a point to Hibs? If Anna knew how he felt about Beth, it wasn't a huge leap to think that Gordon might have sussed it too.

Hibs took a gulp of hot coffee and winced as it hit his throat. Either Gordon was playing a power game with Beth or trying to force Hibs to look at what he was missing. Either way, he wasn't going to give him the satisfaction. What happened last night was only a problem if Hibs had seen it. He would just deny seeing anything.

He took another, more cautious sip of coffee and sighed. She had a boyfriend. Out of bounds. He would just have to live with it.

Beth had finished setting up her experiment by the time Hibs came back. She tensed as he walked behind her and scraped his wooden stool along the floor to the bench. She glanced over her shoulder: he wasn't looking at her.

They worked in silence for a bit and Beth could feel the tension thrumming in the air. She couldn't put up with this much longer.

'Do you want to see last night's results?' She turned to him.

Hibs looked startled. 'I ... yes. Are they any good?' He wasn't making eye contact with her.

She passed across the graphs she'd printed out earlier. 'The pictures are on the computer.'

He took the paper, still not quite looking at her. This was awful. She had to say something: this awkwardness couldn't go on for ever.

'Hibs.'

'Hmm?'

Just the thought of what had happened made her feel all hot. She really, really hoped that Gordon was wrong and Hibs hadn't seen her running around half naked. 'About last night ...'

'Uh huh.'

'I'm sorry about what happened. Gordon—'

He put his hand up to stop her. 'What you and Gordon get up to is none of my business.'

'I know, but ... well, you and Anna ...' She sighed. She was making a hash of this. Just get on with it, Beth. She took a deep breath. 'I don't know how much you saw. I'm so embarrassed.'

There was a pause. Biting her lip, she raised her eyes. He was frowning at his feet.

'I don't want things to get weird,' said Beth.

Hibs finally looked at her. 'I don't either,' he said. 'Don't worry. I didn't ... I got in just as you disappeared. Anna saw— *told* me what happened.'

Oh thank goodness. Beth felt as though a cloud had lifted. At least she could look him in the face without cringing with embarrassment. 'That's great.' She smiled at him. 'I'm glad we've got that out of the way.'

He didn't smile back. 'Actually, there's something else I need to talk to you about.'

'What?'

'Anna and I have split up.'

Ah. The cloud lifted further. 'That's ...' She paused in case the word 'great' slipped out again. Maybe that's why he was so grumpy this morning. 'Are you okay?'

'Yeah.'

He didn't sound okay. Beth had seen Hibs break up with more women than she could remember and she had never, ever seen him look so rough. 'Sure?'

His mouth was still set in a hard line. 'Positive.' He stood up and, grabbing a pair of gloves, strode off in the direction of the cold room.

Beth stared after him until Vik appeared as though from nowhere. 'So that's what's bothering him.'

'Where did you come from?'

'I was lurking over there, by the nitrogen cylinders,' said Vik. 'I figured he might tell you what's wrong.'

'Is nothing sacred?'

'Not really.' Vik grinned. 'Does it matter?'

'I suppose not.' They both looked to the door, where Hibs had disappeared.

'He must have really liked her,' Beth said. 'I've never seen him upset about a girl before.'

'Maybe he's finally fallen in love.'

Beth felt something prickle in her chest.

Chapter Eighteen

Beth spun her office chair round in a celebratory pirouette and hit print. She now had half of the data sets she needed to show that her hypothesis was right. Ideally, she'd wait until she had all the data before she took it to Roger, but his talk was just over a week away and he would need to change his slides. She retrieved the graphs from the printer and leafed through them. There should be enough to convince Roger.

'Hibs?' She turned to him. 'Can you have a quick look at these, please?'

She thrust the papers towards him. He took them and looked through, frowning. After a minute or two, his frown cleared up. 'Hey, these look pretty good. You need another data set, to be sure, but otherwise, pretty good.' He gave the papers back to her and smiled. It was the first smile she'd seen in a while. 'Well done, Beth. Good call.'

Beth felt a small glow in her chest from his praise. When it came to science, Hibs didn't throw his compliments around. If he felt it was a good call, it was a good call.

'I was going to show Roger,' she said. 'So that he's got time to put it in his slides.'

'Do that.' Hibs paused. 'Good luck.'

Still warm from being praised, Beth rapped on Roger's door. He was sitting at his desk, reading.

He looked up, over the top of his reading glasses. 'Yes?'

'Do you have a couple of minutes to discuss some results?'

He perked up with interest. 'Is that the experiment I told you to repeat?' He held out his hand to take her papers.

'No—'

He retracted his hand before Beth could push the documents into it. 'Why not? I told you to do it weeks ago.'

'I'm doing that. This is the other idea I mentioned. I've made some GFP-tagged mutants—'

Roger frowned. 'I didn't tell you to do that. You should have been doing what I explicitly requested.'

'I *am* doing what you explicitly requested ... as well as this.' This conversation was not going as she imagined. She was here to show him her data, but instead they were arguing over something completely irrelevant. Why did this always happen when she tried to talk to Roger? Hibs never had this problem. She took a deep breath. 'Please can you just look at them?' She shoved the papers into his hand. 'I've been tracking the protein localisation as the cell grows. When you look here'—she pointed to one of the photos—'it's obvious that my protein helps hold the other two together—'

Roger gave them the barest glance and then shoved the papers back at her. 'There's not enough data here.'

'Yes, but—'

'Come back when you have enough data.' Roger turned back to his reading. 'And get me those repeat results I asked for.'

Anger boiled inside Beth and her hands began to shake. He was being an arrogant pig. She opened her mouth to argue.

But what if he's right? The thought pricked the hot bubble of righteous anger. Roger knew more about this stuff than she did.

He looked up. 'Are you still here?'

Beth spun round and walked out.

* * *

Hibs looked up when Beth came in and shouted, 'Aaaaargh,' through her teeth. She held the graphs she had just shown him crumpled in a fist and her teeth were clamped so tightly the sinews on her neck stood out. He felt sorry for her: Roger could be brutal.

'Didn't go well then?'

'Ugh.' She threw herself into her chair. He gave her a moment to calm down. When her breathing had slowed, he asked, 'What did he say?'

'He said I was wrong and I should get on with the repeat experiments.'

Even from a few feet away, he could see the tears gathering in the corners of her eyes. Damn. He never knew what to do when girls cried. He always felt he should do something to help. He could go talk to Roger ... but then Beth would never get over this inferiority complex she had. 'So, are you going to?'

She stared into space, her graphs still in her fist, and chewed her lip.

Hibs watched her and willed her not to cry. Come on, Beth. Find some faith in yourself. Don't let Roger keep kicking you. Fight. She stopped biting her lip and looked at her fistful of paper.

'Yes,' she said. 'But I'm also going to finish this data set and show him that I'm right. I know I'm right.'

Atta girl. He wanted to go and clap her on the back or give her a hug or something. Beth had been bullied by men all her life: her father, her boyfriend and now Roger. It had taken a lot for her to even think about defying Roger's authority. It was a small step, but at least it was in the right direction. If she could learn to take one little step at time, maybe she'd finally realise that she didn't need Gordon. Or anyone, for that matter. But especially not Gordon.

She looked up at him. 'You think I'm right, don't you?'

Her lip was all red from being chewed. Hibs realised he was staring at it. He tore his eyes away. 'I do indeed,' he said. 'A good choice. We'll get it all done in time, don't worry.'

She smoothed the papers out on the desk. 'Yeah. We will.' She reached across and put her hand on his arm. 'Thanks, Hibs.'

Her hand felt smooth and warm and he had to resist the urge to turn it over and hold it. 'You're welcome,' he said. When she removed her hand, he waited until he'd walked round the corner before he placed his own hand over the warm afterglow.

Hibs arranged to meet Vik for a drink after work. When he got to the pub he was surprised to find Beth standing at the bar. She hadn't been out with them since Gordon caught her in the pub when she was meant to be in the lab. He grinned at her. 'Evening, stranger.'

'Hi.' She looked pale and tired in the dim light from the bar. 'I've ordered you a pint. I guessed what you'd have.'

'You guessed right.' He reached over and picked up a couple of the drinks, leaving her to pay the barman. 'So, how come you're here? Where's his lordship?'

'Swimming training.' Beth picked up the remaining drinks. 'Actually,' she said, dropping her voice. 'I'm here because Lara didn't want to go straight back home.'

'Oh, okay. How's she doing?'

Beth shrugged. 'She's determined not to have Chris back. But I think she's lonely.'

He nodded. 'Understandable.' He followed her into the nook where Lara was talking to Vik. They looked up when Beth arrived with the drinks and both looked relieved. Hibs smiled. It always took Vik a few drinks to unwind properly. 'Hello, beautiful lady,' Hibs said to Lara as he slipped into the seat next to her.

'How are you?' He tried hard not to do the concerned voice. He'd heard that the concerned voice only made things worse. He did his best to sound merely interested instead.

'I'm good, thanks.' She looked older, he thought, but still perfectly groomed. At least her anally retentive tidiness was back. That much was normal.

'Coping?' He leaned forward.

She nodded. 'Yes. One miserable day at a time.' She smiled and patted his hand. 'Thanks for asking.'

'Ah, what are friends for.' He picked up a cardboard beer mat and started twirling it on its edge.

Across from him, Beth picked up her pint, took a sip and closed her eyes to savour it. 'I haven't had a pint in ages,' she said, as she opened her eyes.

'Why not?' said Hibs.

Beth avoided eye contact and mumbled something about Gordon.

'What? He gets to dictate what you can drink now, does he?' He stopped twirling the table mat. He wasn't sure what angered him more. Gordon for being so controlling. Or Beth for letting him.

Beth looked up. 'Don't start. Please. I just want to have a quiet drink, okay?'

Hibs glanced at Lara, who was watching Beth carefully. She caught his eye and gave a tiny shrug.

'Okay,' he said. 'Sorry.'

There was silence around the table for a moment. Beth looked so small and sad that Hibs wanted to rush round and put his arm around her. He stared at his pint disconsolately.

'So, Vik,' said Beth. 'What happened with the latest woman your aunt set you up with?'

'She thought I was goofy,' Vik said, frowning. 'You guys don't think I'm goofy, do you?'

There was the slightest pause before Beth said, 'Of course not. You're not goofy. You're adorable.'

Vik looked crestfallen. Hibs drew a breath through his teeth.

'Adorable?' said Hibs. 'That's the worst thing you can say to a guy.'

'That's worse than goofy,' Vik said. 'Now I wish I was just goofy.'

Beth looked from one to the other. 'What are you on about?'

'Adorable. And cute. And sweet. All that means that he's pretty much unshaggable,' said Hibs. 'I thought everyone knew that.'

Vik nodded. 'Yeah. Nice guys don't get laid.'

There was a pause and the two women looked at each other.

'I'm not sure that's strictly true,' said Lara.

'Hibs is a nice guy,' Beth pointed out. 'He gets laid.'

'I'm not a nice guy.' Oh no. He wasn't going to be painted into the 'adorable' corner. Beth was out of bounds for now, but if he ended up labelled 'nice' there was absolutely no chance of her seeing him as anything other than a friend.

'You are.'

'No I'm not. I'm a commitment-shy, good-for-nothing bastard.'

Lara leaned forward. 'Have you ever cheated on anyone?'

'I've never been with anyone long enough to cheat

on them,' said Hibs. 'Which brings us nicely back to commitment-shy, good-for-nothing bastard.'

Lara shook her head. 'You never promised to be faithful,' she said. 'You never said you'd stay with someone, for richer, for poorer, in sickness and in health.' Her voice cracked the tiniest bit.

Hibs wished he could go through the floor. He'd been so busy trying to raise his profile with Beth, that he'd forgotten how fragile Lara was at the moment. 'Lara—'

Lara put a hand up to stop him. 'No. You didn't, did you? Which just makes you immature. Chris. Now *he* is a good-for-nothing bastard.'

Beth was glaring at Hibs and Vik was looking frantic. Hibs tried to think of something to say. Lara took a deep breath and let it out, slowly. When she looked up, her gaze was steady. 'But, I have to admit. He does get laid. Apparently.'

'Lara, I didn't mean to—' Hibs began.

'It's okay, Hibs. I need to get used to being with other people and not get upset at every little thing,' said Lara. She held his gaze. 'Relax. I'm okay.'

He sensed the battle inside her: she wanted to conquer the pain. He had to respect that. 'Okay,' he said. 'Just for you, I'll admit to being nice.'

She smiled, an unconvincing, wobbly-at-the-edges smile, and everyone round the table relaxed a bit.

'But I'm not adorable,' Hibs added.

Beth gave a nervous laugh. 'You wish,' she said.

Hibs looked up and was about to challenge her when a timer beeped.

'Oh.' Beth dug her phone out of her pocket and turned the alarm off. She took a large gulp of her drink. 'I'd better head back.'

'Why?' said Hibs. 'You don't have to do a reading for another two hours.'

'Gordon will be finishing training about now. I want to get back to the lab before he twigs that I'm not there.' She took another glug of her drink and stood up. 'I'll see you guys later, okay.'

Vik scrambled to his feet. 'I'll walk with you.'

'What? You're deserting us too?' Hibs wasn't really surprised. Lara's outburst had been uncomfortable for them all. Vik didn't deal with that sort of thing very well.

'I'll see you later,' Beth said to Lara. 'I'm sorry to rush off, but ... well, Gordon would be upset if he thought I'd lied to him.'

Lara waved. 'Don't worry. I'm sure Hibs will keep me company for a bit. Won't you, Hibs?' She nudged him.

'Yeah. What with me being Mr Nice,' he muttered.

Beth smiled and she and Vik left.

Hibs stared at the door for a few moments after she'd gone. 'I don't get it. Why does she let him do that to her?'

He turned back to find Lara watching him, looking at his hand. He followed her gaze down and saw a beer mat was crushed in his fist. He opened his hand and tried to smooth the twisted cardboard down but it wouldn't go back to its flat shape. He looked back up, to find Lara still watching him.

'How long have you felt like that ... about Beth?' she asked softly.

He continued to smooth down the beer mat. He could lie to Lara, he wanted to talk to someone and he sure as hell couldn't tell Beth. 'I don't know. It crept up on me a bit.'

Lara was leaning on her forearms. 'She doesn't know, does she?'

He shook his head. 'She's with Gordon.' He grabbed an edge of the beer mat and started to tear it. 'And he treats her so badly, Lara. Why does she let him do that to her? She's bright, she's pretty, she's outgoing. Why does she let him treat her like dirt? He keeps telling her she's rubbish and she still loves him. How does that work?'

Lara sighed. 'I don't know. I've tried to tell her, but she just doesn't see it.'

'What can we do to make her understand that he's ruining her self-confidence?'

'I don't think there's anything we can do.' Lara shook her head. 'She has to figure it out for herself.'

Hibs snorted. 'She's clearly not going to do that.' He picked up his pint. 'He controls what she can and can't drink for fuck's sake.'

Lara nodded. They sat side by side, staring into space for a moment.

'Hibs,' said Lara. 'If you've liked Beth for so long, how come you haven't told her?'

He took another sip from his drink. 'She's with Gordon,' he repeated.

'But they broke up for six months. You could have said something then.' She narrowed her eyes. 'It's not like you have any problem asking girls out.'

Hibs laughed. 'I haven't actually asked a girl out since I was about eighteen.'

'But—'

'They come to me. Honestly. I'm not bragging or anything. I really haven't asked a girl out in over a decade. I just show them I'm interested and the rest … just happens.'

'Really?' She looked him up and down. 'Huh.'

'Thanks.'

She smiled. 'So, are you going to tell her?'

'I told you. She's with Gordon.'

'Maybe she's with him because she doesn't realise there's an alternative. You could give her someone to run to.'

He hadn't thought of it that way. 'I guess.' But what if she wasn't interested? All he'd have done is scare her away and remove another friend that she could have gone to for help.

'Or are you too scared that she'll turn you down?' said Lara.

He was about to deny it when Lara carried on. 'Sometimes, you have to take a risk,' she said, looking at her wedding ring. 'Even when the outcome isn't what you hoped. You have to find out.' She looked up, her eyes full of tears. 'Because, ultimately, it's better to know. One way or the other.' She wiped the tears away with a finger.

He wasn't sure what to do. It didn't seem right to hug her. She wasn't that close a friend and he certainly didn't want her to think he was hitting on her. He dug a wad of blue tissue out of his pocket and handed it to her. 'It's clean.'

She took it and blew her nose and tucked the tissue into her jeans pocket.

'For what it's worth,' said Hibs, 'I think it's very brave, what you did. And I think sticking to your decision is even braver. It must be hard.'

'It is. But it was the right thing.' Lara sighed. 'My grandmother used to say, "If you want to find out how strong you are, you have to let yourself be vulnerable."'

'She sounds like a wise lady.'

They both picked up their drinks in silence.

'You know, Hibs,' Lara said, 'despite what you said earlier, you really are one of the nice guys.'

He grinned. 'I'm going to pretend I didn't hear that.'

Chapter Nineteen

The lab phone rang – everyone ignored it, hoping someone else would get it. Finally Beth gave in and put down her pipette. 'Fine. I'll get it. Again.' She tossed her gloves in the bin and picked up the receiver.

'Beth?' Anna's voice came down the phone. 'We've got a problem.'

'Aren't you supposed to say, "Houston we have a problem?"'

'What?' There was a puzzled pause. 'Anyway, not important. We have a serious fucking problem. Dan Blackwood's pulled out of the calendar.'

'What? When? Why?'

'He sent an e-mail. His wife objected, apparently. Although I'm suspicious. If his wife had objections, why didn't she say something before? Why now?'

'Oh. Shit.' It was as though someone had tipped water over her. She had been really proud of that calendar. It was the most satisfying thing she had done in ages and those photos were all hers. No one else had helped, or advised in any way. It was something that made her happy and powerful and now it might not come to anything. The thought made her want to cry. 'We have to call Lara and tell her not to send the pictures to the printers.'

'Already done that. I said I'd send them when we found a replacement. Beth, we need a Dr January. We haven't got any backup choices. I've been trying to think of anyone we can ask and all I can come up with is Hibs.'

Beth glanced across the lab to where Hibs was scowling

with concentration as he pipetted blue liquid into tiny little wells. 'He's already said no.'

'Can you ask him again? He might agree if you ask.' Anna gave a little laugh. 'He's certainly not going to do it for me.'

'I don't know ...' As she watched, Hibs stretched, moving his shoulders to get them out of the hunched position he'd been in for the past few minutes. She had a lovely photo of him that she could use. And she could do the interview bit easily. All she needed was for him to say yes. On the other hand, she'd already asked and he'd refused. He headed for the dry area, still rolling his wrists to stretch them.

'Well, he's pretty much all we've got at the moment,' said Anna.

'Maybe we can persuade Dan—'

'Already tried that. No go.'

'I'll try,' Beth said.

She hung up and walked slowly back to her bench. There was another option, of course. There was always Gordon. If she asked him, he'd be sure to agree. But none of the photos that she'd taken of him had the same *presence* that the photo of Hibs had. She was pleased with that photo: she'd captured Hibs perfectly.

Besides, asking Gordon looked like nepotism. The others would think he'd somehow engineered the whole thing to get into the calendar. It irritated her that they thought so little of him.

Beth sighed. If Hibs said no, she would ask Gordon. At least that way they'd know she'd tried to find someone else first.

Hibs sat down to check his e-mails. Beth was on the

phone again. It was probably Gordon. Again. He had started calling Beth on the lab phone – probably another way for him to keep tabs on her. It was creepy how controlling that guy was. And Beth was sliding back to being the nervous wreck she had been when he last had his claws in her. Hibs rubbed the bridge of his nose. He wanted to help her, but she didn't believe she even had a problem. He pulled up Google and typed in 'symptoms emotional abuse' like he'd done so many times before. A quick scan told him all he needed to know. Isolation from friends and support networks – check. Eroded self-esteem – check. Denial that abuser's behaviour is wrong – check. Finding excuses to explain abuse – check. Delusion that she was in love with him? Check.

Hibs sighed. Gordon was systematically destroying Beth, but how could he make her see that? The helplines he'd spoken to had all emphasised the need to be gentle with her rather than risk pushing her away. He couldn't help her until she admitted she had a problem.

He recognised the sound of her footsteps and was just about to close the browser when he had second thoughts. Maybe she would read it over his shoulder or something. She may not think it applied to her, but you never knew what her subconscious might pick up. He swivelled his chair round.

'Beth. It's Friday. You coming to the pub?'

She sat on the desk opposite him. She wasn't even looking at his screen. Bugger. 'Um … no. I have plans,' she said.

'With Gordon, no doubt.' It came out sounding bitter. Get a grip, Hibbotson.

'Hmm.' She was staring at her feet. She looked up. 'Hibs, I need your help.'

Hallelujah! She must have finally realised that Gordon was stifling her. Hibs leaned forward. 'Sure. Anything. What's up?'

'Dan Blackwood's pulled out of the calendar.'

That was not what he had been expecting. 'I thought the whole calendar thing was finished with?' he said, trying to keep the frustration out of his voice.

'It was, almost. But Dan's pulled out now and we're a man short.'

'Right.' He could see what was coming and he really didn't want to be in their calendar. The idea felt ... weird. 'Beth, we've had this conversation before. I don't want to do it.'

'I've got a really nice shot of you. Want me to show you?' She logged into her computer.

'No, because I'm not doing it.'

She turned to look at him. 'Please?' Her eyes looked huge and blue but he couldn't help noticing how tired she looked. The extra work at night and whatever Gordon was making her do in between times were clearly taking their toll. Hibs felt his chest contract. He wanted to hold her. To tell he'd save her if only she'd let him.

'Pretty please?'

But he still didn't want to be in that calendar. There was no way he was going to let Beth and her friends put a goofy picture of him in his lab coat anywhere public.

'No. Sorry.'

She turned back to the computer and pulled up his photo. Hibs was taken aback as a close-up of him filled the screen. Bloody hell. Were those crow's feet by his eyes? When had they appeared? He leaned back and took another look at the image itself. It was a good photo. His face was framed so that it highlighted his cheekbones. If you didn't look too closely, it was actually quite flattering. He looked all moody and mysterious. Not goofy in the slightest. 'No,' he said again, but he was less sure now.

Beth sighed. 'I was afraid you'd say that.' She shut the picture down and stood up to leave. 'I guess I'll have to ask Gordon.'

Wait. What? Gordon? There was no way he was going to let that narcissistic, bullying bastard get in instead. He wouldn't be surprised if Gordon's bullying of Beth was part of an attempt to make it into the calendar. 'I'll do it,' he said.

Beth turned. 'Really?'

He nodded. The relief on her face was enough to convince him he'd done the right thing. He smiled, glad that he had somehow made her world better.

'What changed your mind?'

'The photo,' he said. 'It's really good. I didn't think anyone could take a decent photo of me, but turns out you can.'

The smile she gave him made him wish he'd said it months ago.

Chapter Twenty

Beth let herself into the flat at the end of the day and was surprised by the smell of cooking. She wondered what was going on. Perhaps Anna was treating herself. She popped her head round the kitchen door and found Gordon sitting in the kitchen, humming to himself while he flicked through Anna's *Cause Celeb* magazine.

'Hello,' she said cautiously.

'Babe!' He swept over to her and gave her a big kiss. 'I'm cooking you dinner.'

'You are?' She glanced at the hob. The oven was on and there was a bowl of vegetables on the counter top. She had thought they'd be going out for dinner that evening. 'Why?'

Gordon pulled a face. 'What do you mean why? Can't I treat my favourite girl to a delicious home-cooked meal without having a reason?'

Beth looked back to his face. He seemed hurt. 'Oh. I didn't mean it like that.' She put her arms round his neck. 'It's lovely. It's just a surprise …' He was still looking hurt, so she kissed him. 'Thank you.'

'You're welcome.' He grinned. 'I've got a bottle of wine in the fridge, too.'

The door slammed and Anna came in. 'Hello.'

Damn. Anna. It was going to be hard to have a romantic meal for two with Anna drifting in and out of the kitchen. Beth cast a glance at Gordon, who looked surprisingly unworried.

'Alright, Anna,' he said.

'Gordon.' Anna helped herself to a glass of juice from

the fridge. 'Don't worry. I'll be out of your hair in a minute.'

'Are you going out?' said Beth.

'Yeah. Got a date. I'll disappear in the next half hour so you can have your romantic meal in peace.' Anna gave her a tight little smile.

'See,' said Gordon. 'I've got things all organised.' He slipped his arms around Beth's waist.

'If I don't see you before I go, have a good evening,' Anna said as she finished her juice.

'Oh, we will,' said Gordon.

As Anna disappeared, Gordon gave Beth a squeeze. 'Dinner will be about twenty minutes, if you want to go and get ready. You know, freshen up.'

'Okay.' Beth disentangled herself from his arms and placed a kiss on his cheek. 'I meant it. This really is lovely.'

'You're worth it,' he said.

Beth had a quick shower and changed into a skirt and soft jumper. She dried her hair and checked her reflection. All the late nights were starting to show. There were shadows under her eyes and her skin looked pale. She added a touch of blusher and lipstick. Better.

She felt a flutter of happiness at the fact that he'd taken the time to plan and cook her a meal. It meant a lot – not least because she knew he hated 'all that Jamie Oliver stuff'. In the year she'd been seeing him before, he'd never cooked for her. What had prompted this sudden change? Perhaps it was the conversation with Hibs and Anna a few weeks ago. Beth smiled. Whatever the reason, it was very welcome.

When Beth returned to the kitchen, the table was set for two. A pair of tea light holders that normally lived on the kitchen windowsill now housed candles. Gordon was pouring the wine.

'Hey.' He kissed her and pulled a chair out for her. 'Madam.'

'Thanks.' She sat down and reached for her wine.

'A simple starter,' said Gordon. He placed a bowl of salad in front of her. 'Mango, avocado and prawn salad.'

Beth looked at the plate. Everything was carefully stacked in the middle and drizzled with dressing. 'This must have taken you ages!'

'It did. But I wanted to show you how much you mean to me.'

She reached up and pulled him towards her to kiss him. Gordon grinned and kissed her back before sitting down. He picked up his fork. 'So, how was your day?'

'Okay. Nothing special.'

'Work going okay?'

'Yes, actually, the experiments are showing what I'd hoped.' She sipped the wine and felt it warm her up. 'How about yours?'

'Not bad, actually. I've only got five more months to get this stuff done, but I think I can manage it.'

Five months. That was how long she had him for. Beth's heart descended to her knees. His secondment was for six months. And the first of those was already gone. 'Gordon,' she said. 'What happens when the six months are up?'

He looked up at her, his lips twitching with a suppressed smile. 'That's what we're celebrating,' he said. 'I've had a brainwave.' He paused.

A small flicker of unease. She hoped he wasn't going to suggest she came to the US with him. 'Tell me.'

'I've applied for a postdoc job at the biology department here. It's right in my area. I'm pretty sure I'm going to get it.' He grinned. 'I won't be going back.'

Beth's spirits bungeed back up. 'Oh, Gordon, that's fantastic news!' She left her seat to rush round and hug him. He pulled her onto his lap.

'I know.' He kissed her, pulling her tightly to him. When they finally parted, he said, 'Are you ready for the main course?'

She nodded and slid off his lap. He squeezed her bum as he left his seat.

He had made roast lamb with potatoes and green beans. 'This is really good,' she said as she wiped the last potato round her plate to mop up the juices.

'I told you, I don't cook often, but I can if I want to.' He smiled at her. 'Unfortunately, I didn't have time to make pudding, so I had to buy it.' He fetched a parcel from the counter and ripped off the Marks and Spencer packaging. 'Chocolate mousse,' he said. 'Your favourite.' He put the pot in front of her and sat back down. The candlelight caught his hair and highlighted it with gold. He looked into her eyes and raised his glass. 'To us.'

'To us.' She couldn't take her eyes off him. He looked so gorgeous. And he was applying for a job to stay. It meant he needed her enough to give up his promising career in the US. This changed everything. Beth took another sip of wine and closed her eyes. Happiness suffused her whole body. Gordon loved her. She didn't want this night to ever end.

After dinner they lounged on the sofa, Beth leaning against Gordon's chest, comfortable in his arms. They talked about his trying out for the swimming team again and about how much better life would be when Beth didn't have to do night shifts any more. She was feeling totally relaxed and just starting to nod off.

'How's your calendar going?' Gordon said.

'Actually, we had a bit of a hiccup this morning. One of the guys dropped out.'

'Ah. Why?'

She couldn't be bothered to explain: it would spoil the mood. 'I'm not sure.'

'Have you got a replacement?'

'Umm ...' A spark of discomfort punctured her mellow mood. In the back of her mind, she heard Anna's comment. There was silence for moment. She listened to Gordon's heart beating against her ear and prayed he wouldn't ask. Anna was wrong. Anna was wrong.

'If you haven't,' Gordon said, 'I'd be happy to step in.'

Buggering hell. She lifted her head and looked up at his beautiful face. He was watching her intently and Beth felt some of the alcohol-fuelled comfort burn off. She turned her face away. 'That's nice.'

'Great. Could you do the questions? Or does it have to be Anna.'

'I'm sorry, I didn't mean you could.' She wriggled sideways to look at him.

'But ...' His eyes narrowed. In the dim mood lighting, they seemed to glitter in a disturbing way. 'What do you mean? You need someone for the empty slot now that Dan's pulled out. And I've agreed to fill it for you.'

Hang on – she hadn't told him it was Dan who'd pulled out. 'We don't need you to fill it.' The remnants of Beth's feelings of well-being vanished. Suspicion stirred that he might have prepared this whole evening just to lead her to the question of the calendar. She willed Gordon to let it go. She needed to know that all the lovely stuff he'd said and done were for real and not just put on because he wanted to feed his ego. Please. Please. Please.

'Have you already got a replacement?'

The gentle glow was gone. The whole evening had been a prelude to this. A bribe to get her to put him in her calendar.

'They can't have been that good or you'd have put them in the original calendar. Who is it?' His tone was hard now – she'd made him angry. Shit. She should have spoken to him before she asked Hibs.

'I don't get to choose,' she said, quickly. 'It's up to Anna and Lara. I don't choose.'

'Oh for fuck's sake, Beth. Why do you let those two bully you? You should stand up to them. Demand some respect.'

That was almost the same thing that Hibs had said to her. Only he'd said it about Gordon. Tears threatened. Beth moved her head back against his chest and blinked them back.

Suddenly, Gordon sighed. 'I'm sorry, babe.' He stroked her hair. 'I didn't mean to shout. It just winds me up that people take advantage of you, that's all.' He curled a finger under her chin and tilted her face up to his. 'Okay?'

Beth nodded, not convinced that she was. The sudden change of tactic was more unsettling than him shouting at her. He had apologised. He'd had a lot to drink. They both had, so maybe it had come out all wrong. She sat up and was surprised to find herself a little unstable.

'Tell you what,' said Gordon. 'It's been a lovely evening; let's not spoil it talking about unimportant things.' He reached over for the bottle of wine and topped up his glass. He gestured to hers.

Unimportant things. The calendar was important, but not to him. She drained her glass and held it out for more. The wine sent a burst of warmth through her as she sat back on the sofa. He had cooked her a lovely meal. He'd changed his career plans to be near her. She had to hold on to that.

Beth didn't know how long she'd been asleep for before Gordon gently shook her shoulder and suggested they went to bed. She nodded, still muzzy from sleep and too much wine, and rolled off the sofa, yawning and stretching; Gordon reached up to stroke the exposed inch of tummy between her skirt and top. She lowered her arms to find him smiling up at her, his eyes sparkling.

She looked over at the kitchen, where the washing-up was still stacked up at the side of the sink. 'We should ...'

'We'll do it in the morning.' He was standing next to her now, drawing her slowly into his arms.

Beth glanced past him again at the plates. He kissed her neck. She felt Gordon's lips curve into a smile against her skin. He scooped her up as though she weighed nothing. The wine and the remnants of sleep made everything slightly dreamlike. Beth wrapped her arms round his neck and laid her head against the muscled expanse of his shoulder. Gordon had such comfortingly broad shoulders. Just wide enough for her to rest her head on, like a muscly pillow.

In the dark of her room, Gordon pulled her top over her head.

'I'm so tired,' she murmured. 'I don't want to—'

He interrupted her by kissing her again. He tasted of wine and mint from the lamb. All she wanted was drop into bed and sleep, but she didn't want an argument with Gordon. He had made an effort that evening. He'd think she didn't appreciate it. Her skirt rustled down to her feet and Gordon traced the lines of her body with his fingers, raising goosebumps. A shiver ran through her. In the dim light of her room, she could see the gleam in his eyes and knew he was smiling. She let him lie her down in bed.

While Gordon stripped off his clothes, she shuffled a little to get comfortable. Part of her was so very, very sleepy. Another part of her wanted the comfort of his body next to hers, the warmth of his lips. When his mouth found hers again, she tried to stop thinking and just give in to the moment.

His kisses got more intense and rough, but Beth didn't object. He wasn't hurting her. It was his way of spicing up foreplay. Like that trick a week ago, where he'd held her topless until just before Hibs and Anna came in. He had been really excited by that. Thinking back on it now, the adrenaline had added a little extra zest to their lovemaking afterwards. Gordon's mouth found her nipple and he rolled it between his tongue and his teeth. A thrill ran through her spine. Then he nipped it with his teeth. Beth gasped. 'Ow!' He did it again and she tried to pull away. The slow smoulder of desire turned into something else. 'Stop it. Please.'

He didn't stop. He wrenched her hands up over her head and gripped both wrists with one big hand. Beth tried to protest, but his mouth was on hers again. His free hand pulled her leg to the side and he entered her.

His lips moved away from hers and, as he moved up, his shoulders rose until her face was in his chest. Beth found her nose trapped against his pectoral. She tried to move her face, but couldn't. He was pressing too close for her to even open her mouth. She was trapped and she couldn't breathe. Her chest tightened. With her hands above her head and the rest of her trapped under him, she could barely move. Suddenly everything was amplified. The throb of pain from her nipple, the sound of his breathing, the smell of sweat and body spray from his skin. His body pressed harder into hers. The pressure on her nose was so heavy it hurt. Blood roared in her ears as she struggled, legs flailing, uselessly far away. The darkness got deeper and deeper and then pinpoints of light appeared. Her lungs burned. She no longer had the strength to struggle. She was going to die. Here. Under Gordon.

Gordon let out a groan as he climaxed. Suddenly, space opened out above her. Oxygen rushed into her nose. She gulped down air, panting. She was dimly aware of Gordon releasing her hands. He said something and slid off the bed. She lay there, like a discarded rag doll, unable to do anything apart from breathe, breathe, breathe. She squeezed her eyes shut and felt relief rushing down her arteries, oxygenating her lungs, her arms, her legs. Her head buzzed, as though a bee was trapped inside it.

Gordon returned and slid into bed next to her. Beth tensed, dreading that he'd climb on top of her again.

'Wow,' Gordon whispered in her ear. 'That was amazing.' He kissed her shoulder. She turned her face away, but he didn't seem to notice. 'You're something special. You really are.'

Beth lay very still. Her mouth was so dry she couldn't have spoken, even if she'd wanted to. Gordon gave her shoulder another kiss, nuzzled against her, and fell asleep.

For a long time afterwards, Beth lay there, staring at the darkness, not daring to move. She heard Anna come home and go to bed. Beside her, Gordon slept, his breathing deep and regular.

She looked across at him. He seemed so content. There was no way he could have done it on purpose. She took a deep breath and felt the muscles in her ribs. Muscles she'd barely thought about before. She needed a wee. She needed to sleep. She needed … to be somewhere else. But she couldn't do any of these. She continued staring into the space above her. Glad it was there. Glad it was empty.

Chapter Twenty-One

The next morning, Beth felt ragged. She had eventually fallen asleep, but she still felt tired. Sitting on the bed, she watched Gordon rush around and pull on his clothes. She touched her nose and wondered if she'd imagined the whole episode from the night before.

'Gordon,' she said.

'Yes, babe?' He was leaning over to pull on his socks and she couldn't see his face fully.

'Last night …'

'Mmm?'

'Last night, did …' Beth stopped. 'Did you try to suffocate me' sounded like a ridiculous question. Of course he hadn't. People didn't do that to their girlfriends. If he'd wanted to suffocate her, he'd have used a pillow. He wouldn't have tried to smother her with his chest during sex. The more she thought about it, the sillier it sounded.

Gordon finished putting his socks on. When he turned to look at her, he was smiling. 'Last night was pretty special wasn't it?' He touched her cheek and she resisted the urge to move back. 'I'm glad you enjoyed it too,' he said. 'I could tell from the way you were panting.' He tucked a strand of hair behind her ear and leaned in to plant a kiss just below her earlobe. 'I love you,' he whispered.

Her mind reeled. He'd thought she was just super aroused. That's why he hadn't responded when she struggled. He hadn't meant to harm her. The explanation was there. Right there. It should have helped, but somehow it didn't. She must have done something stupid to cause that lack of communication, but she couldn't figure out what. She hugged her knees, suddenly filled with a weird mixture of shame and fear. All she wanted to do right now was disappear. Tears threatened and she ducked her head so that Gordon didn't see.

'I've got to run off, babe. I'm sorry.' He straightened out his clothes. 'I'll see you later. Don't forget you're coming to the department's annual dinner with me tomorrow.' He planted a kiss on her mouth.

'Yes,' she managed weakly.

'I'll pick you up at seven.' He patted her on the shoulder and left.

Beth continued sitting on the bed, staring into space, for a long time. After a while, Anna's alarm went off, and Beth moved and dragged her feet into the kitchen to find that Gordon had left the washing-up. She sighed and rolled up her sleeves.

Hibs finished his meeting with Roger and got up to leave.

'I'll walk back with you,' Roger said. 'I need to talk to Beth.'

Hibs held the door open and let his boss past. The meeting had gone well. Roger was impressed with the pictures and data from Hibs's portion of the work. He only needed a few more data sets and they could start writing a paper. With the colourful pictures, there was a good chance they could make a cover article in a decent journal. 'Actually,' he said. 'Beth's pictures would make a nice tie-in.'

'What pictures? I asked her to repeat the phenotype data.'

'She has. It's the same as before. Not statistically significant.'

Roger stopped. 'Beth's not exactly the most on-the-ball person, is she?'

Hibs frowned. 'She's very organised and capable. I don't understand what your concern is.' He knew Roger wasn't very supportive, but he'd assumed it was merely down to his being stressed out and a bit depressed. It had never occurred to him that he might doubt Beth's ability to stay the course.

'Well,' said Roger. 'She's vague; she doesn't listen to instructions; she never completes her data sets properly and, let's face it, she's more interested in her extra-curricular activities than in her work.'

Hibs drew a sharp breath. That was unfair. 'Hang on. On what evidence have you formed this conclusion?'

'It's obvious.'

'Not to me, it's not. As far as I know, she's completed every task you've set her. She's been helping me with this last set of experiments. Half the work you just admired is hers.'

Roger looked surprised. 'Is it?'

'Yes.'

'Hmm.' Roger started to move out of the office but Hibs stepped in front of him.

'Roger. Do you have a good reason to believe Beth isn't up to doing a PhD?'

Roger glanced up and down the corridor and leaned conspiratorially towards Hibs. 'She's not exactly brilliant, is she?'

'Why did you take her on then?'

'I didn't have a choice. I only had two viable candidates and the first one didn't want it. The funding was time limited, so it was take the second choice candidate or lose the money. I didn't want to take her, but I couldn't think of a good enough reason not to.'

'You took her on as your student: you have a duty towards helping her. You might want to think about that.'

'Are you threatening me, Hibs?' Roger squared up to him.

'Not at all,' Hibs said, as pleasantly as he could manage. 'Just pointing out some key university policies.' Whatever was going on in Roger's life, he couldn't take it out on the PhD students.

Roger narrowed his eyes at him, but didn't respond.

They strode into the lab in silence. Beth was at her desk, staring at the computer screen, sitting very still.

'Beth, have you got that phenotype data?' said Roger.

Beth turned slowly and looked blankly at him for a moment before replying. 'Yes. Sure.' She turned back to her computer and started clicking through her files.

Roger gave Hibs a 'See what I mean?' glance. Hibs had to admit that Beth wasn't being particularly confidence-inspiring at the moment. She looked even more tired than usual. He'd had to rush into Roger's office first thing, so he hadn't had time to talk to her that morning.

'Here.' Beth centred a graph on-screen and moved out of the way.

Roger looked at it. 'Hmph.'

'Statistically significant?' said Hibs.

'No.' There was a curious flatness to Beth's voice, as though her mind was elsewhere. She was chewing on her lip.

Roger said, 'Hmph,' again. 'Well this isn't much use for my presentation.'

Beth said nothing. Hibs wished she'd speak up for herself.

'I'll just have to leave your work out of my presentation,' said Roger.

Beth still said nothing.

'I'll see if Vik has some of his slides ready.' Roger walked off without any further comment.

When he'd gone, Beth closed the file down, checked her timer and went back to staring blankly at the screen. Worried by her unresponsive behaviour, Hibs perched on the desk next to her. 'Beth, are you okay?'

'Fine,' she said, but she didn't look at him. There were frown lines on her forehead and the bags under her eyes were so dark she looked like a lemur. Her eyes were shot with red and her lip was starting to look raw where she'd chewed on it. Maybe she really needed to get some more sleep.

'You don't look fine.'

'Don't I?' She finally stopped staring at nothing and looked away.

'In fact, you look bloody awful.' He leaned towards her. 'Look, we've only got three more nights of experiments to go. Do you want me to do all of the rest?' He was supposed to be taking a karate class that evening but he could try and change it, see if he could swap with one of the other instructors.

'No.' Her response was a little faster than he'd expected. He didn't believe it for a minute. Whatever was bothering her, she clearly didn't want him to probe her about it.

'I'll be fine. Don't worry about it,' she said. 'I'm just tired. As you say, it's only a few more nights.' For the first time, she made eye contact.

Hibs tensed. Her eyes were too wide, too intense. Something was wrong. What had happened to her to make her so worried? Fear scratched at him.

She seemed to sense that he'd realised and looked away.

'Beth …'

She plugged headphones into her ears and ignored him.

Beth stared out of the window. She was supposed to be writing up her results, but she couldn't concentrate. All she could think about was the night before. There were two possibilities: Gordon had blocked her air supply by accident and mistaken her struggling for enthusiasm. Or he had done it on purpose. Both ideas seemed preposterous. He was her boyfriend; he loved her. He'd cooked her a lovely meal and they'd had such a wonderful evening. He was changing his career plans to be with her. Those weren't the actions of someone vindictive. Okay, sometimes he got annoyed with her and a little intense, but that was just because he loved her so much. He'd said so.

On the other hand, it was pretty difficult to smother someone by accident. Really. She wondered idly if Hibs had ever managed to suffocate someone while making love to them. He didn't have the sort of pecs Gordon did. And she shouldn't be thinking about his pecs anyway. She cast a furtive glance over her shoulder before she reminded herself that Gordon wasn't there. And even if he were he couldn't read her mind. Neither could Hibs.

A third possibility floated up to the surface: she'd imagined it. That morning, Gordon had behaved exactly as normal, as though nothing untoward had happened. And she had been really tired and woozy. Maybe she'd had some sort of anxiety attack and somehow imagined Gordon was squashing her on purpose. She opened up a browser and googled 'panic attack'. From what she read, it seemed it was possible.

Next to her wrist, the timer beeped, making her jump.

She stared at it for a moment before she remembered why it was beeping. It was time to go and check her bacteria to see if they were ready to be set up for tonight's experiment. She closed down her browser and went to the hot room.

When she returned, she slid back into her seat and noted down the time and the reading from the spectrophotometer. She had to check the time twice before she was sure she'd done it right.

The more she thought about it, the more it seemed likely that she'd had some sort of panic attack and just imagined the whole thing with Gordon. It was a relief to stop worrying about whether her boyfriend was some sort of psycho. On the other hand, what was happening to her? Not only had she had a panic attack and imagined an actual attack, she'd almost accused her boyfriend of trying to suffocate her. Which made her paranoid. That could not be a good thing. She bit her lip again and felt it split. She tasted blood. Damn.

She sucked at her lip and felt the sting. It was oddly reassuring. At least she could be sure she wasn't imagining that.

There was the sound of footsteps behind her, but she ignored them.

'Beth.' Hibs leaned on the desk next to her.

'What?'

'Are you sure you're okay?'

No. I'm paranoid. I'm losing the plot. A few nights of broken sleep and I turn into a total nutjob. 'No,' she said.

'What's wrong?' Hibs hunkered down next to her.

She turned to face him. 'Hibs, do you think I'm crazy?'

He said no. But the look on his face … His eyes widened. Frown lines appeared. He looked really … wary. Beth turned back to her computer. 'Huh. You've noticed.'

'No. Beth, what's going on?'

Beth shrugged. 'Dunno.'

Hibs laid a hand on her arm and it was all she could do not to recoil from the contact. 'Beth, I think you need to get some sleep. I'll do the rest of the night shifts. You take some time off.'

'No point,' she said. 'I'll be fine.' She looked at him again. Even with the worry lines, he looked beautiful. His face was level with hers and his hand was burning a hole in her sleeve. If she told him now, what would happen? Hibs had always been kind and friendly. He would listen to her fears, but what would he think of her? Would he be wary of being friends with a crazy person?

She bit her lip again and felt it sting. She couldn't tell him. She couldn't tell anyone. Working this one out was up to her. She removed his hand from her arm and stood up. 'Excuse me.'

Chapter Twenty-Two

Hibs watched Beth leave. Something was definitely wrong. Why did she think she was crazy? What kind of crap was Gordon telling her now? Whatever it was, it must have one hell of a hold on Beth for her to let Roger take her slides out of his presentation. This meeting was a big deal: the whole department would be there and it showcased the lab. Except now it would showcase the lab without Beth's work. He was surprised and disappointed that she'd let him do that without an argument. Something about the way she was, the thousand-yard stare, the vagueness, frightened him. He couldn't just sit there and watch her slide further under Gordon's spell. There had to be something he could do to help.

He hurried down the corridor and out of the security doors to find somewhere quiet and phoned Lara. It went to answerphone so he left a message asking her to call him. Then, unable to leave the problem alone, he called Anna.

'Hello. Didn't expect to hear from you,' Anna said brightly. 'Have you changed your mind then?'

'Actually, I'm phoning about Beth.'

'What about her?' The friendly tone left Anna's voice.

'Have you noticed anything odd about her lately?'

'Let's see? She has massive self-esteem issues and she's going out with a guy who treats her like crap ... Apart from that, no, not really.'

'She's been behaving really oddly today. Can you talk to her?'

There was a pause. 'You're really worried that something's wrong?'

'Yes.' Bloody hell. What did it take to convince her? Why was he the only person who could see the size of the problem?

'Like what?'

'I'm not sure. She's been staring into space and chewing her lip to bits. Then she asked me if I thought she was crazy. Do you know if she had a row with Gordon?'

'They seemed happy enough last night.' Anna paused. 'Although, come to think of it, she didn't say much this morning. Gordon made her this meal last night; he seemed quite pleased with it.'

'Really? Gordon cooked?' Well, that was a turn up. Maybe he had wanted something. His mind whirred. What if he'd asked Beth to do something and she'd refused. Could he have hurt her in some way? Or threatened her? Hibs clenched a fist in anger. If Gordon had actually hurt Beth …

'Could be the lack of sleep thing. You guys have been working crazy hours lately.'

'I suppose.' He wasn't convinced. Tired was one thing; Beth's behaviour was something else. 'Look, can you keep an eye on her?'

Anna sighed. 'Okay. Fine. I'll try.' Another pause. 'Wanna come and help me?'

The comment derailed Hibs's train of thought. He tried to think of a glib answer and failed. 'I've got to go.'

When Beth got home that night, thankfully Anna had already gone to bed. Beth found a bottle of wine on the side – it must have been Anna's, she thought, but poured herself a glass anyway.

She sat at the kitchen table, her hands curved around the glass. If she was going crazy, she needed to think about it. Get her facts straight. Then go to see her GP. There might be pills you could take for paranoia. She needed a plan. She grabbed a pen and looked around for a piece of paper. Seeing none to hand, she went over to the almost-full recycling bin, thinking there must be an envelope or something she could use. She started to remove the magazines and newspapers, without looking at what she was pulling out.

Suddenly, something caught her attention. It was part of the packing from an M&S pre-prepared salad and she could see the words 'mango, avocado'. Frowning, Beth delved back into the box and found the rest: 'and prawn with lemon dressing'. The salad that Gordon had made for her. He'd claimed to have prepared it himself. She laid the two halves on the floor. It could be a coincidence. Maybe Anna had bought the same salad. She returned to the box, hoping not to find anything more. But it took only a few seconds to locate the wrapper showing lamb, minty potatoes and green beans. All prepared. Just pop in the oven.

Beth sat back on the floor and stared at evidence of the meal that Gordon had 'cooked' for her. For a moment, she felt nothing. Then a clamour of emotion. She wouldn't have minded that he'd bought ready-made food. She would have been thrilled just to get the attention. But he'd lied to her. And, worse, he'd thought her so stupid that he hadn't even bothered to hide the packaging where she wouldn't see it. He'd assumed she wouldn't find it. She nearly hadn't. Oh god. She really was as gullible as he thought she was.

Her wonderful romantic meal had been a lie. It was like someone tearing wax strips off her heart. Gordon didn't love her. He was just playing with her. Treating her like an idiot. She thought about the terror of the night before and knew that she hadn't imagined it. He had been trying to suffocate her. Not to kill her, just enough to frighten her. But why? Did he get off on that sort of thing? *Why?* The answer came to her almost before she'd finished the question. Punishment. He was punishing her for not saying he could go in the calendar.

Beth reached up for the glass of wine and found her hands were shaking. It took her a few attempts to take a sip.

So what now?

She stared down at the packaging. She could confront him with it. But what did that prove? Gordon would say it was just some packaging. It didn't mean it was his. She could ask Anna if she'd had the same meal. But then Anna would think she was being weird.

Beth chewed her lip, ignoring the pain. Who could she tell? No one. She needed more information. More proof so that Gordon couldn't claim the benefit of the doubt. But where could she get that?

She carefully gathered up her 'evidence'. She would have to keep it somewhere safe, where Gordon wouldn't find it. As an afterthought, she carefully labelled the backs with the date and where she'd found them.

In her room she crawled under her bed and stuck the bag in the bed slats. Gordon wouldn't find it there. When she climbed into bed, it smelled of Gordon, so she climbed back out and stripped the bedclothes off. She found a new set, slamming the cupboard doors shut as she went. As she was battling to put the duvet cover back on, Anna knocked on her bedroom door.

'What are you doing?' Anna was wearing her little shorty pyjamas and top and looked like she'd just rolled out of bed. 'It's past midnight.'

Beth paused, duvet still in hand. She had forgotten it was so late and hadn't bothered being quiet. 'Sorry,' she said. 'I was just ... changing the bed.' Should she tell Anna her fears?

Anna was watching her carefully. 'Beth, are you okay?'

No. Not Anna. Not yet.

'Yes.'

'Because if there's anything bothering you, you know I'll help you in whatever way I can.'

'I'm fine,' Beth said. 'Just tired. Want to go to bed.'

Anna nodded and shuffled back to her room.

Alone again, Beth finished sorting out the bedclothes and got back into bed. She couldn't talk to Anna. Lara had problems of her own. That just left Hibs. And she didn't want him to think she was an idiot.

Beth didn't sleep much in between trips to the lab to take her readings. She needed more information. If she confronted Gordon with these scraps of ideas, he would just laugh at her until she ended up believing she was wrong.

By the time her experiments were finished, she knew what she had to do. She made a list of all the things that Gordon said which could have been lies. Then, having tucked the list safely under the bed, next to the packaging, she finally fell asleep.

Chapter Twenty-Three

'Afternoon, Tyler,' Hibs said as Beth wandered into the lab. 'You okay?'

It was nearly lunchtime. Once she'd fallen asleep, Beth had slept through her alarm. 'Overslept,' she said. Her eyes felt like they were full of gravel and her head hurt. This was nothing compared to the pain she felt inside. But at least now she knew she wasn't going mad. She avoided eye contact with Hibs and shrugged on her lab coat.

'I set up your cultures for you this morning,' Hibs said. 'I wasn't sure if you were coming in or not.'

'Sorry, like I said, I overslept.'

'I'm not surprised,' he replied. 'I'm having trouble staying awake nowadays.' He leaned his elbows on her bench. 'Tell you what, when all this is finished, you and I both deserve to sleep for a week.'

'Hmm.' Beth examined her lab book and tried to remember what she was supposed to be doing.

'Beth? Is everything okay?'

She turned to find him watching her, his eyes hooded with worry, and she wondered what he'd say if he knew. It would be so shameful to admit the extent to which he had been right. Hibs was one of the few people who still thought well of her. She couldn't lose him. 'Yes,' she lied. 'I'm fine. Thanks.'

Hibs looked like he was about to argue, but his mobile phone rang. He raised an eyebrow at Beth by way of apology and answered it.

When Hibs had turned away, Beth returned to her diary. She'd written 'black tie dinner with Gordon'. Shit.

She'd completely forgotten that she'd said she'd go to this bloody dinner with him. The meal would be okay, but afterwards … What happened when he wanted sex? She thought of their last encounter and goosebumps appeared on her flesh. She didn't want to sleep with him. It was too scary. But could she really refuse him?

She pulled her list out of her pocket. She needed to be sure that she wasn't just being paranoid. First, she needed to check on her bacteria. She grabbed a pair of gloves and set off to the hot room.

Beth found the job vacancies section on the university website and searched for post-doctoral roles in the biology department. Gordon had said it was right in his field of interest, phylogeny, but she thought she'd look at them all, just in case. He'd said he'd just applied, which meant the closing date couldn't have been more than a week ago. She set the search criteria to cover two weeks before and two ahead – four job vacancies came up. She scrolled through. None of them seemed appropriate.

She found the website for Gordon's current supervisor, in case the work there might link to any of the vacancies. No.

Hibs came in.

'Hibs. If you have the perfect candidate for a job, would you be able to give it to them without advertising the post?'

'Not here. HR rules. You have to advertise,' Hibs said. 'Why? Is Roger feeding you some crap about giving a postdoc to someone?'

'No, just wondered.'

She turned back to her screen. So, no job. He'd lied about that too. She wondered why.

'Why are you looking for a job in Biology?' Hibs was reading over her shoulder.

Beth shut the browser down. 'I wasn't. I was just ... nosing around.'

Hibs narrowed his eyes. 'Do you want to work down the corridor from Gordon?'

'No.' She recognised that look. He was going to start quizzing her again. Ordinarily, she would have told him her suspicions, but she couldn't trust him to be objective. He hated Gordon. If she gave him an excuse to doubt him, he'd jump on it. 'I'm going for coffee. Want one?'

She returned, balancing three mugs on a plastic tray, to find Hibs pleading with someone on the phone.

'Please, mate. Greg's not well and I'm working in the lab tonight. I'll do both the classes next week.' He listened, his frown deepening, and then sighed. 'No, no. I understand. I'll think of something. Don't worry, mate. Give my love to Gill. You have a good time.' He hung up and sighed again.

'Problems?' Beth handed him his tea. It was nice to see that she wasn't the only one with problems. Since Hibs had split up with Anna, he was getting grumpier.

'Sort of,' said Hibs. 'Greg's got the flu and Howard's got to go to parents' evening, so there's no one to do this evening's karate class. And Vik's off at some family do, so I can't palm the experiments off on him.'

'Ah.' It was Hibs's night on the microscopes. She thought of her planned evening with Gordon. She didn't want to go – perhaps, this was the excuse she needed. 'I'll do it,' she said.

'What, take a karate class?' He was smiling at her now. Somehow it made him look even more tired.

'No, wally. Your evening readings.'

'That's not fair. It's your night off.'

'I don't mind.'

'What about Gordon?'

She shrugged, in what she hoped was a nonchalant way. 'He won't mind.'

Hibs's gaze explored her face. There was hope in his eyes. 'You're sure?'

'Yes. Enough already. I said I'd do it.'

'Thanks, Beth. You're a real star. I owe you one.' He smiled at her again and looked so relieved she had to fight the urge to hug him. 'Tell you what, if you can do the ten o'clock reading, I'll do the early-morning ones.'

'Sure.' Beth smiled back at him. It felt strange, smiling. She hadn't done that in days now. Hibs thought she was a good person. He didn't think she was a useless nutjob. She needed to hang on to that.

And she needed to get on with her list.

Beth stood next to a potted plant as she waited for Dan Blackwood, ready to duck behind the plant if Gordon showed up. She would have preferred to have met elsewhere, but Dan was busy and this was the only time he could fit it in. She could tell he didn't really want to talk to her, but she had been persistent. Through the leaves of the plant, she saw Dan striding out to reception. She stepped out and smiled.

'Hi, Dan. Thanks for agreeing to see me.'

'That's okay. It's the least I can do. I'm just going to grab a coffee,' he said. 'Want one?'

'No thanks.' She followed him into the big atrium. The Biology building had been refurbished a few years back and now included a small conservatory that served as a coffee shop. She glanced around nervously and was relieved that Gordon wasn't there. He would normally have swimming training about now, but she wasn't sure he even went any more. She had even more reason than Dan to want to keep this brief.

'I was wondering,' said Dan. 'Could you sell me some prints of the photo you took? My wife likes it.'

She was surprised that he wanted the photo, but pleased that he thought it good enough to pay money for. It also meant he owed her a favour. 'Sure. E-mail me what you want and I'll send you a quote.' In a flutter of panic she realised she had no idea what she should charge for them. Not the normal high prices photographers charged, obviously, because she was still an amateur. But if Dan thought the photos were worth paying for … perhaps she should charge something approaching the going rate. How did you decide? Who could she ask?

Dan led her to a table at the far end. 'So, what did you want to talk to me about?' he said, forcing her to focus on her more immediate problem.

'I'm here about the calendar.' She put her hand up as Dan started to protest. 'No, I'm not going to try and persuade you to come back: I respect your decision. I just want to know why.'

'I told you, I didn't think my wife would like it.'

'We discussed that before and you were okay with it. What made you change your mind?'

Dan stirred his tea, not meeting her eye.

'Dan?'

'You're right,' said Dan. 'We were okay with it at the start, but I was chatting to one of my colleagues and he said that people were already talking about it and everyone saw your calendar as guys advertising themselves as available.'

'Okay. Could you tell me which colleague?' She leaned forward. 'Just so that I can have a chat with them and find out why he thinks that.'

'Oh, he said his girlfriend wouldn't let him apply to go in.'

Beth breathed out. Okay. So it wasn't Gordon.

Feeling she had to stick to her original story, she said, 'It's a shame that she feels that way. Could you tell me who they are? Just so that I can set the record straight.'

'Okay. My friend is Gordon Kettering. His girlfriend is Mila … I forget her last name. It's something Eastern European.'

The words were like ice down her spine. Beth sat frozen for a moment before stuttering, 'G-Gordon Kettering?'

'You know him?'

Pull yourself together, Beth. With some effort, she managed to keep her features neutral. 'I know Gordon. I didn't know he had … a … er … girlfriend.'

'They haven't been together very long, I don't think,' said Dan. 'He's only around for a few months anyway, so I don't think it's serious. I don't know much about this stuff, anyhow. Gossip about colleagues is more my wife's area.'

'Yes. I see.' Suddenly, the little conservatory was too small. Beth stood up. 'Thank you for your time, Dan. It was very kind of you to see me.'

'No problem.' He looked up at her through his mess of hair. 'I feel bad that I pulled out on you. Have you found a replacement yet?'

'Yes, we have,' said Beth. 'Thanks again.' She turned and fled before Gordon spotted her there on his home turf.

Chapter Twenty-Four

When she got back to the lab, she phoned Gordon, knowing his phone would be turned off. 'Hi, Gordon, it's me. I can't come to the dinner tonight. Sorry.' She hung up. It was a cowardly way to do it, but it was the only way she could think of.

She put 'Mila' into the people search on the university website. There were three Milas, all with exotic-sounding names. One was an undergraduate – she didn't think even Gordon wouldn't stoop so low as to date an undergrad. Would he? She clicked through to the others. One was a lecturer in philosophy and looked to be in her fifties. The other was a research assistant with mousy brown hair and huge eyes. Beth stared at the picture. It had to be her. She was pretty, but nothing spectacular. She thought of herself. Pretty, but vanilla. Yes, this had to be the girl.

She carefully copied down the e-mail address, even though she had no idea what she was going to do with it.

In the microscope room Beth turned on the red light on and waited for her eyes to adjust to the monochrome before uncovering the microscopes. The light gave everything a surreal edge, like she was in a horror movie. She'd been told that spending too much time in it could lead to hallucinations. Beth pursed her lips and grimaced. Lack of sleep, red light. If she was cracking up, there'd be plenty of possible causes.

She held her breath while she took the images and e-mailed them across to the lab. What did she do now? She needed to confront Gordon, but how?

Having taken the photos, Beth backed slowly out of the

microscope area and secured the curtain before swapping the red lights for the normal ones.

She was still blinking a little from the shock of normal lighting as she went back up to the lab. Her mobile phone was ringing again and Gordon's name flashed up on the screen. She pressed 'Ignore' and returned to her work. There were six messages on her answerphone – all from Gordon. They'd been gathering there since six o'clock, which she guessed was when he'd picked up her message. She didn't listen to them, too terrified of his power over her. He had lied to her and manipulated her. She was obviously too weak to stand up to him. She cast a nervous glance at the phone as another voicemail symbol popped up on the screen.

This was a silly way to do things. He would stop ringing in a bit, when it was time to go to his dinner. After a few seconds, the lab phone rang. It made her slightly panicky, but she ignored that too. It was probably Gordon checking to see where she was. She wondered if he was going to the dinner alone, or whether he was going to take Mila as a last-minute replacement. Was Mila the 'colleague' he'd taken to the opera? How often did he see her? Was that where he was when he was meant to be at swimming practice? Or all those other times when he claimed the biology department had no mobile phone reception? Beth's late-night experiments must have been an absolute godsend to him.

Why hadn't he just asked Mila to go to the dinner in the first place? He'd obviously been showing her off to his colleagues as his girlfriend. Beth frowned. She'd met some of his friends when they'd been going out before. They had mostly been big, shouty men. She hadn't been comfortable around them and slowly she and Gordon had stopped seeing other people. They'd been happy in their own little bubble. Just the two of them.

Her lab timer beeped, making her jump so violently that she banged her knee on the side of the desk. Rubbing her knee, she turned the timer off and limped down to get her samples out of the centrifuge.

The lab phone rang again. It was past nine o'clock now, so Gordon would be at his dinner now. Beth answered it.

'Beth, thank goodness,' said Gordon. 'I was so worried.'

She froze, too surprised to hang up. 'Gordon.' She felt the panic start to gather in her stomach.

'I've been trying to call you all evening. I tried you at home, in the lab, on your mobile. I was going crazy with worry. Are you okay?'

'Y-yes.'

He was going crazy with worry? He certainly sounded worried. Maybe she'd been wrong. Maybe it was all a ghastly mistake. What evidence did she really have? Some discarded wrappers, a job advert she couldn't find, and the say-so of an academic who, by his own admission, didn't really keep up with gossip. It could all be explained away.

'Beth? Are you sure you're all right? You sound ... unwell.'

'I'm okay. I'm in the lab.'

'I know,' he said. 'I'm downstairs.' He was enunciating carefully, as though she were a child. She must sound really spaced out.

She rubbed her eyes. Maybe the lack of sleep and the red light *were* too much for her. Maybe she *was* losing it.

'So ... are you going to come down and let me in?'

'Uh ... yes. Just a minute.'

*   *   *

She always took the stairs down when she was alone in the building – she didn't want to take the lift in case it got stuck – and her footsteps echoed weirdly up the stairwell.

Through the window of the second security door, she could see Gordon. He was wearing black tie and he smiled and waved when he saw her. Beth waved back. The last of the day's light was fading and Gordon, standing in the suffused light from the glass entranceway, glowed. He always looked amazing in a tuxedo. The twinge of pleasure she felt was almost automatic and the unease that followed was unusual. She hesitated. Should she let him in? She reminded herself that she had overreacted before and that it was ridiculous to do so again. Beth pushed the button to open the first security door and checked she had her ID card in her pocket to let them back in again. It wouldn't do to lock herself out.

Gordon peered in through the glass at the end of the corridor. She caught sight of his eyes and suddenly she was afraid. She took a step backward and Gordon waved again. Beth's heartbeat got louder. Hairs at the back of her neck stood up. She should go back. He'd tried to suffocate her. He'd lied to her. She should stay away. But Gordon's gaze locked with hers and she couldn't leave. It was hypnotic – like he'd conditioned her to respond to him. She felt herself inching forward, her arm outstretched to push the door release, as though he were a magnet and she a speck of iron. Her fingers reached the button and she heard the click as the lock released.

Gordon seemed to enter shoulders first, expanding to fill the space, like a spider emerging from a crack. As soon as he was in the door, his face changed. He loomed above her. His shoulders were still broad, but there was nothing comforting about them. 'What the fuck are you playing at?' he roared, veins standing out in his neck. 'You left me standing there, waiting for you, like a lemon.'

Beth backed away. 'I-I'm sorry.' Her voice was a squeak. He was bloody huge. Of course he could suffocate her if he'd wanted to. She was an idiot to have believed anything else.

'Sorry? SORRY? This is the second time you've stood me up you fucking feckless bitch.' His voice thundered, filling the claustrophobia-inducing space. Beth glanced to the CCTV camera mounted above the door. It was behind Gordon. If he killed her here, all they'd have is a picture of his back. What good would that be? Her hand stretched out behind her: if she could touch her ID card to the reader, the door would open. It wouldn't give her a lot of time, but at least she would have somewhere to run.

Gordon's gaze flicked to her hand. 'Oh no you don't.' He lunged towards her but Beth twisted and ducked. The card made contact with the reader and the door mechanism whirred. Gordon grabbed her hand and wrenched her around. His arm came in front of her face. In sheer panic, Beth bit him. His arm moved fast, but her teeth grazed it. He swore. She twisted out of his grip and slipped sideways through the still-opening door. She was much smaller than he was and it would take a few more seconds before he could get his big shoulders through. She raced to the lift and stabbed the button frantically. Gordon burst through the doors just as the lift closed. Beth watched the floors tick by. Would he run up the stairs and catch her at the top? Hibs and Vik often tried to race the lift but neither of them ever made it. Would Gordon, in his rage, be faster than they were?

The lift doors pinged open. There was nobody in the lobby. Without waiting to check the stairs, Beth raced to the door to the lab and punched in the code. She had to hold her breath and pray that her hands were steady enough to get the numbers right. The door clicked open. She slipped in and shut it behind her. She retreated down the corridor until she was in the lab, breathing fast. She knew the number for campus security was on the wall, beside the phone. She could call them if he turned up. But what would she say? Her boyfriend was coming? She stood there, panting. Still no one.

She swallowed the rising panic and tried to force herself to breathe properly. Okay. Think. Think. He wasn't coming after her yet. What was he doing? He was already in the building. Was there any way he could get onto this floor? There were other labs up here. Anyone who worked in them would be able to let him in. Did he know any of them? They would have seen him with her and if he told them he was here to see her, they might let him in.

Beth backed into the lab. What should she do? Pulling out her mobile, she called Hibs. His phone went straight to answerphone and panic clawed up Beth's throat again. 'Hibs, it's me. I'm scared.' She fought down the panic: she needed to focus. What did she need to tell him? 'I'm in the lab. Gordon's outside. I'm scared he might …' He might what? 'I'm just scared. Come and get me. Please.' Her voice rose to a squeak at the end. She held the phone to her ear, willing him to come on the line, until the answerphone beeped again and she was cut off.

She went to the middle of the lab and looked at the windows, eyes darting from one to the next. It was dark outside and there were no lights on in the building opposite. Maybe if she pretended she wasn't here, even if Gordon got to her floor, he might think she'd gone home.

She turned lights off and backed down the lab. At the end of Vik's bench there was a metal clamp stand with several clamps attached. She unscrewed one and hefted it in her hand. It was long and sharp in places, but not very heavy. After a second's thought, she unscrewed the rest of the clamps and picked up the stand itself. Heavy. And long. If she swung it and managed to make contact, that would hurt. She turned off the rest of the lights and crouched down in the shadow on the nitrogen cylinders, so that she could see the door.

It felt like she'd been waiting for years. Her legs were protesting and her back was going stiff from tension. At the click and the *schlup* of the security door opening, all aches were forgotten and Beth gripped the clamp stand with both hands, pressing against the wall to stay hidden. Footsteps in the corridor. Quick strides. No hesitation. Had Gordon found a way in? Beth's jaw throbbed with tension. Someone came into the lab and flicked on the lights.

She tensed, getting ready to strike out. The figure turned and spotted her. She raised the clamp stand to shoulder height.

'Beth?' It wasn't Gordon's voice.

For a moment her brain froze, unable to recognise anything. Then relief. Overwhelming, body-draining, blessed relief. 'Hibs.' Thank goodness. The clamp stand clattered at her feet. Hibs turned, automatically going into a ready stance.

She threw herself into him. 'Hibs. Oh god, it's you.'

'Hey.' His arms closed around her. 'It's okay.'

Beth shook her head and realised she was shaking all over. 'I thought you were Gordon. I didn't want to go home, in case he was waiting for me. I was worried he'd get in and ...' The tears suddenly broke through. She put her head against his shoulder and sobbed.

Hibs's arms stayed loosely wrapped around her for a moment before they tightened, drawing her close. He stroked her hair and repeated, 'It's okay, it's okay,' until the worst passed. It took a few minutes before Beth was able to appreciate the gesture. Hibs. Her friend who was always there for her. Right now there was no one else who could make her feel safer. Thank heavens for Hibs. Finally, her tears almost spent, Beth sniffed and raised her face.

'Want to tell me what happened?' He was still holding her. She realised she didn't want him to let go.

'I was supposed to be at a dinner with Gordon.'

'Why did you offer to swap with me if you had to be somewhere?'

'I didn't want to go.' Beth wiped her hand across her face.

Hibs frowned. 'Okay. I won't ask. I guess that's between you and Gordon.'

Beth sniffed again and Hibs moved away to fetch a length of blue paper towel from above the sink. Immediately, she felt the chill of his absence. She took the tissue paper from him and blew her nose.

'Wait.' Hibs took her arm and turned the wrist over. An angry red weal was developing where she'd twisted out of Gordon's grip. 'Did Gordon do that to you?' Beth nodded and stared at her wrist. How had she not noticed the pain before? Hibs ran a finger next to the bruise. 'Can you move your wrist properly?'

She put the wrist through its range of movement and winced. 'I can manage,' she said.

'Let's get some ice on that. Here, sit down.' He took her over to the desk area and motioned for her to sit, and then he picked up an ice bucket from the lab. 'Stay there,' he said. 'I'll be two seconds. If Gordon turns up, I'll brain him with the ice bucket on my way back. Okay?'

She managed a little smile. Now that someone else was here, some of the adrenaline that had been keeping her upright sagged out of her. She leaned back in the chair and tipped her head back. Her legs felt wobbly. Hearing Hibs come back, she looked at the door. He was in his karate clothes, with a denim jacket thrown over them, pouring ice into a latex glove. The whole thing looked weird, but somehow that made her feel better.

He hunkered down in front of her and wrapped the ice-filled glove round her wrist. 'There we go. That should help with the swelling.' He looked up at her, his face full of concern. This was what it was like when someone genuinely cared. How could she ever have thought that Gordon gave a damn about her? 'How are you feeling now? Better?'

'Yes.' She paused. 'Doesn't protocol demand you get me a hot beverage?'

'Don't push your luck.'

She gave a little giggle. Hibs smiled at her and leaned his forehead against hers. They sat together, foreheads touching for a moment, in comfortable silence.

Beth wasn't sure when comfort turned to attraction. Suddenly, she was aware that he smelled nice – a combination of fresh laundry and sweat. There was a slight gap where the fabric of his karate top gaped enough to expose a tiny bit of lean chest. He was too close. Her breath caught in her throat. She looked up, moving back a little, and her gaze met his. She was close enough to see his pupils dilate and hear the change in his breathing. If he kissed her now, she knew she wouldn't hesitate to kiss him back.

The moment seemed to stretch. If she moved, just a little bit, she could kiss him. She turned the idea over in her mind. She hadn't kissed anyone other than Gordon in years. After all those days and years of friendship, what would it be like to kiss that mouth? To feel those gentle fingers touching her? All she had to do was lean forward.

Hibs took a deep breath and looked down at her wrist. 'How's this doing now?' he said, leaning back, putting a safe distance between them.

Beth felt a wrench of disappointment. Why had he done that?

'It looks like the swelling's gone down,' said Hibs, talking faster than usual. 'Flex those fingers for me.'

Obediently, she moved her fingers.

'Okay. That's good.' He stood up, not making eye contact. 'I'll just get rid of this ice pack.' He waved the ice packed glove in front of her and practically ran to the other end of the lab.

Without the ice on one side and Hibs's hand on the other, Beth's wrist felt extra vulnerable. She placed it on her lap. What was wrong with her? She had called Hibs to come and help her and she was about to jump on him. Beth groaned. What was she turning into?

Hibs stood over the sink, staring at the ice chips. A cold shower. That's what he needed. The girl was upset and there he was thinking about kissing her.

'Dickhead,' he muttered. He ran some hot water into the sink and watched the ice chips disappear. At least the mark on her wrist wouldn't be so bad now. His jaw tightened as he thought of the reddened skin. Worse, the state of terror she'd been in when he'd arrived. If he ever saw Gordon, he'd kill him. What kind of a monster was he to frighten Beth like that?

And what kind of a git would he, Hibs, be to take advantage of her when she was so shaken up. He gave himself a stern talking to and returned to find Beth sitting where he'd left her, staring into space. Jesus, she really was in a bad way. He could look after her physically and make sure she was okay, but he was way out of his depth with the psychological side of things. Whatever Gordon had done to her, hurting her wrist was only a minor part of it. He seemed to have taken away something that animated her.

'Beth, shall I take you home?'

She seemed to return to the present. 'What if he's waiting for me?' The fear in her voice tore his heart.

'If he is, I'll make sure he doesn't get near you.'

She nodded. Her faith in him was touching. He was slimmer than Gordon, but he was faster and well trained. He could take Gordon any day. He knew that, but it was nice that Beth seemed to know it too.

'Come on then,' he said.

'What?'

'Home.' He made shooing motions with his hands. 'It's getting late, Tyler, and you look like crap on a stick. Let's get you home.'

She glared at him, but there was no intensity to it. 'Thanks,' she said, flatly.

'Always happy to give you a reality check.'

'No, that's not what I mean.' She shrugged. 'I meant for coming to get me.'

He wanted to throw caution out of the window and

gather her up in his arms. He wanted to cuddle her and stroke her hair and tell her nothing, nothing would harm her again. But she was damaged and confused and fragile. So he smiled and said, 'That's okay. Nothing your average superhero wouldn't do.'

He was rewarded with a weak smile.

Chapter Twenty-Five

Beth cranked her eyes open and groped around to turn off her alarm. Light glowed through the gap where her curtains hadn't been properly closed. It was another day already. With a groan, she pulled her arm back under the covers. She didn't want to get up. Not today. To get up and leave her room would make everything real.

The last time she'd been alone in this bed, she'd been in love with Gordon. In the space of a day, she'd gone from contented to bonkers to petrified. And now? She tried to sort out the clamour of emotion in her head. She felt betrayed and sore and angry. But somewhere in there was something else. Something light in the heavy darkness. Beth frowned. She was possibly going nuts. Her boyfriend had tried to attack her at least once, maybe twice. Her boss thought she was lousy at her job. What was there to be pleased about?

She turned on her bedside lamp and examined her wrist. The bruise was visible now. Gordon had hurt her but for once it wasn't invisible. Hibs had made her take a photo of it so that she had tangible evidence that he'd hurt her. She wasn't crazy. She prodded the bruise and winced. It was real alright.

How could she have been so stupid? Gordon had lied to her at every turn and she'd fallen for every single word of it. The dinner he'd put on for her had been a masterclass in seduction. The food, the plans for the future, the warmth, that feeling of being treasured. It had all been made up. Taken out of its wrapping and reheated for her. And she'd taken it all on faith.

His job application had been a lie too. She knew, with absolute conviction, that he was going to go back to America, just as he'd originally planned. And that girl, Mila. How long had he been seeing her? She wondered if any of his so-called swimming training sessions were real. Perhaps none of them. Yet he always called her on the nights when she was working.

She felt a sudden chill in her stomach when she remembered how he often made a call for a few minutes when they were together. He must have been checking up on Mila. And when he'd turned off his phone, Beth had thought it was because he wanted to concentrate on her. How had she fallen for all that?

She tried to think back to how things had been when she'd first started going out with him. Surely, she hadn't been so gullible then? In the beginning, things had been normal. It had started with little things. Laughing at her insecurities. Little jokes about her work. All tiny, tiny little things that had added up to a big fat hole in her self-esteem. It had happened so slowly that she hadn't even realised she was changing. Bastard.

Beth looked at her wrist again. Did Mila have any idea what he was doing to her? Poor girl. Perhaps she should warn her.

Beth's mobile phone rang. Her first thought was that it was Gordon, and she felt a stab of panic. Despite her pep talk to herself, she couldn't talk to him. He still had power over her. She stared at the wall for a moment, wanting to crawl back under her duvet and hide, but then shook her head. That would lead to her sliding back under Gordon's spell. She had to do something to get out. She picked up the phone to reject the call. But the name on the screen was Hibs. Puzzled, she answered.

'Good morning. I'm just giving you a heads-up that I'm coming round,' he said.

Beth sat up. 'Why?'

'To walk you to work. I thought you might appreciate some company on the way in.'

'Uh, I was thinking I might not go into work today …'

'Why not?' There was rustling as he moved the phone. 'Just a minute. Tell me in person.' He hung up and the doorbell rang.

Beth jumped out of bed and pulled on a dressing gown. She heard Anna go to the door. A muffled conversation outside was followed by a rap on her bedroom door. She opened it, to find Hibs holding his backpack in one hand and a carrier bag in the other. 'Are you feeling okay?' he said. 'I mean, after yesterday.'

She was so pleased to see him she could have hugged him. The idea of going back into her life was frightening, but here was Hibs. Ready to stand behind her.

Hibs waved a bag in front of his face. 'I picked up some cake. I figure we deserve it after all the fun and games last night. Come on, Tyler. Up and at 'em.'

She managed a small smile.

'That's better,' said Hibs. 'Now, hurry up and get ready. It's Roger's big presentation today. You don't want to miss that.'

'Fine. Fine. I'm coming.' She pushed the door shut, leaving him outside in the hallway. 'Fine.'

They walked in slowly. It was the sort of morning that made the world seem like a new place. The dawn mist had all but burned off, leaving everything covered in sparkling dew. It was Hibs's favourite part of the year, when summer was just past its heady best and starting to slide gracefully into autumn. While it was still definitely summer, there was something that hinted at change, just waiting to turn. A bird swooped past, making them both look up.

'What a beautiful morning. The sun's shining,' Beth said.

Hibs frowned. As far as he could tell, the weather was pretty much how it had been yesterday. 'It's summer,' he said. 'It's been pretty sunny all week.'

'Really?' She looked around again. 'How come I never noticed?'

She had been so focused on Gordon and keeping him happy that she'd stopped noticing everything else. Still, if she was noticing now, it could only be a good thing. 'Perhaps you had other things on your mind,' he suggested.

Beth nodded. 'I guess.'

They walked along in silence. Beth was frowning and Hibs hoped she was thinking about Gordon and how wrong they were together. She looked smaller somehow, as though the scare last night had taken something away from her. Hibs wondered what it would be like to take her hand, to be her boyfriend, rather than being the work friend who hung out with her. To touch her and hold her. He had a sudden memory of her running away, clutching her bra to her as Gordon chased her. The wave of anger at Gordon was so strong it made him catch his breath. He gripped his bag tighter. Much as he wanted to hunt Gordon down and break every single one of his limbs, this was about Beth. He had to let her decide to let go of Gordon. *Then* he would hunt him down and break his every limb.

'Hibs?' Beth was staring into the middle distance.

'Yes?' Whatever she wanted of him, he would do it. He wondered what she was going to ask. Something about last night, or maybe – please – a request to make Gordon swallow his own teeth …

'Why do you like being a scientist?'

Okay, that was not what he'd been expecting. He forced himself to think about the question though. 'I find it … interesting.'

'But why?'

This was going to require a full answer. Hibs took a deep breath and let it out. 'Beth, I'm the third of three boys. My oldest brother is Jedediah Hibbotson the second, named after my great-grandfather. My other brother is Alfred Hibbotson the second, named after my grandfather.'

Beth smiled. 'Are you James Hibbotson the second? I didn't know that.'

'No,' he said. 'I'm not. I'm just James Hibbotson. I'm not named after anybody.'

'What has that got to do with science?'

'My brothers were meant to take over the family business. They were groomed from when they were young. They took degrees relevant to the business. They're both very clever guys and between them they know everything there is to know about business and logistics. That's what my dad wanted. Two sons to take on his empire. I was a mistake. So I wasn't meant for anything. I could do whatever I wanted. Science was interesting enough to engage me, so I decided to do that. Turns out, I'm good at it. No one in my family understands what I do, but they understand that I'm good at it. That's what keeps me coming back, contract after contract.'

Beth was quiet for a moment. 'I'm still not sure I understand.'

What was wrong with him? He could talk for England normally, but when it came to talking to Beth, he was a complete babbling idiot. He decided to try again. 'I do it for the buzz of being good at it. That thrill you get when things fall into place and then, suddenly, you've discovered something no one else has ever known before. It doesn't happen often, but when it does, it's incredible.'

Beth's face fell. 'I've never had that feeling. Does that mean I'm not that good?'

Bugger. That wasn't what he'd meant to happen. 'No. I'm not say—'

Beth held up a hand. 'It's okay, Hibs. I know what you mean. You love it because you're good at it. You're good at it because you're interested. I don't think I'm interested any more. I used to be. Now, I'm not so sure.' She sighed. 'I hate to say it, but I think Roger might have a point.'

'No he doesn't. He's a wanker.'

A slight twitch of her mouth gave away that she was amused. 'He is. But he's hit on something.' She turned and looked him in the eye for the first time that morning. 'I'm going to quit.'

He touched her arm and made her stop. 'Beth, you're upset right now. Don't do anything you'll regret later. Maybe you should talk to Lara.'

'I've done a lot of thinking, Hibs. I feel like I'm thinking clearly for the first time in a long time. I'm not happy, and that's made me insecure. I need to do something different.'

He felt panic in his veins. If she left now, he'd lose her. He wouldn't be able to see her every day and talk to her. He wouldn't be there when she was finally free of Gordon. 'No.'

It came out too frantic and Beth looked up, surprised.

'Promise me you won't do anything rash,' he said,

trying to think of something to say that could change her mind. 'You're two-thirds of the way through. You can start writing up soon. It would be a shame to throw it away so close to the finish.'

He noticed the narrowing of her eyes and the tightening of her mouth. She had already made up her mind. How come when he gave her good advice she could ignore it, but if Gordon said roll over, she did it? 'Beth, at least give yourself some time to get over this Gordon thing first.'

She sighed and nodded.

Okay. That bought him some more time. They were within sight of the department now. He had to tell her how he felt. Otherwise she would never include it in her thoughts. 'Beth.'

She turned and looked at him. A strand of hair blew across her face. She pushed it back. The bruise on her arm was big and ugly. He couldn't add to her problems right now. She needed to split up with Gordon first. Then move on. Hibs sighed. 'Nothing. Just ... good luck.'

Chapter Twenty-Six

Beth and Vik sat together for Roger's talk. Hibs was late coming into the hall, so was sitting at the back. Roger rattled through his introduction to the lab and presented Hibs's work. Beth sneaked a glance at her watch. They were only twenty minutes into the session. She wondered what Roger would use to pad out the presentation. She listened to him describe a bit of what he was hoping Vik would do and as Roger got to the end, Beth heard Vik let out a long breath.

'And last, but not least'—Roger moved on to a new slide and Beth recognised her graphs, with their massive error margins. He thought they showed something important and was going to ignore everything she'd sent him and present his theory instead. She groaned quietly and sank lower in her seat.

As Roger came to his conclusions, a hand went up. It was the head of department. Roger stopped. 'Yes?'

'Those don't look very convincing,' the head of department said.

'Yes, the error bars are quite large,' Roger conceded. 'Beth, whose work this is, is repeating them.'

'And are the repeats showing anything more consistent?'

'I believe they might be,' said Roger.

Beth put her hand up. Roger ignored her.

'Have you considered the alternative possibility that what you have there is an artefact? Have you tried looking to see if the deletion of that gene causes any other disruption?'

'Actually,' Roger began. He was going to blame Beth, she just knew it.

She'd had enough of this. She was going to quit and she didn't need to put up with this crap any more. Roger already hated her, so there was nothing for her to lose.

'Excuse me,' Beth said, loudly. Beside her, Vik cowered and tried to disappear. She glanced at him. Even if she didn't do this for herself, she had to face Roger down for Vik. Otherwise Vik would end up as demoralised as she was.

The head of department turned and raised an eyebrow.

'I … er … I'm Beth Tyler. Those are my results,' she gestured towards the screen. 'I just wanted to say that I've repeated those experiments and it's not clear that there's a trend.' Roger was glowering at her, as though he were about to explode. She held his gaze, defiant. 'I have repeated them and even with more results, there is no significant difference.' All heads had turned towards her now and her legs started to shake. She clenched her fists and carried on. 'We have considered that the protein might be involved in something more structural. In fact, we repeated the experiment you mentioned earlier, but with the protein missing.' She glanced at Roger, hoping he'd put Hibs's slides up – he didn't, but she carried on and described their results anyway. 'So,' she concluded, 'we think our protein may be holding the others in place.'

There was a moment of silence when the room felt enormous. She focused on the head of department, who narrowed his eyes and examined her for a moment. Finally, he nodded. 'Good. Will you be writing this up?'

Beth opened her mouth to reply, but Roger beat her to it.

'Yes. With the GFP images, we might even be able to

get on the front cover of a journal.' He grinned. 'The results go against the current dogma, so it should make it into a fairly high-impact journal.'

Roger was talking as though he was in complete agreement with Beth. She wasn't having that. Someone asked a question and she jumped in before Roger could answer. This made it easier to field the next question and then the next. Roger cleared his throat, the noise made even louder by the microphone. Everyone's attention went back to Roger. Beth sank back into her seat and clamped her knees together to stop them knocking. Beth didn't pay attention as Roger finished off the last few slides and concluded the presentation. She had seen murder in Roger's eyes. She was in so much trouble. But she'd had to do it. She couldn't let Roger misrepresent her work like that. Vik nudged her in the ribs and gave her a thumbs-up under the desk. She gave him a weak smile. Yes, she decided, she had done the right thing.

As the lecture theatre emptied, she hung back and watched the head of department stop Roger.

'Good lecture,' he said. 'That's some nice innovative work with the protein deletions. It's a shame the results weren't ready in time for the presentation.'

Roger beamed. 'Oh yes. We had hoped to have it all done in good time, but you know how it is.'

Beth gasped. Having told her not to bother, Roger was now claiming he supported her work all along. She made her way to the front to join them – she had to say something. Roger ignored her.

'Excuse me.'

'Yes, Beth, I can manage here. I'll see you back in the lab,' Roger said, before returning to his conversation with the head of department.

'I just wanted to ask if you'd like to see the latest results now,' she said, pointedly.

Both men looked at her. Lowly graduate students weren't supposed to interrupt members of faculty like that, but Beth stood her ground. It was her work they were discussing. She had every right to be included.

'We should put some time in the diary to talk.' The head of department shook hands with Roger. He nodded to Beth. 'Good work.'

She stared, surprised to be acknowledged by him.

'It's good to stand up for your work. If you don't believe in it, no one else will.' He smiled. 'Keep it up.' He gave her nod of farewell and strode out of the lecture theatre.

Beth caught Roger's eye. 'The head of department was impressed with my work.'

Roger looked as though he was about to retort, but didn't. He looked down at his laptop and back up at a spot behind her and said, 'Yes. Well done.' With that, he stormed off.

Beth smiled and followed him out.

As Roger stomped past the tea room, Vik peered out. He beckoned Beth in.

'Well done!' said Vik. 'That was amazing.'

Beth's smile spread into a grin. 'Thanks.'

Hibs was looking at her with a strange expression on his face. His eyes sparkled. 'Well done, Tyler. I'm so proud of you I could burst.'

'Thanks.' His praise bolstered her already buoyant spirits and she couldn't stop grinning. She still had a long way to go before she was free of Roger, but at least she'd made a start. The decision to leave after her PhD was liberating. It was almost as though she were stepping out of a chrysalis.

'I don't think I could have stood up in front of the whole department and contradicted Roger like that,' said Vik.

'You could. Especially if you knew you were right,' said Hibs.

Beth looked at Vik. He had lost some of his sparkle lately. Perhaps Roger was getting to him too. She had always assumed the problem had been with her, but if he was picking on Vik too, perhaps the problem was with Roger.

She'd been so tied up with her own problems she'd almost stopped noticing Vik.

'Do you guys want to go to the pub this evening?' she said.

'On a week day?' said Hibs, with mock surprise. 'Tyler, you rebel.'

'Haven't you got to go out with Gordon?' said Vik.

The silence that followed the question went on a little too long. Beth's heart began to crescendo. She was not going out with Gordon. She had no intention of ever seeing Gordon again. But she hadn't seen or spoken to him since the night before. Technically, she was still his girlfriend.

Hibs raised an eyebrow at Beth.

'No,' she said. 'I'm not going out with Gordon any more.'

Vik's eyes widened. His face tried on several expressions before settling on sympathetic. 'What happened? Are you okay?'

She looked at Hibs, who said nothing. 'We had a disagreement,' said Beth. 'I don't think he … I don't think he treats me very well and I don't think I should be with him.'

Vik blew out his breath. 'Wow. Good for you. I mean, you can do so much better than him.' He gave her a tight smile. 'Really. You can.' He reached forward and gave her an awkward pat on the arm. 'You're okay, aren't you?'

Ah, Vik. He was quite sweet in his little-boy-lost kind of way. 'Yes, thanks, Vik. I'm okay.' She looked from one man to the other. These guys knew her better than anyone and didn't think she was stupid. Her friends. How could she ever have thought that someone who kept her away from her boys could be good for her? 'So ... pub tonight then?'

'That'd be good. I can't stay late though, I've got plans,' said Vik.

'Plans?' Since when did Vik have plans that didn't involve her and Hibs? Things must have moved on while she was with Gordon.

'I've got a Skype call with a girl from America.'

'Ooh. One of the girls your mum's trying to set you up with?' She hadn't been following the saga of Vik's parents' matchmaking efforts. 'Is this one promising?'

'I guess I'll tell you tomorrow.' He didn't look optimistic.

'What about you, Hibs?'

He held up a lab timer. 'Science is a cruel mistress.' He smiled. 'And I promised I'd meet one of the karate guys for a drink before the ten o'clock reading. Sorry, Beth. I can do tomorrow though.'

She looked from one to the other, slightly disappointed that they couldn't make it to the pub when she wanted them to.

'It's a pity I can't come,' Hibs said. 'I'm looking forward to hearing exactly how Gordon reacted when you dumped him.'

Chapter Twenty-Seven

Beth sat at the kitchen table, her mobile phone cradled in her hands. Anna had gone out and the front door was locked with the security chain pulled across. She'd had a couple of glasses of wine to build up her courage. It was a good time to call Gordon.

There were several messages from him on her phone. She deleted them and then brought up his number. Her heart sped up and her chest constricted when she pressed call. It would probably go to answerphone. It rang once. Twice. He answered.

'Beth. Thank goodness. I've been so worried.'

The mere sound of his voice froze her. She couldn't move. She sat still, holding the phone to her ear, while her heartbeat filled her skull. Her throat closed up and it was difficult to speak. She tried to say something, but all that came out was an anguished croak.

'I've been trying to call you all day but you weren't answering. I even tried the lab phone. I've been worried sick.' He paused, apparently waiting for her to respond. When she said nothing, he carried on. 'Beth, about yesterday. I just wanted to say I'm sorry. I didn't mean to get cross. I just … I waited for you for ages. You can understand how I'd be a little bit miffed.'

A little bit miffed? The indignation was enough to make her find her voice. 'You attacked me.'

There was a pause. 'I wouldn't do that. What are you talking about?'

Gordon's response took her by surprise. He had attacked her. Hadn't he?

'I would never hurt you, babe. You know that.'

But he had. She hadn't imagined it, had she? Doubt stirred. The word 'paranoid' popped into her mind. What if …

'Beth, are you sure you're okay? You've been acting a bit weird lately,' Gordon said, his voice all concern.

Slowly, Beth brought her wrist up in front of her face. Her sleeve slid back, revealing the red mark. It was starting to go yellow at the edges. She hadn't imagined that. Gordon was playing with her mind. He was poison. She had to get away from him.

'It's over, Gordon. I don't ever want to hear from you again. Goodbye.' When she tried to hang up, it took her two goes because she was shaking so badly. She sank into her chair, clutching her bruised wrist.

The phone rang again. She pressed 'Cancel' so that it went to answerphone and went to her room. Kneeling on the floor, she reached under the bed for the cardboard wrappers she'd stored there. This was what had set it all off. If she hadn't found these in the recycling, she would still be under Gordon's power and convinced she was going mad. And somehow she'd be feeling guilty about that too. It was hard to believe how much influence Gordon had had over her. Even now, just thinking about how angry he would be made her heart pound. He made her pulse race and she had thought it was love. Now she knew it was fear. How had she got so mixed up?

In the beginning she had been so in love. Gordon was gorgeous and charismatic and had that powerful swimmer's body. She had a sudden vision of those same powerful shoulders pressing down on her and shuddered. She had to take a couple of deep breaths to remind herself that there was still air in the room.

Her phone rang again. Gordon would keep trying. He didn't know she knew about Mila. He still thought he could talk her round. She hit cancel again. There would be messages, each one of them toxic. She would delete them without listening to him. Everything he ever said was a lie.

She laid the wrappers out on the floor, one by one. Something else fell out – a bundle of fabric, the Pluto T-shirt that Gordon had thrown away. She smoothed the picture down and thought of Vik and Hibs on her birthday. Hibs had chosen this for her. It had made her happy on a day she'd given up to disappointment. Thank goodness for Hibs, with his ready smile and gentle hands.

She traced the edge of the crying Pluto with a finger. Hibs. She may as well stop pretending she didn't fancy him. If Gordon hadn't returned and picked up their relationship as though he'd never been away, she might have kissed Hibs. Slept with him, even. She thought of him holding ice on her wrist, his face too close to hers. She had wanted him so badly just then. But she couldn't do anything about it because she was still with Gordon.

Well, she wasn't now. She wanted comfort. If there was one thing she could be sure of, it was that Hibs would be happy to offer it. There was nothing to stop them getting together. She pulled off her T-shirt and replaced it with the Pluto one.

The phone rang again and Beth picked it up. Gordon's name was flashing on the caller ID. He was just going to keep ringing unless she did something. The more she avoided him, the more he would think he still had power over her. She stood up, feet firmly planted, took a deep breath and answered it.

'Beth, I don't know what's got into you—' Gordon began.

'Gordon, leave me alone. I have nothing more to say to you.' Her voice came out with barely a tremor. She needed to do this if she was to ever be free of him. 'If you contact me again, I will report you to the police.'

'Babe, you've got completely the wrong end of the stick.'

'Oh just … just fuck off.' She hung up and turned her phone off for good measure. God, that felt good. Now, she just needed to go tell Hibs. She smiled and ran downstairs to get her bike.

Hibs called up the microscope photos he'd just taken and started systematically filing them in the correct folders. It was a repetitive task that he usually saved for the morning, but since he wasn't in any hurry to go home, he'd decided to do it that night.

Someone entered the corridor and he could tell that it was Beth. Was it sad that he recognised her footsteps? Probably. Lara was right: he had it bad.

He looked up when she entered. Her hair was tousled from the cycle helmet, her cheeks were tinged pink and her eyes were unusually bright. 'Hey, you okay? Has Gordon been bothering you?' He stood up, mentally preparing himself for battle. Personally, he would be delighted to stamp that smug bastard's face into the ground. All he needed was an excuse.

'Not really. Well yes, but I've dealt with it.' She was so full of nervous energy, she looked like she was about to take off.

'What happened?' Whatever it was, it must have been something big to get Beth so keyed up. At least she wasn't in tears.

She shifted her weight from foot to foot. 'I told him it was over. Then I turned my phone off.'

Finally! His smile was almost as big as hers. That must have taken some courage. No wonder she looked wired. 'Well done, Beth. That couldn't have been an easy thing to do.'

He closed the gap between them and gave her a quick hug. 'I'm proud of you.' Then, because holding her made him think of other things that were well outside the realms of friendship, he released her. 'How are you feeling?'

'Not sure,' she said. 'Relieved, excited, sad. All at once.'

Hibs smiled. 'You know what I do when I feel like that.'

Her eyes narrowed. 'Get laid?'

He laughed. 'Very funny. I was going to say get drunk.'

He sensed the change in atmosphere before she said anything.

'We could do both,' she said.

She stood on tiptoes and kissed him and all thought disappeared as his blood supply headed south. His world was filled with the sensation of her mouth on his. The soft press of her breasts. The pressure of her fingers behind his neck. He had fantasised about kissing Beth hundreds of times and nothing he'd imagined came close to the real thing. There was nothing, nothing, he wanted more than this. He put his hand on her hip and felt a response shimmer through her.

It took a few moments for his brain to recover from the sudden rush of blood to the groin. This was Beth. This wasn't how he'd wanted to start a relationship with her. He could sleep with her now and she'd think it meant nothing to him. He couldn't bear that. He pulled away. 'Beth. I don't—'

The shock in her face nearly broke his heart.

She stepped back from him, tears already brimming.

He had always been so good at speaking his mind. He was always confident with women. Now, when he needed it the most, his brain wouldn't work. He wanted to tell her he wanted her for always, not just for a one-night comfort shag, but the words just wouldn't come fast enough. 'Beth.'

She turned and ran out of the lab.

'Fuck.' He ran after her. Halfway down the corridor, he remembered he'd left his Bunsen burner on. He swore again and ran back to turn the gas off and kill the flame. Still swearing, he thundered down the corridor after her.

Her footsteps echoed in the stairwell. Looking over the side, he could see she was several floors below him. He took the steps down two at a time. Not for the first time he wished there was a fireman's pole installed in the middle.

He got to the bottom of the stairs in time to see her run out of the glass doors.

Beth unlocked her bike and wrenched it away from the wall. She could barely see for the tears. How could she have been so stupid? She'd kissed Hibs. And Hibs, the man who slept with just about anything female, had turned her down. She'd always assumed he'd never tried it on with her because she was a colleague and a friend, but perhaps it was because he didn't fancy her. She heard him calling her name, somewhere behind her. She jumped on her bike and started pedalling.

But Hibs was too fast for her. He grabbed the handlebars of her bike. 'Beth, stop.'

'Leave me alone, Hibs. I'm embarrassed enough as it is.'

'For fuck's sake, will you stop for a moment and listen.'

She stopped trying to push the bike forward. She'd never push past him. Tears streamed down her face. Whatever humiliation was coming, she would have to face it until he let go of her bike. She knew he'd try to let her down gently. That only made things worse. She couldn't look at him. 'I'm sorry.'

He put a hand under her chin and lifted her face up until she was looking at him. She tried to look away.

'Beth. I pulled away because I didn't want you to get the wrong idea.' He moved closer until he made eye contact.

Beth wrenched away from him. 'You don't want anything serious and we work together so you don't want a one-night stand either. I get it. Now let me go.'

'See. I told you you'd get the wrong idea.'

She must have heard him wrong. She looked up. Through the blur of tears, she was aware that he wore an expression she'd never seen before. If she didn't know better, she'd have called it fear. But this was Hibs: he wasn't afraid of anything.

'I've loved you since … Jesus, Beth, I don't even know how long. Since the day I met you.' He squeezed his eyes shut and reopened them. 'I stopped you just now because I don't want things to happen like this. You're not like the others. You're special. I want to do things properly.' He frowned. 'Am I making sense?'

'No.' She had no idea what he was going on about. But she'd heard him right. He'd just said he loved her. Suddenly hundreds of little things fell into place. The gestures of incredible kindness. The total antipathy to Gordon. The flirting in the pub the night Gordon came back. This was Hibs trying to tell her he loved her. The first rush of happiness made her head spin. He wanted her! She hadn't made an idiot of herself. But a little voice niggled. If he loved her so much, why hadn't he just asked her out? It's not like he was shy or anything.

'I've been with lots of girls, Beth. None of them have made me feel the way you do. I don't want to just sleep with you; I want to spend every minute of every day with you. I want to have a proper relationship with you.' He moved his hands as though he was desperate to do something with them but didn't know what. He gave an exasperated-sounding *tsch*. 'Look, can I take you out to dinner or something?'

He was in his lab coat, his face flushed from running down the stairs. He still had that slightly panicky edge to his voice. And he appeared to be asking her out on a date. It all felt so surreal that Beth felt the sudden urge to giggle. 'And do what?' she said. 'Get to know each other?'

Hibs let go of her bike and rubbed the bridge of his nose. 'Give me a break, Tyler. I'm trying to do the right thing here.'

She recognised the familiar rush she felt. She wanted him. Of course she did. Did she love him? Had she just mistaken love for friendship? Right now, she wanted to be with him, to be warm and loved and safe. But she wasn't sure if there was anything more than that. It wasn't fair to let him think there was.

'Hibs. I'm not sure ...'

Hibs shook his head. 'I'm not asking you to love me, Beth. You've just split up with Gordon. You're not ready – I get that. I just didn't want you to think that you're another notch on the bedpost.'

She nodded as though she understood. 'So. What happens now?'

Hibs frowned. 'I'm not sure.' His eyes locked on hers and he leaned closer. 'How about we start here?' He kissed her. It wasn't a slightly stunned kiss like before, but a proper kiss, warm and wanting. Beth felt it in the depths of her, heating her up from the pit of her stomach. She slid her hand up to his face, her thumb brushing his cheekbone, and he responded by pulling her closer. Beth gave herself up to feelings she'd forgotten how to have. She felt wanted and excited and ... protected. When he finally drew back, she was surprised she hadn't melted into a puddle. If he could reduce her to mush just with a kiss, she definitely wanted more. But ...

'How about a trial period,' said Hibs. 'No commitment.'

'How is that different to all your other women?'

'Because I promise to hang around for as long as you want me. The lack of commitment is all on your side. Deal?'

Beth laughed. 'Tell you what, how about you buy me a cup of coffee and we'll take it from there?'

'Deal.' He gave her an apologetic smile. 'I just need to finish up in the lab ...'

Beth nodded. He didn't need to explain that to her. 'Science is a cruel mistress, huh?'

'Exactly.'

She got off her bike and turned it round. 'I'll help you.'

Hibs took the bike from her and wheeled it along with one hand. They walked side by side.

Beth realised that she was smiling. Somehow, she felt lighter than before. Happy, in some indefinable way. She glanced over at Hibs and saw that he was smiling too. She reached across and took his free hand. His fingers wrapped around hers. They walked back to the lab hand in hand, and it felt like the most natural thing in the world.

Chapter Twenty-Eight

By the time they finished up in the lab, most coffee places were shut. 'I can make you a coffee,' Hibs suggested. 'Your place or mine?'

'Yours.' There was always the risk of running into Anna if they went back to her flat.

Hibs's house was only a tiny one-bedroomed place, but still a real grown-up house. The front door opened straight into the living room, which had hardly any furniture in it. The only evidence of regular use was a fleece lying on the table and a stack of papers on the sofa.

Beth had been there before; it was nice, homely, if a little spartan for her taste.

Hibs drew the curtains and returned to Beth. 'So, what can I get you? Tea, coffee, hot Ribena?'

'You're serious about this coffee thing?'

'Of course. That's what we came here for. I wouldn't want to have brought you here under false pretences.' He was very close to her now; she looked into his grey eyes and saw the laughter in them.

'Oh shut up.' She reached up and put her arms around his neck.

He laughed and pulled her to him. There was no hesitation in his kiss. Beth felt as though her whole body were liquid. She kissed him back, wanting him more and more with each second. She found the hairband that was keeping his hair back and tugged it off. His hair smelled of expensive shampoo and it slid over her hands, soft and heavy. The sensation was incredibly arousing. Beth gave a little moan.

Hibs took her hand and led her up the narrow staircase and into his bedroom.

She helped him pull off his T-shirt. His body was lean and toned. Beth ran her hand over the smattering of hair on his chest. Gordon's chest had been smooth where he'd removed his body hair to reduce drag in the pool. She'd forgotten what honest body hair looked like. They shed the rest of their clothes and Hibs pulled her to him, kissing her. His hair fell onto her shoulder like an extra caress.

They kissed for what seemed like hours, yet not long enough. By the time Hibs laid her on the bed, she wanted him so much she thought she'd explode. He moved on top of her and, suddenly, she was reminded of Gordon crushing her. The flashback was so vivid she let out an involuntary cry.

Hibs froze. 'What's wrong?' He moved off her and rolled onto his side, next to her. 'Beth?'

'Nothing. It's nothing.' She reached for him. No, no, no. She'd had the chance to have something good and she'd ruined it. She wanted him so much but she'd blown it. She felt a wave of self-pity well up inside her. The happy buzz vanished and tears threatened.

He sat up and turned on the lamp. 'Beth? What's the matter?'

With the light on, she was suddenly terribly aware of her nakedness. She was lying on top of the duvet and there was nothing to cover herself with. Feeling exposed and vulnerable, she scrambled into a sitting position, pulling her knees up in front of her.

'Tell me what's bothering you. If you don't tell me, I can't help.' Hibs reached across and picked up his T-shirt. He passed it to her.

Beth took it in both hands. It was as though he'd read her mind. The simple act of kindness was like a raindrop after a drought. He hadn't even paused to think, just handed her the T-shirt because he saw she felt exposed. How had she forgotten what normal people did for each other? She pulled the T-shirt on and felt its comforting warmth cover her. Hibs was watching her, sitting naked on the bed, his face creased with worry. Suddenly it was all too much. The emotions she'd been keeping at bay burst over her in one massive sob.

Hibs gathered her to him and held her. 'Shhh.' He rocked her gently and kissed her hair until the sobbing subsided. 'Tell me what's wrong.' He sounded worried and flustered. 'I can't help if you don't tell me.'

Curled up against him, with her face buried in the hollow of his neck, she told him. When she got to the bit where Gordon suffocated her, she felt him draw a sharp breath and go very still. The feelings of fear and shame that she'd felt the morning after Gordon's attack came back. What was Hibs thinking? Gordon would have told her it was her fault – did Hibs think the same? She looked up. His jaw was clenched so hard that a vein was throbbing in his neck. He was angry. With her?

'Hibs?'

He looked down. At the sight of her, his face softened. 'Oh, Beth. I had no idea. If I'd known I wouldn't have …' He planted a kiss on her forehead. His arms tightened around her and he rested his cheek against the top of her head. 'Beth? Have you considered going to the police?'

She looked up. 'The police?'

He stared at her with a puzzled frown. 'He raped you,' he said, as though it were obvious. Rape? She hadn't thought of it like that. She had focused so much on the fact that she couldn't breathe. She had asked Gordon to stop. Hadn't she?

'He was my boyfriend,' she said, carefully. 'We were having sex. No one will believe that I didn't consent.' He would lie. He would be charming and disarming and she would be a dithering mess. No one would believe her. She sighed. 'I should have said "no" clearer. I should have—'

'Should have nothing,' Hibs said. 'No one has the right to treat another human being like that. He isolated you from your friends. He tried to control everything in your life. I bet he's done little things to you before like that – to punish you for breaking some arbitrary rule. Am I right?'

She thought about the past few weeks with Gordon. She went to the pub without telling him and he made her late for the lab meeting. Saying no to putting him in the calendar led to him half killing her. She thought about the episode with the T-shirt and wondered what had prompted that. What had happened before? They'd had a conversation about Hibs fancying her. Had she somehow let on that she was attracted to him? Perhaps Gordon had seen the way Hibs felt about her. He was still holding her tight, and she looked up at him. Hibs moved to meet her gaze.

'Do you remember that day when Gordon and I were messing around in the kitchen ...?'

'When I got back from the cinema with Anna? Oh I remember that all right.' He nodded. 'He wanted to make sure I saw you.'

'You saw?' Gordon hadn't just been trying to humiliate her. He'd been using her to show Hibs who was boss. Gordon had wanted show Hibs that Beth belonged to him and would have made sure that Hibs had seen her. 'Oh god. I thought you hadn't seen. You said ...'

'He grinned at me before he followed you into the

room,' Hibs said. 'I figured the fact that he wanted me to see you was a good enough reason to pretend I hadn't.'

Beth groaned and curled around herself.

'I'll come with you to the police,' Hibs said.

She shook her head. Apart from everything else, she would have to tell people what Gordon had done. What she'd allowed him to do. She felt small and stupid.

A loud beeping interrupted her thoughts. Hibs groaned, untangled himself and slipped off the bed to retrieve the lab timer from the pocket of his jeans.

'Two o'clock already?'

Hibs stood in the middle of the floor, looking from his timer to Beth and back again. 'Screw it.' He threw the timer on the floor and got back in the bed.

'But your time point.'

'I'll just have to redo the experiment tomorrow. I can't leave you now.'

She knew better than anyone what that meant. He would have another night of work, and they'd both been mentally counting down the days until they could have a proper night's sleep. Besides, Hibs was married to his work. That he'd even considered missing his reading because of her was incredible. She felt a little bubble of happiness that he cared enough for her to do that. 'What happened to "science is a cruel mistress"?'

'But you're upset. This is more important than an experiment. It's more important than anything.'

She gave him a push. 'I'm okay. I'll still be here when you get back.' He hesitated and she could almost feel the pull of his choices. Hibs always put his work first; she didn't want to get in the way of that. 'You mean to tell me,' she said, 'you'd mess up a scientific experiment because you were too busy getting laid?'

His eyes wrinkled up in a smile. 'Well, when you put it like that ...' He slid out of bed. 'You're sure you'll be okay?'

She nodded. Oddly, she knew she would. She felt safe here in his house, in his bed, wearing his T-shirt. It was funny that it had taken her all this time to realise that Hibs made her feel safe. She snuggled down under the duvet and watched him pull his clothes back on. Now that she was properly tucked up, the day caught up with her. She hadn't slept properly in weeks.

He knelt on the floor beside the bed and brought his face level with hers. 'Thank you.'

She wondered sleepily what he was thanking her for.

Hibs got back to the house and let himself in. It didn't look any different to normal. For one scary moment, he thought perhaps he's imagined kissing Beth. He took the stairs two at a time and rushed to his bedroom. Beth was curled into a ball in the middle of his bed, fast asleep. He sat and watched her sleep for a moment. Poor Beth. He thought about how spaced out she'd been after Gordon had attacked her. He'd known something was wrong, but he hadn't pushed her hard enough to tell him. How did you cope with stuff like that? Nothing in his experience had prepared him for this. He wanted to help, but he had no idea how. He was completely out of his depth. He checked the time. It was three in the morning and everyone he could think of was asleep now. He would talk to Lara in the morning. She might know what to do.

He climbed into bed next to Beth. She stirred, but didn't wake as he tucked an arm around her and fell asleep.

Chapter Twenty-Nine

Beth hummed to herself as she worked. Next to her, the Bunsen flame hissed straight and blue. She labelled some petri dishes and started inoculating them. Behind her, Hibs was doing his own work. She felt acutely aware of him. Every so often, they would make eye contact and smile.

Roger stomped in. He stood at the end of the bay and watched. Beth stopped what she was doing and turned to look at him.

Roger cleared his throat. 'I've just been looking at those results you sent me.'

Beth put the lids back on her dishes and turned the Bunsen flame down to yellow. At the other side of the bay, she sensed Hibs had paused to listen.

'What do you think?' She reasoned that if he thought they were plain wrong, he wouldn't hesitate to say so.

'Very persuasive,' said Roger. 'I think we have enough to write that up as a paper.'

'Really?'

'Mmm. Get a draft to me in the next few weeks.' He left abruptly.

Beth stared at the space he'd just vacated. Wow. Coming from Roger, that was a vote of confidence. She turned to Hibs. 'You heard that, right?'

'Yep.'

'Vik?' She crouched to look through the space between the benches and overhead shelves.

'I heard,' Vik said. 'Well done. You've broken the wall.'

'See. I told you you're good,' said Hibs.

Beth grinned. It was nice to be taken seriously by her supervisor. After all the crap that she'd had in her life, things were suddenly taking a turn for the better. She had a feeling it was all down to Hibs. She watched him for a moment, admiring the speed and grace with which he worked. As though feeling her eyes on him, he paused and turned. 'What?'

'Just wanted to say thank you.'

'I didn't do anything.'

'You helped me with the experiments and stood up for me when Roger rubbished them.'

His eyes met hers. 'It was my pleasure, Tyler. My pleasure.'

Beth felt a little flip in her stomach. Being with Hibs was very different from being with Gordon. She felt relaxed and happy. He never made her feel small or weak or silly. She even liked that he still called her Tyler, which just highlighted that while some things had changed, the good stuff had stayed the same. She stood there, grinning like a madwoman at him, until he gestured towards her petri dishes. Right. Work. Of course. She turned her attention back to her neglected experiments.

Chapter Thirty

Someone shook her shoulder. Beth hadn't even realised that she'd fallen asleep.

'Man, you really are tired,' said Vik. 'Do you want to go home and get some rest?'

She blinked. 'I ... er ... I guess I could.'

'You and Hibs both need to take some time off.'

Beth wondered if it was that obvious that they'd spent the night together. 'What?'

'You guys have been working nights and doing seven-day weeks. You really need to catch up on your sleep,' Vik continued. He was busy stapling together articles that he'd printed out. He didn't look at her. 'I don't think you're really safe to be in the lab.'

Okay. So he thought they were just tired. 'Hmm.'

'You're both so tired and so loved up,' said Vik.

Her head snapped up.

'Oh, come on,' said Vik. 'You think I haven't noticed? A blind person would notice.' He smiled at her. 'You know what you're doing, right?'

Beth said nothing. Did she know what she was doing? It had been a crazy few weeks. She'd gone from abject terror of one boyfriend to being deliriously happy with a new one, but she still couldn't relax enough to sleep with him. That didn't sound much like someone who knew what she was doing.

Vik sat down in front of her. 'Beth, I know I'm not an expert, but are you sure this is the right thing for you? You went out with Gordon for ages and the idea of being single can't be easy. And Hibs is ... well, he's Hibs. Are you sure you're okay with having a short fling? I don't want to see you get hurt again.'

'Vik ...' What could she say to him? How could she make him understand that this wasn't a rebound thing? She'd wanted Hibs for ages. 'It's not a fling.'

'Are you sure he knows that?'

'What?'

Vik sighed. 'You know Hibs tends to see relationships as being just for sex. I don't want that to happen to you.' He looked up, his brown eyes full of concern. 'You're my friend.'

Beth was touched. How could she have lost sight of all these people who cared about her? What power had Gordon wielded to make her push them away? Much as she loved Vik, she couldn't tell him that the one thing Hibs didn't get from her, yet, was sex. 'Don't worry, Vik. He's not using me. He ... I think he really, genuinely loves me.'

Vik didn't look convinced.

She patted his hand. 'Don't worry, I'll be okay. Honestly.' She stood up and stretched. 'Although, I think you might have a point about getting some sleep.'

Tidying up her bench before going home, she took her samples into the cold room to put them on ice. Vik had a point. She wasn't okay. She should talk to someone. The air of the cold room gripped her as she thought about the word 'rape'. That's what Hibs had called it. Rape was something that happened to other people. Not her. But now that Hibs had pointed it out, she knew that was exactly what had happened.

Just giving the horror a name had somehow made it more solid. She hadn't imagined it. She hadn't overreacted. She wasn't sure how knowing that helped, but somehow it did. Hibs believed her. She hadn't expected him to. She'd expected disbelief, repulsion or blame. Instead he'd given her sympathy and kindness and love.

She knew about date rape. She *knew*. Yet Gordon had her so brainwashed that she didn't recognise it.

The cold wormed its way through her clothes. Goosebumps appeared on her skin. She shivered. Who was she trying to kid? She wasn't okay. She rubbed her arms and left the cold room. The warmth seeped back in from the minute she kicked the door shut behind her. She owed it to Hibs to try and get herself sorted out. She owed it to herself.

She pulled off her lab coat and gloves and ran down to the tea room before she could change her mind. On the noticeboard, crowded out by all the other notices and adverts from people selling bikes or computers, was one for the university's counselling service. She tore off a phone number, stepped outside and made the call.

Beth checked through the post that Anna had left piled up on the kitchen table, while Hibs made them tea. It was strange being in the flat with Hibs there as more than a friend. If anything it was weirder than seeing him at work. At least in the lab she knew she couldn't touch him.

'Vik had a go at me earlier,' Hibs said.

'Really? About what?'

'I think he's worried I'll hurt you. He's quite protective of you, you know.' Hibs slid her tea across the table.

Beth blinked. She turned the mug carefully. 'How exactly did he think you'd hurt me?' She turned it back again.

'Emotionally.'

'Right. That's ... sweet. I think.'

Hibs came round to stand next to her. 'Beth?'

When she looked up, he took her hands in his. 'Are *you* worried I'll hurt you?'

She looked into his eyes and saw fear and concern. It was strange seeing them there. Gordon would never have bothered to ask her about her fears. He would have just told her she was wrong. Did she worry that Hibs would hurt her? She realised she wasn't worried at all. It wasn't that she'd never considered it, like when she was with Gordon. She now knew the risk. She'd weighed it up and genuinely didn't think he would hurt her. He'd been her support for so long, before either of them had even realised it.

'Beth?' He was waiting for an answer.

'No. I'm not worried you'll hurt me.'

The relief on his face was touching.

'Actually, there's something I need to tell you,' she said.

He looked slightly panicked.

'I called the counselling service. You're right: I can't carry on pretending something nasty hasn't happened.' She stopped him as he started to speak. 'Please don't ask me to go to the police. They'll never believe me. And I don't want to face him again.'

Hibs nodded. 'Okay. I understand. At least, I think I do.' He pulled her to him. 'I'm glad you decided to see a counsellor. I can't help you and they might be able to.'

She pulled a strand of his hair loose and twirled it in her fingers. 'It kills you that you can't fix things, doesn't it?' she teased.

'It does.'

'You're such a bloke.'

'Are you complaining?'

When she shook her head, he kissed her.

They were still kissing when Anna arrived. Beth instinctively sprang back, but Hibs was still holding her hand.

Anna said, 'Oh,' when she saw Hibs. Her gaze slid to their hands.

Beth braced herself. She still wasn't sure how Anna felt about Hibs. If she still had feelings for him, this could be very awkward.

Anna looked from Beth's face to Hibs. 'You told her?' she said. 'Finally.'

Beth looked at Hibs in confusion. He nodded and looked slightly sheepish.

'About bloody time,' said Anna. 'Well, congratulations.' She gave Beth a grin. 'I'll get out of your hair.'

'Actually, we'll be clearing off in a few minutes. We're going to my place,' Hibs said.

'Your place? Gosh. Push the boat out.' Anna shook her head. 'Anyways, I've got to go have a shower. Got a hot date.' She winked at Beth and left.

Beth watched her go. 'What was that all about?'

He was still looking sheepish. 'Uh, the reason she and I ended it was … well, basically, I was too in love with you to be with someone else.'

'Oh.' Beth looked down the corridor. 'Poor Anna. That must have been so hard for her.'

'So hard for her? How do you think I felt? I had to put up with seeing you being mauled by Gordon.'

Beth shook her head. 'Show some empathy, Hibbotson.'

Hibs kissed her. 'You're a nice person, Beth. I like that about you.'

She smiled. 'But I have to realise that not everyone else plays fair, right?'

'Exactly.'

Chapter Thirty-One

Beth looked around the bar in the staff club. It was still early and there was no one there. She had just finished her first session with the counsellor and was still feeling raw and exposed. It had been odd talking to a stranger about the things that Gordon did. It was reassuring that the counsellor had listened carefully and told her, in clear terms, that yes, Gordon had been bullying her and she was absolutely right to leave him. Hibs and Lara had been telling her the same thing for a long time, but it helped to hear it from someone outside of her social sphere. Someone with no vested interest in any of them.

Hibs was joining her there for a drink. She quickly checked the decking outside, but it was too overcast for anyone to be sitting out there. She was early and rather than sit in the bar by herself, she decided to go the lounge to see what was on TV.

The lounge was at the other end of the building and she had to pass the front entrance to get to it. A quick glance at the doorway told her Hibs wasn't there. She walked briskly past the various doors to the snooker room and toilets. She was almost there when she heard a sound behind her. Some sixth sense made her tense.

'Beth,' said Gordon. 'At last.'

Her heart raced. She hadn't seen Gordon since the night she'd run from him. She forced herself to take a deep breath and turn round. He was behind her, closer than she'd thought. 'Gordon. What—'

'I saw you come past. I followed you.' He examined

her face, as though working out the weakest spot. 'You haven't been returning my calls.'

Beth's throat felt like it was closing up. She cleared it. 'Yes.'

'Why? What's happened?'

She shook her head. It was hard to speak to him when her heart was trying to escape through her neck. How could she have ever found him attractive? The mouth that she'd thought so beautiful was twisted into a sneer. His eyes were thin and malevolent. Suddenly, she was acutely aware of how empty the place was. If she screamed, how long would it be before someone came running?

'Look, Beth. I'm worried about you. You need help. You're turning away from your boyfriend—'

Beth clenched her fists. 'You're not my boyfriend.'

'Babe. See what I mean?'

She took a step back, petrified of him. While he still made her feel this way, she would never be free. 'I'm not paranoid,' she said. 'You ... you abused me.'

He laughed. 'I never did anything you didn't want me to do to you.'

'You raped me.' She wanted to shout it, but it came out in a whisper.

'That's slander,' said Gordon, his voice irritatingly reasonable. 'And mental. You're having those paranoid delusions again. You should get some help for that. Maybe speak to your GP?'

He was doing it again. For a small, insane moment, she believed what he was saying.

'I should have mentioned to your supervisor about your mental condition,' Gordon continued. 'Maybe I still should.'

It was the mention of her work that did it. Something

inside Beth clicked. 'You used me. You bullied me, harassed me for weeks. And when I didn't do what you wanted, you raped me.' Her voice was stronger now. This was how Gordon operated. He said his piece with such conviction that she believed him. Well not any more. Hibs was right. He did it because he could get away with it. There was only one way to stop it. 'There's a term for that, you know. It's called abuse. I'm going to report you to the police.'

Gordon sneered. 'Don't be silly.'

Behind Gordon the light changed. Beth glanced over his shoulder to see Hibs enter the corridor, very quietly. Relief flooded her body. She glared at Gordon. 'We'll let the authorities decide that.'

Gordon's arm drew back. Hibs moved so fast that Beth could barely work out what happened. Suddenly Gordon was on the floor, his arm twisted behind him, with Hibs leaning over him.

'Oh. I should have guessed. The nerd in shining armour.' Gordon sneered.

'I don't think you're in any position to be insulting people,' said Hibs. He looked up at Beth. 'Okay?'

'Yes.' She took a step towards Gordon. 'Stay away from me, Gordon. And if you do anything to Mila, or anyone else, I will support them in pressing charges. They may not believe one of us, but two ...'

'I don't know what you're talking about, you mental bitch.'

'Now, now.' Hibs moved and Gordon's face twisted with pain. 'Apologise.'

Gordon growled through clenched teeth. Hibs moved Gordon's arm a fraction. 'I can break your arm, you know,' he said conversationally. 'Now apologise.'

Gordon said nothing and Beth saw Hibs's face harden. His jaw was clenched. She felt a flash of panic that he would make good his threat. Gordon deserved everything he got, but Hibs had never hurt anyone on purpose. She couldn't let him start now.

'Hibs.' She shook her head.

There was a moment before Hibs blinked. It was as though he was seeing through a mist. He inclined his head to show he'd understood.

'The only reason I'm not breaking your arm right now is because Beth wouldn't like it.' Hibs twisted, making Gordon grunt. 'Now, if I find that you've been anywhere near her again, I will come back and finish the job. Understand?' When Gordon didn't respond, he moved the arm some more. 'Understand?'

Gordon gasped and nodded. Hibs motioned Beth to get behind him. She moved quickly. Hibs let go of Gordon and stepped back. Gordon stood up, rubbing his wrist. 'I could do you for assault.'

'What assault?' said Hibs. 'I didn't see anything, did you, Beth?'

'No.' She kept her eyes on Gordon. She didn't trust him not to leap at her.

Gordon's eyes flicked as he checked for CCTV cameras and witnesses. There were none. Beth realised that he had deliberately chosen this place to threaten her so that he wouldn't be seen. It had worked against him.

Hibs's mouth curved into a smile, but his eyes didn't change. 'Well, I wish I could say it was nice seeing you, Gordon, but it wasn't. Let's hope we don't see you again.' He turned to Beth. 'What say we go somewhere else for that drink? I've gone off the atmosphere in this place.'

'Yes. Me too.'

They turned and walked back to the main doors. It was all Beth could do not to break into a run. Hibs strode along beside her. Neither of them looked back. It was only when they were out of the door that Hibs said, 'Are you all right?'

She felt better than she had done in ages. Okay, Hibs had come to rescue her, but she had faced Gordon down. She would go to the police. Gordon should not be allowed to do this to anyone else. 'I'm fine. You?'

Hibs didn't say anything as he unlocked his bike. She could see a pulse in his jaw, and the tension in the set of his shoulders. He was angry, but she wasn't frightened like she would have been with Gordon. 'Do you want to go for a drink somewhere else?'

Hibs shook his head. 'I'm sorry, Beth. I'm not sure I'd be good company today. Maybe it's best if I just head home. I need to calm down a bit.'

She put her hand on his arm. 'I'll come with you.'

By the time they got back to his house, the shock of confronting Gordon had eased and Beth was practically dancing with the adrenaline rush. 'You were amazing,' she told Hibs.

'Thank you.' He held the door open for her and followed her in. 'I think you were doing pretty well by yourself.'

'You think?'

'If he'd tried to hit you, you would have run away, right?'

She thought back to the terrible, paralysing fear. Would she have run? She realised that yes, she would have at least tried. But she hadn't needed to. She was no longer afraid of Gordon. She was finally free from living under his shadow. She felt like she'd been let out of prison.

'First rule of self-defence,' said Hibs. 'If you have the chance to run away, get the hell out.' He took out glasses and a bottle of wine.

Beth nodded. She didn't know what else to say. Hibs clearly didn't share her sense of exhilaration.

She watched him carefully as he poured two glasses of wine. He slid one towards her and took a large gulp from the other. He was scowling. She could see the tension still in his jaw.

'Hibs. Are you okay?'

He didn't look at her. 'I'm okay.' He closed his eyes and pinched the bridge of his nose. 'I'm sorry, Beth. I'm just fighting the urge to go back and hunt that bastard down. If I hadn't got there when I did … I just …' He opened his eyes and Beth saw the confusion of feelings in them. 'If he'd hurt you, I would have broken his arms.' He took another gulp of wine.

Seeing Hibs, who was normally so unflappable, fighting to regain composure shocked Beth. Anger shot through her. Bloody Gordon. Bad enough he threatened her. But he had no right to affect Hibs like this. Her Hibs. Who was always there when she needed him. Who made her feel safe and wanted and strong. She was so angry she had a good mind to track down Gordon and beat him up herself. The strength of feeling surprised her. Why was she so protective of Hibs? The answer was there, waiting for her to find it. She loved him. She had loved him for months. Gordon's influence had masked it, but the attraction to Hibs had always been there. She had mistaken it for friendship.

Hibs finished his glass of wine and sighed. He seemed to be getting back to his normal self now. He leaned against the work surface, his long legs stretched out. Beth stepped into the gap between them and gave him a hug. Hibs wrapped his arms around her and kissed the top of her head. She could hear his heart beating against her ear. 'I love you,' she said.

Hibs went still. 'Pardon?'

She leaned back so that she could look at him. 'I love you,' she repeated.

The smile on his face could have melted an iceberg. Beth laughed. She took his face in her hands and kissed him. He kissed her back with ferocity. She reached inside his T-shirt and felt the sleek muscles underneath. A little shiver ran through him at her touch. She pulled at his top and he helped her pull it off him. Then he did the same with hers.

Still kissing, he moved her backwards into the living room until she landed on his sofa, displacing a pile of papers. He moved away from her lips and kissed his way down her body. Beth relaxed and let him work his magic. When he had carefully kissed, stroked and explored every part of her, he pulled her on top of him. Beth closed her eyes and felt the world explode in her head.

Chapter Thirty-Two

Clarissa had organised wine and nibbles for the launch of the WIS calendar. The bar in the Staff Club was crowded. All the men featured had been invited and Anna had arranged a display on one of the chrome tables so that she could sell the calendars.

Beth was apprehensive that Gordon might come to the event. She hadn't seen or heard from him since the incident in the corridor a few weeks before. She hoped she'd seen the last of him, but she kept an eye on the door anyway, just in case.

Clarissa wafted over and handed her a glass of wine. 'Well done, Beth. I have to admit, I didn't think you'd manage it, but you've done a good job.'

Beth wondered if Clarissa realised how patronising that sounded. 'Well thank you for your resounding endorsement.' She waited for Clarissa to move off, but she seemed to have something on her mind. 'Can I help you with something?'

Clarissa looked down at her glass. 'Well, actually, I was wondering if ... er ... is Dr April single? Do you know?'

The naked guy? 'I think he is, let me ask Anna.'

'No. No. Don't.' Clarissa's face flushed with what looked like panic. 'It's okay.'

'He's over there,' said Beth. 'You could talk to him. Do you want me to introduce you?'

'I ...' Clarissa cast a quick glance across to where Dr April was chatting to Lara and, judging by Lara's polite expression, boring her.

'Better to regret something you've done than something

you haven't,' Beth said. Seeing Clarissa hesitate, she grabbed her arm. 'Come on. He's really nice.'

She dragged Clarissa across the room. 'Hi, Nick,' she said.

'Oh, hello.' Dr April smiled, showing his even teeth.

'Nick, this is Clarissa.' Beth steered her over. 'She's the chairwoman of WIS. She works on hormones. Nick's work is on kinase cascades.'

'I know,' Clarissa said. 'I read the blurb on the calendar.'

'Oh. Okay. I'll leave you to connect up the two parts of the signalling pathway, then. I'll just borrow Lara for a minute.'

As they walked off, Lara leaned in and whispered, 'Thanks.'

'You're welcome.' She studied her friend, noting that she looked a lot less teary than she had done in the weeks before. 'How are things with you? You look … better.'

Lara nodded to acknowledge what she'd said, but didn't smile. 'I'm improving,' she said. 'It's hard. I miss him. But I'm getting better at living without him.'

Beth put a hand on Lara's arm and gave it a little squeeze. 'It was the right thing to do then.'

Lara nodded. 'Painful, but right. Yes.' She gave Beth a small smile. 'I'll be okay. I'm getting on with stuff.'

They passed Anna, who was chatting up a random punter, persuading him to buy a calendar from her. 'You could give it to your mum as a Christmas present,' she said.

The guy laughed. 'Tell you what; I'll buy a calendar if you give me your phone number.'

'Deal.'

Beth shook her head as Anna scribbled her number on a piece of paper. 'Shameless.'

'Seems to keep her happy.' Lara turned and studied her. 'And you? How are you coping?'

'I'm okay, actually. I've started writing up my thesis. I feel so much better about everything now that I know I'm not going to be stuck in Roger's lab forever.'

'And how are things going with Hibs?' said Lara.

Beth smiled and glanced over to where Hibs was chatting to one of the other men from the calendar. 'He holds my hand.'

Turning back, she saw that Lara looked puzzled. She had to explain. 'When Gordon and I walked anywhere, he used to put his arm around my waist and sort of pull me to him.' She clamped her elbow to her waist to demonstrate. 'It was really uncomfortable. Hibs doesn't do that.' She looked over to him again. 'He holds my hand.'

'You mean, he doesn't treat you like you belong to him,' said Lara. 'It's called respect, Beth. I don't think you had much of that from Gordon.'

'I know. I can't believe I didn't realise.' Beth shook her head.

'At least you're rid of him now.'

Beth cast a quick glance towards the door as another group of people came in. 'Although, I'm a bit concerned that Gordon might show up today.'

'He wouldn't dare try anything here. Not with all those people around. Just don't go anywhere by yourself. Not even the loo, okay?'

Beth nodded. 'I know.'

She spotted Dan Blackwood enter the room, closely followed by a teenaged girl. Beth caught his eye and waved. He came over.

'I've got your prints for you,' she said when he'd come

near. She retrieved the bag from behind Anna's stall and handed it to him.

'Thank you.' He handed her an envelope. 'There's your cheque.'

'Come on, Dad, open it.'

Beth turned her attention to Dan's daughter. Now that she'd figured out who she was, Beth could see the resemblance. She peered around Dan at the photos.

'Wow. Did you take those?' she asked Beth.

'I did.'

'They're great.' She nudged her father. 'Dad, they make you look kinda dashing and Indiana Jones. No wonder Mum didn't want you in the calendar.'

Dan tutted and rolled his eyes. 'I'll get you a drink. What do you want?'

'Rum and Coke?'

'You can have just Coke.' He headed for the bar, leaving his daughter standing next to Beth, holding the photos.

'Dad was really disappointed when Mum told him he had to pull out,' the girl said. 'I'm glad we've at least got the photos.'

'I'm sorry your mother felt that way. It really isn't that sort of calendar.'

'Oh, I know,' said the girl. 'These guys are all, like, old.'

Beth tried not to laugh. To a teenager, they probably did look ancient.

'Do you do events?' said the girl suddenly.

The change of direction in the conversation threw Beth. 'Pardon?'

The girl gave an impatient tut. 'Do you do wedding photographs?' she said, slowly and clearly.

Did she? Why not. She supposed she could.

'My uncle's getting married in the autumn,' the girl continued. 'They need a wedding photographer and if you can make Dad look all cool and brooding, then you can probably make Uncle Tom look like sex god of the year.'

Beth borrowed Anna's pen and wrote her e-mail address out on a piece of paper. 'Here. Just ask him to e-mail me.'

Beth watched the girl make her way back over to her father. A new avenue to explore. Maybe even a new career – this time doing something she knew she genuinely enjoyed and was good at. A grin forced itself onto her face.

'What was that all about?' said Anna.

'I think I might have just been approached for my first commission,' Beth said, still grinning.

'Cool.'

'Do you want to take a break? I'll do the calendar stall for a bit.'

'Really? Oh brilliant. I've been dying to get out there and circulate.' Anna scanned the room. She gestured, discreetly, to a handsome man by the bar. 'So I think I'll start over there.'

Beth laughed. 'Good luck.'

It was fun standing behind the stall. People came up to her and asked her questions or complimented her about her photography. She accepted the compliments without denying them like she normally would have done. A few of the women came to ask her about the guys in the photos. She politely deflected them saying all she knew was what was on the calendars. Despite her and Anna's good intentions, the calendar seemed to have acted as a singles ad. She glanced over at Dr April, now deep in conversation with Clarissa, and Dr August, surrounded by a small crowd and clearly loving all the attention. No one seemed to be complaining.

A girl approached, holding a glass of wine. Beth's heart gave a lurch of recognition. It was Mila, Gordon's other girlfriend. No. Gordon's girlfriend. There was no 'other' about it now.

Mila examined the calendar, leafing through the sample, and Beth took the opportunity to study her. She was slim and pretty, just like in her picture on the website. Up close, Beth could see she was also petite and had an air of vulnerability about her. Yes. She was Gordon's type. Beth wondered if she had any suspicions of Gordon's other life. The one he'd pretended to share with Beth.

'Would you like to buy a calendar?' said Beth.

Mila looked up, her eyes big and apologetic. 'I'd love to, but I don't think my boyfriend would approve.'

'Really? Why not?'

Mila looked away. 'He thinks the men who agreed to do this are all posers.'

Did he now? She wondered what he would have said if he'd managed to smarm her into including him in it. 'What do you think?'

Mila's gaze drifted back to the calendars stacked up on the table. She made eye contact for the first time. 'I think it's just a bit of fun.'

'You should buy one then.'

Mila shook her head. 'Probably not a good idea, no.' She gave Beth a little smile and ambled off.

Beth stared after her. Mila clearly had no idea about her. Gordon had been lying and cheating on her all this time and now he was doing the same to Mila. She thought about what else Gordon had done and a shiver ran down her spine. She couldn't let someone else go through that. 'Wait!' she shouted. But Mila was already on her way out.

Beth caught the eye of one of the other women from the group and waved her over. 'Can you take over for a bit,' she said. 'I'll be back in five minutes.' Weaving through the people in the room, she ran after Mila.

Mila was already half way down the corridor on her way out.

'Mila!' Beth shouted. Mila stopped and turned. 'There's something I need to tell you.'

'How do you know my name?' Mila was looking at her sideways, with suspicion.

'Doesn't matter.' She was out of breath from running. 'Listen. I need to tell you something. About Gordon.'

'Gordon?' Mila's big eyes widened further. 'Who are you?'

'My name's Beth Tyler. I'm …' What could she say? Perhaps the truth was easiest. 'I'm Gordon's other girlfriend. Or was, anyway.'

'What?'

'Until recently, until two weeks ago, I was going out with Gordon. I had no idea about you. Gordon told me he was at swimming training every evening when he wasn't with me. I was at work so I didn't think to check.'

'Look,' said Mila. 'If this is some sort of joke, it's not very funny.'

'It's no joke. Honestly. I—'

'I don't have to listen to this.' She turned to go but Beth grabbed her arm.

'Please. You don't have to believe me, but please listen to me. I went out with Gordon for a long time until he went to the US. When he came back, we got back together. A few weeks ago. I had no idea about you. He lied to me and manipulated me. He did stuff and then pretended I'd imagined it.'

Mila's eyes darted around, looking for rescue.

'He tried to ...' She couldn't bring herself to mention him suffocating her. It was too weird. Too intimate. 'I was supposed to go to the department dinner with him two weeks ago and I cancelled. He was so angry he attacked me.' She was speaking as fast as possible. 'I've reported him to the police. I've got a non-molestation order—'

'Let go of me.' Mila's voice was pleading. 'Please.' She sounded frightened.

Oh god, Gordon was going to wreck this girl. 'Mila, Gordon's a bully. He gets off on intimidating people more vulnerable than he is. He tried to kill me. And then he tried to make out I was getting paranoid. I thought I was going crazy. He—'

Mila prised Beth's fingers off her arm and turned and fled. Beth didn't follow her. As Mila pushed through the door, Beth saw her look over her shoulder at her. Then she was gone.

Mila had been frightened by her. She probably thought Beth was some sort of nutter. But at least she'd tried to warn her. And if Mila ever got to the point where she doubted her own sanity, she might now consider that there was another explanation.

Footsteps came down the corridor. Beth tensed and turned, half expecting to see Gordon.

It was Hibs. He put a hand on Beth's shoulder. 'I heard. Well done.'

'She's going to tell Gordon,' said Beth.

'You never know. She might have recognised enough in what you said to keep it to herself.'

'I tried,' said Beth.

'I know.' Hibs gave her a hug. 'Well done, Tyler. I'm proud of you.'

Beth smiled into his shoulder. 'Thanks. I'm proud of me too.'

'Do you feel up to going back in?'

'Yes.' They turned and walked side by side down the corridor. As they reached the door, he took her hand.

Chapter Thirty-Three

Beth lay in a warm post-coital glow, her head on Hibs's chest, listening to his heartbeat. The past few weeks had been a rollercoaster. Now, suddenly, she was more in charge of her work and the rest of her world. She still found it hard to believe that she'd stood up to Gordon. She knew that the catalyst for all this change was the man who was currently tracing patterns on her shoulder with his finger.

She lifted her head to look at him. He smiled at her. 'Hello.'

'Hibs, I've decided that I don't want to stay in academia. I've made an appointment to see a careers advisor.'

He stared at her, his face serious. The finger on her shoulder stopped moving. He didn't say anything.

'I'm going to finish my PhD first,' she added.

He nodded, but still didn't reply. She rested her chin on his chest. 'Say something.'

Hibs looked away for a moment before he looked back into her eyes. 'I'm just thinking that if having sex leads to this kind of announcement, you and I should never sleep together ever again.'

She poked him in the side. 'Be serious. What do you think?'

'Is it what you want to do?'

'Yes.'

'In that case, go for it.' He reached across and stroked her cheek. 'I'll support you in whatever way I can.'

She laid her head back on his chest and let the feeling of contentment wrap around her. 'Where have you been all my life, Dr Hibbotson?'

'Right here,' he said. 'Just waiting for you to notice me.'

Somehow, it was the most perfect thing he could have said.

About the Author

Rhoda Baxter writes contemporary romantic comedies. She has lived all over the world, including the Pacific island of Yap, Nigeria, Sri Lanka and Didcot. She now lives in East Yorkshire with one husband, two children and no pets or carnivorous plants.

Rhoda studied at the University of Oxford and holds a DPhil in microbiology. When choosing a pen name, she got nostalgic about the bacteria she used to study (Rhodobacter species) and named herself Rhoda Baxter after them.

Now her day job involves protecting and commercialising intellectual property generated by university research. This allows her to stay in touch with cutting edge scientific research without having to spend long hours in the lab.

Rhoda is a member of the Romantic Novelists' Association. *Doctor January* is her first novel published in paperback with Choc Lit. She also has a novel published by Choc Lit Lite, *Girl on the Run*, which is available online.

www.rhodabaxter.com/
www.twitter.com/RhodaBaxter
www.facebook.com/RhodaBaxterAuthor

More Choc Lit

From Rhoda Baxter

Girl on the Run

Outrunning her past was never going to be easy ...

A job in a patent law firm is a far cry from the glamorous existence of a popstar's girlfriend. But it's just what Jane Porter needs to distance herself from her cheating ex, Ashby, and the press furore that surrounds the wreckage of her love life.

In a new city with a new look, Jane sets about rebuilding her confidence, and after Ashby's betrayal, she resolves that this will be something she does alone.

That is until she meets patent lawyer, Marshall Winfield. Sweet, clever and dealing with the aftermath of his own romantic disaster, Marsh could be the perfect cure for Jane's broken heart.

But with the paparazzi still hot on Jane's heels and an office troublemaker hell-bent on making things difficult, do Jane and Marsh stand any chance of finding happiness together?

Visit www.choc-lit.com for more details, or simply scan barcode using your mobile phone QR reader.

More from Choc Lit

If you enjoyed Rhoda's story, you'll enjoy the
rest of our selection. Here's a sample:

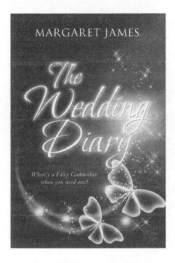

The Wedding Diary
Margaret James

**Where's a Fairy Godmother
when you need one?**

If you won a fairy-tale
wedding in a luxury hotel,
you'd be delighted – right? But
what if you didn't have anyone
to marry? Cat Aston did have
a fiancé, but now it looks like
her Prince Charming has done
a runner.

Adam Lawley was left devastated when his girlfriend turned
down his heartfelt proposal. He's made a vow never to fall
in love again.

So – when Cat and Adam meet, they shouldn't even consider
falling in love. After all, they're both broken hearted. But for
some reason they can't stop thinking about each other. Is this
their second chance for happiness, or are some things just
too good to be true?

Visit www.choc-lit.com for more details
including the first two chapters and
reviews, or simply scan barcode using
your mobile phone QR reader.

Please don't stop the music
Jane Lovering

 Winner of the 2012 Best Romantic Comedy Novel of the Year

 Winner of the 2012 Romantic Novel of the Year

How much can you hide?

Jemima Hutton is determined to build a successful new life and keep her past a dark secret. Trouble is, her jewellery business looks set to fail – until enigmatic Ben Davies offers to stock her handmade belt buckles in his guitar shop and things start looking up, on all fronts.

But Ben has secrets too. When Jemima finds out he used to be the front man of hugely successful Indie rock band Willow Down, she wants to know more. Why did he desert the band on their US tour? Why is he now a semi-recluse?

And the curiosity is mutual – which means that her own secret is no longer safe …

Visit www.choc-lit.com for more details including the first two chapters and reviews, or simply scan barcode using your mobile phone QR reader.

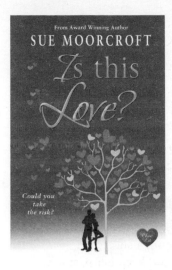

Is this Love?
Sue Moorcroft

How many ways can one woman love?

When Tamara Rix's sister Lyddie is involved in a hit-and-run accident that leaves her in need of constant care, Tamara resolves to remain in the village she grew up in. Tamara would do anything for her sister, even sacrifice a long-term relationship.

But when Lyddie's teenage sweetheart Jed Cassius returns to Middledip, he brings news that shakes the Rix family to their core. Jed's life is shrouded in mystery, particularly his job, but despite his strange background, Tamara can't help being intrigued by him.

Can Tamara find a balance between her love for Lyddie and growing feelings for Jed, or will she discover that some kinds of love just don't mix?

Visit www.choc-lit.com for more details including the first two chapters and reviews, or simply scan barcode using your mobile phone QR reader.

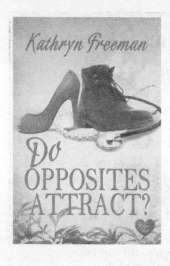

Do Opposites Attract?
Kathryn Freeman

There's no such thing as a class divide – until you're on separate sides

Brianna Worthington has beauty, privilege and a very healthy trust fund. The only hardship she's ever witnessed has been on the television. Yet when she's invited to see how her mother's charity, Medic SOS, is dealing with the aftermath of a tornado in South America, even Brianna is surprised when she accepts.

Mitch McBride, Chief Medical Officer, doesn't need the patron's daughter disrupting his work. He's from the wrong side of the tracks and has led life on the edge, but he's not about to risk losing his job for a pretty face.

Poles apart, dynamite together, but can Brianna and Mitch ever bridge the gap separating them?

Visit www.choc-lit.com for more details including the first two chapters and reviews, or simply scan barcode using your mobile phone QR reader.

CLAIM YOUR FREE EBOOK

of

DOCTOR
JANUARY

You may wish to have a choice of how you read
Doctor January. Perhaps you'd like a digital
version for when you're out and about, so that
you can read it on your ereader, iPad or even a
Smartphone. For a limited period, we're including
a **FREE** ebook version along with this paperback.

To claim, simply visit ebooks.choc-lit.com
or scan the QR Code.

You'll need to enter the following code:

Q211405

Introducing Choc Lit

We're an independent publisher creating
a delicious selection of fiction.
Where heroes are like chocolate – irresistible!
Quality stories with a romance at the heart.

Choc Lit novels are selected by genuine readers like yourself.
We only publish stories our Choc Lit Tasting Panel want to
see in print. Our reviews and awards speak for themselves.

We'd love to hear how you enjoyed *Doctor January*.
Just visit www.choc-lit.com and give your feedback.
Describe Hibs in terms of chocolate
and you could win a Choc Lit novel in our
Flavour of the Month competition.

Available in paperback and as ebooks from most stores.

Visit: www.choc-lit.com for more details.

Keep in touch:
Sign up for our monthly newsletter Choc Lit Spread for
all the latest news and offers: www.spread.choc-lit.com.
Follow us on Twitter: @ChocLituk and Facebook: Choc Lit.

Or simply scan barcode using your mobile phone QR reader:

*Choc Lit
Spread*

Twitter

Facebook